AVA'S CRUCIBLE

BOOK THREE: UNITED WE STAND

BESTSELLING AUTHOR
MARK GOODWIN

ACKNOWLEDGMENTS

I would like to thank my Editor in Chief Catherine Goodwin, as well as the rest of my fantastic editing team, Jeff Markland, Frank Shackleford, Stacey Glemboski, Sherrill Hesler, Paul Davison, and Claudine Allison.

CHAPTER 1

I came to send fire on the earth, and how I wish it were already kindled! But I have a baptism to be baptized with, and how distressed I am till it is accomplished! Do you suppose that I came to give peace on earth? I tell you, not at all, but rather division. For from now on five in one house will be divided: three against two, and two against three. Father will be divided against son and son against father, mother against daughter and daughter against mother, mother-in-law against her daughter-in-law and daughter-in-law against her mother-in-law.

Luke 12:49-53

Ava's breath steamed out of her mouth like fog in the crisp morning air. She held her AR-15 on the hood of the GMC Sierra, peering through the scope at the people on the opposite side of the Red River. Her green tactical vest filled with extra magazines pressed tightly against the side of the vehicle. Slight flurries of snow melted instantly upon landing on the warm hood of the pickup truck. "It sure doesn't feel like Christmas."

"Let's see what you say after we get Foley back." Ulysses jerked his prisoner out of the back of the truck.

Heavy steel trusses supported the long, two-lane bridge which crossed over the shallow but extremely wide section of the river. On the other side of the slender roadway was Texas, the place Ava had called home for thirty years. But no longer; her home state had fallen. Oklahoma was where she laid her head at night. It was where she lived with her father and best friend.

If the trade to get Foley back transpired without a hitch, she'd have everyone that mattered to her . . . in Oklahoma. It still wouldn't be Texas, but it would have to do.

Roughly twenty-five Oklahoma militia members were entrenched along the banks on either side of Ava. They kept their rifles trained on a similar number of communist militants who lined the far side of the river. The Social Justice Legion fighters wore their standardized black hoodies and red armbands, pointing their AK-47s at the patriots positioned on Ava's flanks. The tension in the midst of this Mexican standoff could not have been more elevated.

Ava took a deep breath to still her anxiety and turned to her father. "You don't think they're going to try anything, do you?"

Ulysses tightened the zip ties on Chip's wrists, then spun duct tape around his mouth. "For Chip's sake, I sure hope they don't." Ulysses patted the backpack on Chip's shoulders. "He's got two bricks of shrapnel-coated C-4 strapped to him. Wouldn't be anything left of him but a smear on the pavement." Ulysses pulled the detonator out of his pocket and placed it on the hood of the truck. "The catfish in the river below would have a heyday. It'd be like manna from heaven to them."

Ava knew he was trying to lighten the mood for her, but it wasn't working. Her heart was heavy. If the exchange went as planned, it would be a first. Nothing ever went as planned. And this time, the stakes were higher than ever before.

For three days, she'd thought Foley was dead. Even though she wasn't yet married to him, she'd mourned like no widow ever could. Then, when she'd learned that he was alive, hope sprang to life in her innermost being. Yet, at this moment in time, that very same hope hung like the Sword of Damocles above her head, an ominous instrument of destruction, which threatened to destroy her. If the exchange turned sour and Foley died, she'd have to mourn him all over again.

Ava muttered to herself. "Hope is a fickle thing; it has the power of life and death. I don't think I could survive losing him again."

Her phone vibrated. She pulled it out of her jacket pocket and read the text aloud. "It's Raquel. She said to send Chip out now."

Ulysses shoved the prisoner toward the front of the truck. He said to Ava, "Keep your eye on that scope. I'm not going to let him start walking until they send Foley out."

Ava closed one eye and looked longingly through the rifle's optics. Her heart sank when she saw Foley. He was a long way off, but she could see that his face was badly bruised and he needed crutches to walk. She let the rifle rest on the hood of the truck. "Dad, I've got to go help him across!"

"No, Ava. I understand that this is emotional for you. It's emotional for me, too. But we have to be smart. It's the best thing you can do for Foley."

Ulysses slapped Chip in the back of the head. "Start walking—nice and slow. Keep that backpack on until we're gone. Make sure your friends don't do anything that might make me nervous. That wouldn't be good for your health."

Chip nodded and began his lengthy trek over the bridge.

"And thanks for the information. Don't mention what you told me to your friends and I promise to keep things hush-hush on my end. We both know you're a coward and only in it for the money, but that can be our little secret." Ulysses smiled.

The prisoner paused to turn and look at him, his eyes filled with anger and defeat. He nodded in capitulation.

Ava watched while Chip walked away. "Do you

honestly think he won't tell them about all the information he gave up?"

Ulysses shook his head. "He doesn't want to admit to handing over all of that, even though he knows we'll use the intelligence. People like Chip are more concerned with their status than the actual outcome of the conflict."

"If we win, his status will be a war criminal."

Ulysses nodded. "That's a real possibility to Chip. But if he fesses up to what he gave me, he may very well be executed by the Markovich regime. Staying quiet about it is his least-bad option."

Ava studied Foley through her scope. She looked on in anguish, unable to assist the man she loved so much. In the distance, Foley seemed weak, swinging his good leg forward and wincing each time he had to put his weight back on the crutches beneath his arms.

"Come on, come on, come on!" Ava said the words as if they might grant strength and comfort to her returning lover. Of course, it didn't help. Foley's progress across the bridge was pained and sluggish, but she just wanted to get him out of harm's way and back home.

"Please, Foley, try to hurry," she whispered to herself.

She saw the black-hooded SJL fighters begin to peel off the opposite bank into the shrubbery behind them. "Dad, why are they withdrawing so soon? The exchange hasn't taken place yet."

Ulysses held his binoculars to his eyes. "Something's not right."

Ava thought she heard a noise in the distant sky. She lifted her rifle to scan above the horizon. "Is that a helicopter coming in from the Texas side?"

Ulysses followed her finger. "Three choppers." He dropped his field glasses and let them dangle around his neck. Ulysses picked up his radio and called out to the militia members assisting him and Ava with the trade. "This thing is going pear-shaped. Everybody, be ready to engage on my command."

Ulysses quickly transitioned from the radio to the bullhorn with which he addressed the enemy forces on the other side of the bridge. "I'm going to let you guys in on a couple of little secrets. For one, we've got backup forces on your side of the river. Also, your beloved Chip there has two bricks of C-4 in his carry-on luggage. Both are coated in generous layers of lead shot and nails.

"So basically, if we don't go home, you don't go home. Whoever your commanding officer is, he needs to tell those choppers to turn around right now. Chip has one minute for the birds to be out of sight or I'll disperse his fragments evenly between Texas and Oklahoma."

Chip turned to look at Ulysses with an expression of horror, then turned to begin running toward the Texas side of the bridge.

Ava yelled to Foley who was near the halfway point. "Come on, Foley! Try to hurry!"

Ava's hope faded into fear, watching Foley struggle just to stay upright on the crutches. "Dad, we have to get him off the bridge. They're obviously trying to pull a fast one on us."

Ulysses held the detonator in his hand. "Wait a few more seconds. I'm hoping those choppers are going to turn around."

Ava looked at the three black objects in the sky getting closer. "I don't think they believe you about the reinforcements from Byers being behind them. And I'm not sure they really care about Chip. We need to get Foley, and we need to do it now!"

Ulysses held his binoculars up one last time. "They're not turning. Come on, let's go. You drive. I'll ride in the back of the truck and help Foley into the bed. Back up to Foley's location. That way you can gun it once he's in the truck."

Ava already had the driver's side door open. "Let me hold the detonator. If you get in a firefight while you're picking up Foley, you won't be able to get to it. If they shoot at us, I don't want that piece of garbage getting away."

Ulysses hesitated but tossed her the detonator before getting in the back of the truck.

Ava started the engine and began slowly backing up toward Foley. She could hear the sound of the helicopters' rotors slicing the air. The sound grew louder.

Ava was still a few yards away from Foley when she heard the first wave of gunfire coming from the choppers as they flew over and peppered the militia members on the Oklahoma side of the river. She gunned the engine pushing the back bumper to within inches of Foley. "Hurry!" She watched as Ulysses helped him into the back of the truck.

Ulysses yelled over the radio to the militia, "Target the engines of the helicopters. We've got no surface to air weapons. It's our only hope. Everyone shooting 5.56, focus on the hostiles on the ground. Anyone with 7.62 or larger, direct your fire toward the choppers."

Ava slammed the shifter into gear and stomped the gas pedal. The back tires spun and smoked, propelling the truck forward, toward the Oklahoma side of the bridge. The choppers made another pass overhead, raining down a hail of bullets ahead of their path.

TINK, TINK, PLUNK! Several rounds hit the Sierra when the helicopters passed over. Ava growled with anger at having been double-crossed yet again by Raquel and the Social Justice Legion. "You're not keeping up your end of the bargain, then neither am I!"

She glanced up at the rearview, first to see if Foley was okay. He was lying down in the back and she could not see him. She could see her father returning fire on the hostiles at the other end of the bridge. She could also make out a team of three people working desperately to get the backpack off of Chip.

"I told you to stay down and leave me alone. You should have listened, Chip." She held the detonator high in the air to ensure the signal would have the best position for transmission.

Click.

BOOOOM!

Ava glanced up to see the fireball in the rearview, a pillar of smoke reaching toward the sky. The van near where Chip had been standing was charred, missing the windshield, and spattered with soot and singed blood.

Her mind was focused on the task at hand, on getting Foley and her father out of danger. Yet she still noted how different she felt after watching Chip being disintegrated compared to the demonstrator at the stadium. Previously, she'd been frozen in horror at the thought of her own barbarity. This time, however, she found herself fighting back a certain sense of satisfaction. "This is not who I want to be." She remembered her father's warnings, that war would change her, and that once that part of her was lost, she could never get it back.

Ulysses banged on the rear window and shouted, "Drive past the guardrails, then turn off-road and head back toward the river. The bridge itself is our only cover from the helicopters."

Ava huffed, knowing the direction of the river was also the direction of the hostiles on the ground. But her father was right. Outrunning the helicopters couldn't even be considered. Fighting them from a position of cover was their only hope.

CHAPTER 2

In You, O Lord, I put my trust; Let me never be ashamed; deliver me in Your righteousness. Bow down Your ear to me, deliver me speedily; be my rock of refuge, a fortress of defense to save me. For You are my rock and my fortress; therefore, for Your name's sake, lead me and guide me. Pull me out of the net which they have secretly laid for me, for You are my strength. Into Your hand I commit my spirit; You have redeemed me, O Lord God of truth.

Psalm 31:1-5

Ava sped down the dirt path which ran alongside

the bridge. At the first section tall enough for the truck to fit under, she parked beneath the cover of the roadway.

Ulysses jumped out of the back. "Help me get Foley under the truck. Choppers could still fly low and spray the truck with gunfire. He's in no condition to move fast."

Ava hurried out of the cab and around to the back, complying with her father's instructions. When she saw Foley's face, battered and bruised, a knot formed in her throat. But this was not the time for a breakdown. Crying would have to wait, or she might have a whole lot more to cry about.

"Hey!" She forced a smile in an effort to keep his spirits up.

His reply was weak and labored. "Hey, yourself."

"It's good to see you." She clenched her jaw to keep her lip from quivering.

"It's good to be seen." He grimaced in pain as Ulysses and Ava hoisted him out of the truck bed and onto the ground.

Once he'd managed to squirm under the truck, she gave his hand a squeeze. "I'll be right back."

"Got an extra rifle?" he asked.

"Let us take this one."

"I can still pull a trigger. Trust me, I'm not going to try and play hero, but a little cover fire might come in handy."

Ava nodded and removed the strap of her AR-15 from her shoulder. "Here."

He reached up and took the rifle. "What are you going to shoot?"

"I've got an AK in the back seat of the truck. Dad thinks it'll have a better chance of taking down a chopper anyway." She pulled the spare AR magazines from her vest and placed them on the ground beside Foley.

Foley nodded and closed his eyes, as if he were saving his strength for an engagement with the enemy.

Ulysses called over the radio, "Get under the bridge! It's the best cover we have."

Several of the Oklahoma militia members emerged from the surrounding bushes and charged toward the bridge.

"Ava, look alive. They're coming around for another pass!" Ulysses took aim at the helicopters coming toward them.

Ava quickly retrieved the AK-47 and the extra magazines. She hurried to stuff the mags into the pouches on her vest and took up a position behind one of the concrete pillars under the bridge. Rifle fire rang out from behind her. She heard bullets buzzing by her ear from the direction of the river. "We still have to worry about the hostiles on the ground!"

"Roger that! Keep your sights on the choppers. Wait till you can see the pilot's face to fire." POW, POW, POW! Ulysses spun around to engage the Social Justice Legion fighters on the opposite bank.

Ava fought the urge to tuck down behind the concrete support and hide until the chopper had passed by. When she could make out the pilot, she opened fire. Ta, Ta, Ta, Ta, Ta! She aimed toward the windshield and the top engine cover.

Ulysses looked up at two large spider-web cracks on the front windshield of the chopper. "Good job. You at least made it hard for them to see."

The next chopper flew by and the machine gunner unleashed a barrage of fifty-caliber gunfire toward Ava and Ulysses.

"Get down! Get down!" Ulysses ran toward her and pushed her to the ground. Bullets struck inches from her face.

Ava watched the dust being kicked up by the giant lead projectiles striking the ground by her head. As soon as the chopper had passed by, she jumped back up and emptied her magazine on the rear of the aircraft. Several of her rounds struck the tail of the helicopter and the rear rotor ceased from spinning. "I think I hit it!"

Ulysses joined several of the other nearby militia members in a gunfight with the remaining Social Justice Legion fighters. He picked up his radio. "Byers Militia, looks like that chopper is going to have to set down over by you. Why don't y'all send a welcoming committee to meet them?"

"Roger," a man replied over the radio.

"The other two choppers are coming back!" yelled a militia member kneeling behind a concrete support several yards away from Ava.

She changed magazines and took aim. The first helicopter came in low. The fifty-cal ripped through several of the militia members. Their screams of agony were muffled by the roar of the helicopter's engine.

Ava directed her fire at the massive war machine as long as she could, but when the bullets came too close, she was forced to jump behind the cover of the pickup truck. She looked beneath the Sierra to see Foley crawling toward the edge of the truck and leveling his AR-15. Bang, Bang, Bang! He fired at the chopper. Soon after, Ava witnessed the chopper's nose dive down toward the ground. Evidently, Foley had struck the pilot. She watched the copilot try to bring the chopper back up, but the craft was too near the ground. The rotor blades cut into the soft earth of the river bank and the chopper smashed into the ground, exploding on impact.

She turned to him and smiled. "Nice work, cowboy."

"Never been a very good spectator." His voice was very frail.

"Watch out!" Ulysses screamed as he ran toward Ava.

Fifty-caliber gunfire pulsed out of the third helicopter as it charged in Ava's direction. She rushed to change her magazine, but it was coming in too fast. Ulysses lunged toward her, pulling her behind the concrete piling. "Awwww!"

Ava saw an explosion of blood spray out of Ulysses' leg as the bullet passed through. "Dad!"

He rolled on the ground in torment. "Keep fighting. Take out that other chopper first, then worry about me."

She completed her magazine change and forced herself to redirect her attention to the battle at hand. Ava saw only six remaining Oklahoma militia members of the original twenty-five who'd accompanied her to the battle site. Bodies from both sides lay strewn about the river banks with many of the corpses staining the river a murky crimson. Still, sporadic enemy fire continued to assault them from the Texas side of the river. Ava kept herself hidden from the SJL ground forces and waited for the chopper to make another pass.

Ulysses ignored the gaping hole in his calf muscle and put out another call over the radio. "Byers Militia, if you folks can close in on the hostiles from your side of the river, it would be a great help. We're getting thinned out over here."

A voice replied over the walkie-talkie, "Our team has been slaughtered. I'm down to four guys who can walk on their own and operate a gun. I put in a call to the base up in Altus, but it could be a while. We may have to sit tight."

"No can do. Altus is sixty miles out. Sitting tight is a guaranteed ticket to the other side. We have to keep pressing them." Ulysses' face showed his concern over the dire situation. "Besides, this is an unauthorized militia engagement. I'm not so sure the Alliance States will even want to get involved."

The voice of the man in the Byers Militia replied. "Oh, they're coming. Militia or not, regime choppers crossed the border and fired on targets in Oklahoma. That's a violation of sovereignty that can't go unchecked."

Ulysses looked unsure. "I hope you're right."

Ava pressed the butt of her rifle against her shoulder. "Here he comes!" She lined up her sights with the helicopter's cockpit.

Ulysses' face contorted in anguish as he moved his injured leg to get into a fighting position. Likewise, he raised his rifle. "As soon as you see the gunner, take him out. He's gotta go before we can worry about the aircraft."

Ava nodded, but she knew she could at least crack the windshield while she was waiting for the side shot necessary to hit the machine gunner. She took four quick shots at the front of the chopper, all of which connected with the cockpit windshield. She crouched low behind the concrete support and opened fire at the side door where the fifty-caliber was barking out shells at her and the remaining militia members.

Ulysses also took shots at the gunner. "He's hit! Aim for that tail rotor. We've got a few seconds before they can come back around and assault us from the other side.

Ava emptied her magazine but to no avail. "Missed him."

"That's okay, reload and get ready for the next pass." Ulysses slapped a fresh magazine into the mag well of his rifle.

Gunfire rang out from the direction of the river. Ava turned to see three more militiamen being cut down by seven SJL fighters who were wading across the shallow river with their AK-47s held high. "Dad! We've got company coming!"

Ulysses let out a grunt of disappointment. "Be selective about your shots. The chopper will be back any second. Work on these guys until you hear the chopper. Then focus on the aircraft and I'll do what I can to hold the ground troops back until it passes."

Foley crawled out from beneath the truck, rifle in hand. Sweat droplets covered his forehead, drool was running down into his beard. His skin was pale, and his eyes were half shut. "I'll help with the chopper when it comes."

Ava knew the symptoms of septic shock and Foley looked horrible. "You need to rest."

He replied in a feeble voice, "If we don't survive the next few minutes, rest isn't going to do me any good. I've gotta fight."

"He's right." Ulysses' eyebrows were low and his jaw was clenched. "We're in a tough spot here."

Ava already knew that to be true, but she'd not seen her father this worried before now. If he was so distraught, the situation had to be grim. Ava quickly fired several bursts at the enemy fighters, who were coming up out of the water and onto the bank. They shot back in unison and took prone positions. Ava watched the remaining militia members fall one by one, taking two of the SJL assailants with them.

The black-hooded aggressors took up a position behind one of the far supports of the bridge, using it as cover.

"Checkmate." Ava's voice echoed the defeat in her soul. "When the chopper circles back, we'll be forced to duck behind the barrier, which will expose us to the ground troops. I don't see any way out of this."

A quivering smile crept across Ulysses' face. His voice cracked. "It ain't over till it's over. You just keep shooting, sweetheart. And remember that I'll always love you."

"The chopper is coming." Foley's thin voice was barely loud enough to be heard over the incoming helicopter.

"I love you, too, Dad. And you, Foley." Ava dried her eyes with her sleeve and took aim at the approaching aircraft.

TA, TA, TA, TA, Tat! The fifty-caliber shells from the chopper plowed through the earth, throwing sand violently into the air. Each shell grew closer and closer to Ava, her father, and Foley. The three of them returned fire but continued to miss the replacement machine gunner who maintained the assault.

KABOOM! The helicopter erupted in a massive sphere of flame and debris.

Ava looked up in amazement as two F-16s appeared from behind the smoke left by the exploding chopper. "Alliance fighter jets!" Ava squealed with excitement.

Ulysses nodded with a renewed look of optimism. "Yeah, that's great, but we've still got these pinheads slipping up on us.

Ava quickly looked around the concrete support. The five remaining hostiles were using the diversion as an opportunity to close in on her team and finish them off. She fired three rounds, dropping one of the SJL assailants. Then, her trigger clicked. "Empty! Rats!"

"Just reload." Ulysses continued firing and killed two more SJL troops.

Ava's hands shook from the adrenaline coursing through her veins. She dropped her spent magazine, replaced it with one from her vest, and racked the bolt. She took aim and began firing just as she heard Ulysses' bolt lock open.

Ava killed two more hostiles. "The last two are holed up behind the concrete piling."

Ulysses turned to Foley whose skin seemed to be turning grayer than pale. "Think you could put down one magazine's worth of cover fire?"

He nodded.

Ulysses turned his attention to Ava. "And I'll put down cover from the other side. We need you to run up toward them and flank them. Foley and I will keep them pinned down. Be slow and deliberate. Chest shots, then double tap them in the head when you get to close range. Do you think you can do that?"

Ava looked at her injured father and her dying fiancé. She had no other choice. She nodded.

"Put in a fresh magazine and tuck down on your approach. Keep your profile low." Ulysses' eyes showed a mix of pride and distress for his daughter. "You'll do fine."

Ava took several deep breaths as she mentally prepared herself to run directly into the line of fire. She imagined what the two remaining hostiles looked like crouched behind the cover of the support. She pictured her rifle firing and cutting them down. She exhaled. "I'm ready."

"Okay. You call it. Say *go* and run right for them."

She nodded, pressed the butt of the AK into her shoulder, set her feet and yelled, "Go!"

CHAPTER 3

And it came to pass, that as he was come nigh unto Jericho, a certain blind man sat by the way side begging: And hearing the multitude pass by, he asked what it meant. And they told him, that Jesus of Nazareth passeth by. And he cried, saying, Jesus, thou son of David, have mercy on me. And they which went before rebuked him, that he should hold his peace: but he cried so much the more, Thou son of David, have mercy on me.

Luke 18:35-39

Foley opened fire on the right side of the

support, while Ulysses put down suppressive fire on the left. Ava sprung from cover to the left of the concrete pillar beneath the bridge, her legs pumping hard against the soft sand. She raised her AK-47, taking aim at the edge of the far support where the enemy troops were hiding. Foley and Ulysses continued to shoot steady streams of cover fire. Ava saw the shoulder of the first SJL fighter. She took up the slack in her trigger and took two more steps to the left.

BANG, BANG, BANG! Blood sprayed out from the chest and stomach of the unsuspecting hostile. The second SJL trooper raised his rifle. Ava couldn't afford a shot to the center of mass which might have allowed the man to pull his trigger. She quickly centered the bead of her iron sight between his eyes and squeezed. POW!

The man dropped to the ground. She rushed toward the first downed hostile and placed two more rounds in his head. Next, she shot the second hostile in the face once more for good measure.

Smoke slipped serenely from the barrel of her gun, dissipating in the light breeze. Ava took a breath, looked around, then seeing no other immediate threats, collapsed on the ground from exhaustion. She simply wanted to sit in the sand for a few minutes, to breathe, and give her mind a chance to catch up with what just happened. But that was not to be. Instantly, the momentary silence was disrupted by the sound of more helicopters.

Ava shook her head. "No, no, no. It can't be! God, please help us! We can't fight off another wave. Dad is shot, Foley is at the end of his rope, and I'm utterly wiped out. Please, God!" she begged.

Despite her condition, she reloaded and scanned the skyline for the helicopters. The Alliance fighter jets were nowhere to be seen. Had they abandoned them so soon? Suddenly, she realized the sound of the helicopters were coming from behind. First, she saw four green helicopters, Black Hawks, perhaps. Behind them were two more choppers, bigger than the first four, with two top rotors each. "Chinooks. Please let them be Alliance helicopters!"

Soldiers repelled from the sides of the Black Hawks. Ava was able to recognize the new Alliance States insignia on the side of the aircraft when it turned sideways.

"Thank you, Jesus!" She sighed and fell back into the sand.

Ulysses called out. "Over here! We need a medic for this man!"

Ava could not rest. Not yet. She needed to make sure Foley would get the attention he needed. She forced herself to stand, hand up and weapon dangling from the single-point sling as she returned to her father and Foley. She watched as the Chinooks landed and more soldiers poured out.

The first wave of Alliance soldiers reached their position. One of them quickly unzipped a pouch on his vest. "Let's see what we can do for that leg." He bent down next to Ulysses.

"Don't mind me, this man is going into shock," Ulysses said.

The soldier called on his radio. "I need a stretcher to the bridge, and I need an antibiotic IV.

Hurry!"

"Can you fly him back to base?" Ava pleaded.

The soldier nodded. "We'll have him good as gold in no time, ma'am."

"Thank you, can I ride along?" she asked.

The soldier looked at the carnage surrounding him. "Are you responsible for this mess?"

"Some of it."

"You look familiar. You wouldn't happen to be the girl who caused all that ruckus at the firearm collection points in Austin, would you?"

"That's her. She's the troublemaker in chief," Ulysses winced as another soldier wrapped his leg to get him ready for transport.

The first soldier smiled at Ava and nodded. "Then we'll make room for you, even if I have to give up my seat and walk back."

She took Foley's limp hand. "Thank you, thank you so much."

Late Christmas night, Ava sat up on the waiting area couch after a short and fitful nap. The makeshift military hospital was located in a hangar at Altus Air Force Base where the Oklahoma National Guard had assumed control. The field-expedient medical center appeared to be well-supplied and adequately staffed, but it had no permanent walls. Temporary partitions allowed sound to travel easily from one section of the hospital to the next.

Ulysses rolled out from behind one of the thin partitions in a wheelchair with his leg elevated.

"Dad!" She stood up to help him. "You're out of surgery?"

"Please don't make a fuss over me. I didn't even want a wheelchair. Crutches would have been sufficient." He rolled the chair to the couch where she'd been sitting.

She hesitated before returning to her seat. "Shouldn't you be in bed?"

"Flesh wound. I'll be fine. What did the doctor say about Foley?"

She sighed and reached out to take her father's hand. "I'm still waiting to hear."

"Did they feed you?"

"They offered, but I'm not going to eat until I hear about Foley."

"You need to eat. You've been through a lot."

She shook her head. "I had some water and a Gatorade, but I'm fasting—for Foley. I'm begging God to heal him."

Ulysses conceded. "If that's your conviction, then you should go with it."

A doctor came from behind the petition followed by a soldier in dress uniform. "Ms.Wilson?"

She looked at her father then stood up, "I actually go by Adams now, but yes, that's me."

"Oh, sorry. You actually came to be something of a hero around here when the regime was hunting down Ava Wilson. So please don't be offended if I'm not the last person on the base to call you *Ms. Wilson.*"

Ulysses smirked. "Don't get used to it. She'll be going by Mrs. Mitchem soon enough."

She smiled politely at the doctor. "I'm flattered, but Ava is fine. Any news on Foley Mitchem?"

"Yes, ma'am. His condition is stable, for now."

"For now?"

"It seems he was shot four days ago and never received the proper medical attention. His infection is bad. We're pumping him full of antibiotics which is pretty tough on his system. But it's the only chance we have of saving him. We're going to have to keep him sedated for at least twenty-four hours. After that, we'll know more about how his body is reacting to the antibiotics."

"But he's going to live, right?"

The doctor paused and took a long breath. "We're doing all we can."

"Please, doctor, don't sugarcoat it. What are his odds of survival?"

"For most people, I'd say not good. But I can tell he's a fighter. I'd give him a fifty-fifty shot."

Ava nodded optimistically. The answer was by no means what she'd hoped to hear, but it could have been worse.

The doctor continued speaking, "But, if we're able to control the infection and get him stabilized, we'll probably have to take the leg where he was shot. We can only expect so much from antibiotics. The tissue around the wound is severely damaged."

Ava bit her finger and looked down at the concrete floor. She imagined growing old with Foley, waiting on him in his wheelchair. As long as God would allow him to live, she'd take it. She glanced back up at the doctor and nodded. "I understand. Thank you for your efforts. I really appreciate it."

The doctor turned to the soldier behind him. "This is Sergeant Griffith. He'll escort you and your father to one of the furnished guest houses on the base. It should be stocked with towels, toiletries, snacks, and all the basics.

"Like I said, you're a hero around here, so if you need anything, anything at all, please don't hesitate to ask. It is our honor to serve you in any way that we can.

"Sergeant Griffith will give you some passes which will get you in the dining facility, commissary, or most anywhere else you want to go around the base. If you don't feel like being around people, the sergeant will bring your meals to you. I believe you have coffee, tea, milk, and cereal in the house. We want you to be comfortable while we take care of your friend. And we want you to rest up from the gunfight you were just in. I hear it was a rough one."

Ulysses spun the wheelchair around to face the doctor. "How many survivors were you able to save from the injured Oklahoma Militia members?"

"They brought in fourteen. One died on the flight here. We lost two on the table. Three others are touch and go. The other eight should be released to go home in the morning."

"Thank you." Ulysses looked pensively at his bandaged leg.

"I have a van parked in front of the hangar. I can give you a lift over to the guest house whenever you are ready," said Sergeant Griffith.

Ava looked at the doctor. "Can I see Foley? I'd at least like to say good night."

His face reflected his empathy. "He's in the ICU. We're not really allowed to have visitors in there."

She pushed her hands into her jean pockets, glanced down then back up at his eyes. "I promise I'll never play the hero-card again, but could you make an exception for me? Just this once?"

The doctor exhaled, then nodded softly. "Just this once; for you. But we have to make it quick."

"Thanks." She smiled then said to Ulysses, "I'll be right back, Dad."

"I'll be here with the sergeant. Take your time."

Ava followed the doctor to the Intensive Care Unit. She walked past the other three militia members who'd been injured in the battle. They were all heavily bandaged and attached to various cords and machines which beeped, displaying lights and numbers.

She came to Foley's bedside. Ava barely recognized him. He looked so vulnerable, the mighty warrior who'd saved her from the first Antifa attack at her church before she'd even known his name. He lay in a hospital bed on the precipice of death. Breathing tubes were in his nose. An IV dripped fluids and antibiotics through a long plastic tube and into a needle inserted into his arm. She took his hand, held it for a moment before the rush of emotions overflowed and the tears began to streak down the sides of her face. Her mouth frowned and she gasped for air over the strong wave of sorrow. "Please don't leave me," she whispered through the sobs.

But Foley couldn't hear her. And for the most part, that choice was not up to him. She dried her eyes and looked up to the One who could affect the outcome of this situation. "Please, God! You know how much I love him. Please don't let him die. Heal his infection, give him strength to fight this. Bring him back from the edge."

She paused for a moment to hold Foley's hand, then said, "But if you have to take him home, please, Lord, let him go in peace and comfort. Thy will be done."

The doctor put his hand on her shoulder. "We need to be going."

She nodded, then bent down to kiss Foley softly on his lips. "Sweet dreams, my love. I'll be praying for you."

She followed the doctor back to the waiting area.

CHAPTER 4

Wherefore hear the word of the Lord, ye scornful men, that rule this people which is in Jerusalem. Because ye have said, We have made a covenant with death, and with hell are we at agreement; when the overflowing scourge shall pass through, it shall not come unto us: for we have made lies our refuge, and under falsehood have we hid ourselves.

Isaiah 28:14-15

Ava awoke to the sound of her father knocking on the bedroom door of the guest house.

"The sergeant is on the phone. He's asking if you'd like him to bring breakfast. They'll make anything you want, but the dining facility will be closing soon. They need to start prepping for lunch."

She couldn't remember falling asleep. She'd tossed and turned all night, thinking only the worst of Foley's precarious condition. Ava had tried so hard to have faith, to stay vigilant in prayer all night, but her imagination had gotten the best of her. Yet she purposed in her very soul to maintain her fast until his infection improved or until God called him home. "No, thanks."

She heard Ulysses' muffled voice placing an order over the phone. A few minutes later, he returned to her door. "How about some coffee?"

"Maybe later. I think I just need to be quiet for a while before I get up."

"I'll see you when I see you, then." Ulysses' voice faded as he moved away from the door.

Ava heard him clunking about on the crutches which he'd requested from Sergeant Griffith— against the doctor's orders to stay in the wheelchair for at least seventy-two hours.

Ava spent the next hour praying, begging God to heal Foley. Once she felt she'd wrung her soul out completely, she got out of bed, got dressed and walked out into the living room.

The base guest house was very nice but nothing extraordinarily fancy. The sergeant had told her it was typically reserved for visiting colonels and above. The three-bedroom home was exceptionally clean if nothing else. The kitchen had granite counters and stainless-steel appliances but wasn't over the top. Her room was spacious, and the bed was very comfortable. Large, navy-blue, overstuffed couches with ottomans flanked a high-end media center with a giant-screen television.

Ulysses sat on the couch watching TV with his bandaged leg elevated on one of the ottomans. He placed his coffee cup on a coaster atop the end table.

"Good morning," she said. Despite Foley's desperate circumstances, Ava was exceedingly happy that her father had not been killed in the previous day's action.

"Good afternoon," he replied with a smile.

Ava looked at the clock on the microwave. "Afternoon?"

"Relax, we've got nothing else to do today except take it easy. No use getting an early start on that."

"I know, but I need to call Charity and let her know we're okay. She must be worried sick."

Ulysses lowered the volume of the television. "Could you send her a text instead?"

"We've got burner phones. Why can't I call her?"

"Stingrays."

"Stingrays are local. We're in Alliance territory. So is Charity. Besides, if they've intercepted our phones, they could get the text just the same as a voice call."

"Enemy agents could set up Stingray devices inside Oklahoma or any other Alliance State. Intercepted calls could be passed through NSA's voice recognition system. Once they identify your voice, then they'll have your phone. Texting doesn't have that vulnerability."

"Okay." Ava pulled out her phone.

"And keep it short. No names, no places. You could say, I'm good, Dad is good, boyfriend is sick but stable. Be home in a few days. That's really all she needs to know, and you're not tipping your hand by giving out too much information."

Ava nodded and sent the abbreviated text.

Seconds later, she chuckled at the reply.

"What did she say?"

"She's trying to one-up me on the whole short-and-sweet thing." Ava read the response. "K. Dog miss u. I miss u."

Ulysses smiled. "I had the sergeant bring you some ham and biscuits. I figured if you got some good news about Foley and wanted to break your fast, it would be here. If not, I'll eat them."

Ava poured herself a cup of coffee and came to sit down next to her father. "I don't guess you've heard from the doctor?"

Ulysses shook his head. "I know it's tough, but he said they wouldn't know anything for at least twenty-four hours."

"But what if he takes a turn for the worse? Do you think the doctor will call me?"

"You're a superstar around here. I'm sure he'll let you know."

"I'm going to call him—on the house's landline." She stood up and walked to the kitchen. She called Sergeant Griffith first. In her dismay the evening before, she'd completely forgotten to get the doctor's name, much less his contact information. The sergeant informed her that the doctor was Captain Murphy and passed along his personal cell number.

Ava dialed the number. "Captain Murphy? Hi, it's Ava. I know you're busy but I just wanted to see if anything had changed with Foley."

"He's still stable, which is good news. The fact that he didn't take a turn for the worse overnight is very promising, but we still need some more time."

"So, if that's good news, could you reevaluate his odds?"

The doctor sighed. "Odds are very speculative. Once we feel like we've got him where he has a decent chance of making it through surgery, we'll still have that hurdle to cross."

"But what would you put his chances of survival at—right now, I mean?"

He paused for a moment. "I could say sixty percent since we got through the night. But realize that it's little more than an arbitrary number. A lot of things could still go wrong. I don't want you to get your hopes too high."

"I understand, Captain. But it's something—for me anyway. I really needed to hear that."

"I'm glad I could give you a positive report. I'll call you if anything changes."

"Thanks again, bye." She placed the phone on the receiver.

Ulysses patted the couch cushion next to where he was sitting. Ava plopped down beside him. "What are you watching?"

"The regime news. They're reporting on the incident yesterday."

"Turn it up. I'd like to hear their spin on it."

Carter Lellouche, the afternoon anchor for the mainstream news network, was interviewing the new White House Press Secretary, Mary Snow.

Snow said, "Carter, the administration has been as tolerant as possible, but our restraint has been met with belligerence and violence at every step of the way. Turner Blackwell hasn't even been elected president of his so-called Alliance States, yet he refers to himself as the commander- in-chief. All the while, accusing President Markovich of being a dictator.

"Yesterday's actions can only be described as an act of war. Blackwell sent F-16s to shoot down four United States helicopters, which were only there to watch over a small foot patrol who were trying to defend Texas from an influx of weapons from Oklahoma."

Carter shook his head as if perplexed. "On Christmas Day, no less. I don't understand how Blackwell and these, these, these zealots have been allowed to take this thing so far. We all appreciate that our good leader is trying to avoid a bloody conflict, but a rogue extremist faction is essentially holding nine states hostage. I can't believe the inhabitants of these states actually want this, but the heads of this movement are largely people they've elected."

Snow pursed her lips. "Carter, these states are vast territories of tiny remote towns and isolated communities. Many of these people are disconnected from the rest of America. They haven't engaged with popular culture and have allowed themselves to be left behind by forward thinking. In some ways, they are to be pitied. But you're right. We can't allow the desire of a few, who want to wallow in ignorance, to bring down the entire country.

"For now, President Markovich is firming up the borders of the majority states who are in compliance with the new firearms laws. Many of the compliant states still have a high percentage of residents who subscribe to these superstitions about religion. They hold radical ideologies and are easily manipulated into being domestic terrorists by people like Blackwell. We can't allow firearms to move freely across the borders and enable them to kill or injure law-abiding citizens.

"However, I can assure you, President Markovich, Defense Secretary Coleman, and DHS Secretary Douglas are designing strategies to put an end to the madness. When they do, it will be absolute, and we'll no longer be two Americas."

Lellouche quizzed her further. "Can you elaborate on those strategies?"

"I think you know that I can't, Carter. But I understand that you had to ask."

"I respect your answer. I wouldn't want to be responsible for compromising those plans, but you're right, I had to ask," he said with a wink.

"What I can tell you, Carter, is that acts of aggression like we saw yesterday will not be tolerated. From this moment forward, force will be met with force."

"Press Secretary Mary Snow, thank you so much for making time for us."

"Thank you, Carter."

The split screen vanished and the camera panned in for a close up of Lellouche. "Up next, Shane Lawrence will be with us to discuss the situation around the country. He's hinted at how the new Social Justice Legion will help to winnow the wheat from the chaff, but when we come back, he'll lay out the plan in detail. You won't want to miss this next segment, so stay tuned!"

Ava finished her coffee. "Always the victims. They'll never admit that they were the ones who started it."

Ulysses shook his head. "Oh no, they'll never admit that."

The commercial, which was a highly-stylized call for leftist youth to join the military, finally ended, and Carter Lellouche's show continued. "Thank you for staying with us. As I promised, Shane Lawrence is in the studio with us today."

The camera panned out to include Lawrence in the shot. "Shane, thanks for being with us."

"I'm delighted to be here," Lawrence gave a devilish smile.

Carter placed his finger on his lip. "You were on Ophelia's show not long ago, and you mentioned that the Social Justice Legion would be going through social media posts to determine who was a friend of America and who was a potential foe. I understand the system is set up and will begin assessments this week. I don't mean to steal your thunder, why don't I let you tell us about it?"

Lawrence chuckled. "Yeah, thanks. It's called the Social Value Audit, and it's a collective effort, Carter. This is everyone's program. We have to get rid of this notion of private ownership and private recognition. We've tried that system, and it has failed miserably.

"Citizens will be graded on a sliding scale, from one to ten. We initially developed the program to assess active military personnel, but the president liked it so much that he's asked George and myself to roll it out for the entire population."

"Have I been audited yet?" Carter asked.

Lawrence smiled sheepishly, as if the interview weren't totally scripted and he wasn't expecting such a direct inquiry about the program. "Yes, you have. You got a ten."

Carter feigned a look of concern. "And that's good—I hope?"

Lawrence laughed. "Yes, Carter. It's the highest ranking. A ten is considered most-highly favored citizen status. It means you would be welcomed into any government service field you want."

Ava huffed. "As if this network weren't a proxy of the Markovich regime."

"I'm flattered!" Carter held his hand to his chest. "So, like what? The military? The Social Justice Legion? Could I be an auditor for the Social Value Audit program?"

"Anything you want. But I'll have to admit, I'd miss hearing you deliver the afternoon news."

Carter chortled. "You are kind to say so. Thank

you. But seriously, what about a person who scores a nine?"

"A nine is good. Very good in fact. That person is still a fantastic candidate for military service and many government jobs."

"But not the SVA program?"

Lawrence grinned. "Citizens who score a ten have displayed that they have an acute understanding of the values we cherish. So they make the best applicants for the Social Value Audit program."

"That makes sense. What level ranking becomes a cause for concern?"

"Obviously, we'd like everyone to be a ten, but citizens who score a five or above have nothing to worry about."

"And those who score below a five? What happens to them?"

"Social values are learned. We can't necessarily fault citizens who haven't been taught what it means to be a productive member of an advanced society.

"We'll be instituting education centers to help foster productive social values."

"Once people have been educated, can their rank increase? And also, are these education centers mandatory or voluntary?"

"Great question, Carter. For people who score below a five, social education is compulsory. And yes, the entire purpose of the education program is to bring up the ranking of our citizens. Once a citizen advances to a rank of five, they can choose if they would like to continue their education."

"Is anyone considered too-far-gone?"

"We hope not. Educational facilities for people who score ones and twos will be residential. People ranked as ones may find their accommodations somewhat restrictive, but that's for their safety and for the safety of society. Those who show a willingness to learn will quickly advance to a level-two facility, which will be less austere. Once a citizen's rank has been raised, that citizen will have a much easier time of things."

"Talk to us about threes? How are they educated?"

"They'll be required to attend classes five days a week. They'll be allowed to live on their own as long as they report to class regularly and show a willingness to improve. Otherwise, they'll be demoted and be assigned to a residential facility."

"Oh, so you can be demoted." Carter seemed genuinely surprised by this revelation.

"I doubt you ever would be, Carter. But yes, theoretically, citizens could allow themselves to read the wrong types of literature or be around the wrong types of people, which could hurt their rank."

"You said the wrong type of literature. What do you mean by that?"

"I think we can all agree that the Bible has been instrumental in causing more than its fair share of pain and discord."

"Yes, but everyone doesn't take it as literally as Blackwell and his cultish followers. What about people who just read it for enjoyment and inspiration?"

Lawrence looked at Carter Lellouche as if he

were being naive. "Carter, we've got some very inspiring literary works that inspire and bring enjoyment. If getting rid of this one book can bring healing to our society, don't you think it's worth the sacrifice? We're talking about racism, homophobia, violence, transphobia, xenophobia, hatred of others because of their beliefs; all of this pain can be traced back to one single book. Can't they just read something else for inspiration and enjoyment?"

Carter lifted his hands as if to praise Lawrence for his wisdom. "What a compelling explanation. Thank you for enlightening us. But you see how deeply rooted this brainwashing goes, don't you?"

Lawrence nodded. "That's why we're building the education centers."

"So, will the Bible be banned? Will people be incarcerated for owning one?"

"Whether it is legally banned or not will be up to Congress, but I can tell you that anyone caught with a copy will be immediately sent to a residential education center. Possession of a Bible is the dictionary definition of someone who isn't grasping what it means to be part a forward-thinking society."

Ava turned to her father. "Can you imagine all of the Christians who are in the regime states listening to this right now? They have to be freaking out!"

Ulysses adjusted his leg on the ottoman. "They shouldn't be surprised. In every communist revolution around the world, freedom of religion has been taken away in the very next breath after the guns are gone. In fact, every Christian who turned in his gun at one of the collection points should have handed in his Bible at the same time. It would have saved him a trip."

Ava smirked. "Yeah. I guess all those pastors who told their congregations to turn in their guns will be looking for a new line of work."

Ulysses sipped his coffee. "I'd imagine most of them are ranked pretty close to a ten on the SVA scale. They can go to a voluntary re-education camp until they get an even ten. They'll all make fine Social Value Auditors."

CHAPTER 5

And when he had fasted forty days and forty nights, he was afterward an hungred. And when the tempter came to him, he said, If thou be the Son of God, command that these stones be made bread. But he answered and said, It is written, Man shall not live by bread alone, but by every word that proceedeth out of the mouth of God.

Matthew 4:2-4

Ava felt weak Friday morning as she made her way to the living room. "Did you go to bed last night?"

Ulysses was sitting in the same place on the overstuffed couch. "Yeah, but my leg was bothering me, so I got up."

"You need rest for your wound to heal."

"And you need food. It's been forty-eight hours since you ate."

Ava filled a glass with water. "I'll have some milk or juice today if Foley doesn't get better."

She drank the entire glass of water, then picked up the phone and dialed the doctor. "Captain Murphy, hi, it's Ava."

"I was just getting ready to call you."

"Oh?" Her voice betrayed her worry.

"Relax, good news. Mostly."

"Mostly?"

"Foley's fever is completely gone. His system is functioning strongly, and all his vital signs are normalized."

"That's great! What's the catch?"

"I need to get him into surgery this morning."

"To take his leg?"

"Yes. I would have preferred to give the antibiotics another day, but resources around here are about to be stretched thin. Refugees are flooding out of Texas because of what Shane Lawrence said about the Bible yesterday. Blackwell is asking all Alliance military bases near borders of regime states to set up relief camps."

"That won't affect the hospital, will it?"

"I think it will. At best, we'll have folks coming in who are dehydrated, with various scrapes and bruises. Worst case scenario, we'll have combat casualties.

"I doubt Markovich is going to just let them walk out the door. If he does, he'll be the first communist dictator in history to allow a mass exodus of people who don't agree with his politics. They wouldn't be setting up re-education camps if they were planning on giving people a choice of staying or going.

"The Alliance States will be flying sorties along the borders for the next two weeks. We'll engage any troops or aircraft we see harassing the refugees trying to flee.

"Since Altus is so close to Texas, I'm sure we'll have lots of folks coming here over the next few days."

Ava listened closely, then replied, "I understand. When will he come out of surgery?"

"He should be waking up around noon. It would be good if you could be in the recovery room. He's been out for two days, plus he'll be waking up to one less leg than he had. It's going to be tough on his mind. A friendly face might help him cope."

"I'll be there, of course! You think the surgery will go okay?"

"Like I said, I wish we could have given the antibiotics another day, but I promise, I'll do my best. See you at twelve."

"Thank you." Ava placed the phone on the cradle.

"What did he say?" Ulysses inquired.

Ava relayed the information to her father, including the part about the refugees who were coming to the base.

"You'll eat? After Foley comes out of surgery?" Ulysses' eyes showed his concern.

Ava nodded. "If he comes through okay, and

he's stable, that's all I'm asking for. I'll consider that an answer to my prayers. Maybe I'll wheel you down to the recovery room, and we can all have dinner tonight."

"I can get over to the medical hangar on my crutches."

"You're not even supposed to have crutches. Why don't you let me push you in the chair? You wouldn't want to get Sergeant Griffith in trouble for going against the doctor's orders."

Ulysses grimaced to convey his displeasure. "I can wheel myself."

Ava took a shower, got dressed, and fixed herself up so she'd look nice for Foley. She said goodbye to Ulysses and began walking over to the hangar at 11:00 AM. On the way, she watched several giant C-17s land. Some were already on the tarmac and being offloaded. She mumbled to herself, "They must be bringing in supplies from other bases for the relief center."

Multiple cargo trucks filled with equipment drove by Ava before she reached the hangar. Once there, the building was buzzing with activity. She checked in with the front desk. "Hi, Captain Murphy told me to come by. I'm sure he's in surgery right now, but can you send him a text and let him know that Ava is here waiting when he's finished?"

"Yes, ma'am. It's my privilege." The young private behind the desk quickly sent the text.

"Thank you." She took a seat on a modest couch. A small television sat atop a simple metal storage shelf, which was backed up to a thin partition. Power was provided by heavy-gauge extension cords, which ran along the ground. Duct tape covered the electrical cords and secured them to the floor to mitigate tripping hazards.

The television played a live-streaming newscast produced from inside the Alliance States. Ava quickly recognized the broadcast as being supportive of Blackwell and the patriot states.

A manicured young man in a suit and tie delivered a report from a modern desk in front of a professional studio background. "Acting President of the Alliance States, Turner Blackwell, is requesting challengers to throw their names into the hat for a special presidential election for the Alliance States. Since he was appointed to the vice-presidency by President Ross, he does not want there to be any doubt about the legitimacy of his leadership role in the Alliance States.

"He has said that if he does prevail in the special election, he vows to step aside and resume his role as vice-president when President Ross is returned from his illegal incarceration by the Markovich regime."

"All eight of the other Alliance States governors held a vote of confidence yesterday evening in which they unanimously signaled their support for Acting-President Blackwell.

"In other news, the eastern half of Washington State has declared itself free and independent from the western portion of the state. The new state, which has joined the Alliance States, is called the

State of Liberty. Liberty has tried unsuccessfully in the past to break off from the western half of Washington, but now that shots have already been fired, residents of the eastern side no longer have to worry about triggering a second civil war.

"Acting-President Blackwell welcomed Liberty with open arms. The move not only strengthens the Alliance States but also shields the upper panhandle of Idaho from sharing that portion of its border with a state complicit with the rogue Markovich regime."

Ava smiled at the word choices of the reporter. She was pleased to hear him use terminology that acknowledged the Alliance States as the legitimate government and condemned Markovich's administration as the traitorous regime. Far too long had the right played fair while letting the left act with impunity in the political world, particularly when it came to the media.

"Ava." The doctor came from behind the partition.

"Captain Murphy, how did it go?" She stood up and waited in hopes of good news.

The doctor's expression did nothing to reassure her. He shook his head as if perplexed. "I don't know what to say."

"Is Foley okay? Is he alive?" Her forehead puckered, and she held her breath in anticipation.

Murphy quickly closed the space between them and put his hand on her shoulder. "Yes, he's fine. But his leg, I've never seen anything like it."

"You had to remove more than you thought?" Ava felt concerned, but as long as Foley was alive, she could handle it.

"No, no." He shook his head, his face still showing his confusion. "I probed his leg on Wednesday when he came in. I took out the bullet. The tissue inside was irreparable. I saw it for myself. I've even got photographs."

"I don't understand what you're telling me, doctor?"

"The wound channel—in his leg—it's nearly healed up. I didn't do anything."

Ava looked skeptically at the captain. "So, he might not have to lose his leg?"

"Oh, he'll definitely keep the leg. The only question is whether I let him walk out of here on it tonight."

Tears of joy flooded Ava's eyes. Emotion rushed through her stomach, heart, and throat. She covered her mouth with her hands. "Are you serious?"

"I would never joke about such a thing. But I really don't have any way of explaining it other than a miracle."

She looked upward. "Thank you, Jesus. Thank you, God!"

Ava brought her gaze back to earth. "Is he awake?"

"I've cut off the sedatives. He'll be coming around soon. Come on. I'll take you back to him."

She followed Captain Murphy. "When can we leave? To go home?"

"I'd like to see Foley and your dad a couple more times, but things are going to get hectic around here. Bring them both in tomorrow morning. As long as everything looks good, you can all go home after that. Your truck is down in motor pool."

"We left our truck at the battle site."

"Right. Two of the men drove it back here. Motor pool took the liberty of cleaning it up for you. Tune-up, oil change, the works. I think I mentioned that you're something of a celebrity."

"Yeah, you did. Wow. That's so fantastic. I suppose I could hang around if you guys need help with the refugees."

The doctor shook his head. "We don't have a vetting process in place for the refugees yet. In all likelihood, Markovich will have spies mixed in, wolves among the sheep. Given your notoriety, I think it would be better if you kept your distance. But thanks for offering."

Captain Murphy pulled back a curtain to reveal Foley sleeping on a bed. All the tubes and monitors had been removed from him.

"Thank you again for all you've done."

"Glad I could help with the infection, but the leg, I can't take credit for that." He waved and walked away.

Ava stood at Foley's bedside for the next half hour. His eyelids moved from time to time and his head shifted, but he did not wake up.

An orderly brought her a chair. "Here you go, ma'am. It might be a while. I can keep an eye on him and call you when he wakes up if you need to take a break."

"No, the chair is fine, thanks." Ava took a seat and held Foley's hand for another forty minutes.

Finally, he gripped her hand. His head turned

toward her. His eyes opened slightly.

"Hey there. How you feelin'?" She smiled gently at him.

His eyes opened wider, and he returned the smile. "Thirsty."

Ava took the small sippy cup on the stand next to his bed and held it to his lips. "Here. Drink."

Foley took a shallow sip. "Thanks. How long have I been out?"

"Four years. The war is over."

"Are you serious? Who won?"

She giggled and kissed him on the cheek. "I'm kidding. You've only been out for two days."

He chuckled. "You're cruel."

"If I were cruel, I'd have kept it up. I'd have told you Markovich won."

He put his head down and closed his eyes. "I knew you were kidding anyway."

"Oh yeah? How?"

"You've still got that silly ring on. No way you'd wait four years for me."

She kissed him. "I'd wait forty years for you. And don't ever call my ring silly."

"What did I miss?"

"You just rest and take it easy for now. I'll fill you in later. Once the doctor releases you, we'll all go have dinner together in the dining facility— you, Dad, and me."

"Dining facility? You mean like a DFAC? Where are we?"

"Altus Air Force Base, Oklahoma."

"Near your dad's home?"

"Not far; it's about five hours from here. And it's

our home—at least for now."

"I thought you said Texas would always be your home."

She held his hand tight. "Wherever you, Dad, Buckley, and Charity are; that's my home."

CHAPTER 6

Thine hand shall find out all thine enemies: thy right hand shall find out those that hate thee. Thou shalt make them as a fiery oven in the time of thine anger: the Lord shall swallow them up in his wrath, and the fire shall devour them. Their fruit shalt thou destroy from the earth, and their seed from among the children of men. For they intended evil against thee: they imagined a mischievous device, which they are not able to perform. Therefore shalt thou make them turn their back, when thou shalt make ready thine arrows upon thy strings against the face of them. Be thou exalted, Lord, in thine own strength: so will we sing and praise thy power.

Psalm 21:8-13

In a small ceremony at Ulysses' farm, Ava and Foley were married on New Year's Day. Many weeks passed and March arrived. With it came the first mild days in northeastern Oklahoma.

Ava sat at the foot of the bed watching Foley pack his rucksack. "If your militia team leaves, who'll guard the border?"

Foley did not look up. "Markovich would never hit Oklahoma from the Missouri border."

"I wouldn't be so sure about that. If he were to target Tulsa, he'd have to come across the Missouri border. Arkansas, like the other southern states, is neutral. If he launched an attack across the Arkansas border, he'd risk tipping them over to the Alliance."

Foley packed several pairs of socks and dark-colored tee-shirts into the mouth of the pack. "That whole neutral thing isn't going to last long. The fight is getting bloodier by the day. Sooner or later, the south is going to have to pick a side. Iowa and Minnesota thought they'd remain neutral as well, but the SJL is using them to launch border skirmishes against Nebraska and the Dakotas."

She crossed her arms. "Which validates my point about you being needed here, to guard our border with Minnesota."

"The militia is strong. They'll still be able to hold the border without my team. When Markovich makes his play, experienced soldiers like us will be needed to counter the attack. The intelligence on this assault is good. Markovich will be moving in the next few days. My team has to be ready to mobilize the moment we know where he's taking the fight."

Ava fiddled with the simple gold wedding band on her finger. She wore the homemade wire engagement ring on a thin chain around her neck. It was too fragile for daily wear. She thought back to the days when she'd worried if Foley was going to pull through and survive the infection. Ava realized many more days enduring a heart heavy with concern awaited her.

God had healed Foley's leg, although she hadn't specifically prayed for such a miracle. She'd only requested that He spare Foley's life. She'd not asked for God to heal his leg because she'd thought it too great a thing for which to petition. But sitting in their small bedroom at her father's house, watching Foley pack for war, she wondered. *Had I known that God would heal his leg, would I have asked Him to? If he'd lost his leg, he wouldn't be running off to war. Yes, I'd be waiting on him hand and foot, but he'd be here, with me; safe—and done with fighting.*

Ava recognized her terrible selfishness in the thought, but she couldn't help it. No matter, God had done as He so desired, and Foley would follow his heart into the battle. Ava could change neither of those things. Her duty was only to accept them as they came. However, she didn't have to like it.

The bedroom door creaked open. Buckley nudged his way into the room, tail wagging.

"You won't leave me, will you, Buck?" Ava patted the bed, signaling for the dog to join her.

Foley dropped his pack on the ground, came to her and embraced her face for a long, passionate kiss. "I'm not leaving you. I'll be back. I promise."

She believed him, at least as far as it depended on him. But she was not so naive as to think the circumstances were very much under his control. After the kiss she pressed his head to her chest, caressing his hair with her fingers. "It would be so much easier if you'd just stay."

He lay next to her, motionless for a few stolen minutes. "Easy has never been my way of doing things. And you, of all people, should understand what it's like to have this conviction. You dragged your dad and your friends into the fight because you knew it was the right thing to do, and that it had to be done."

She wondered if she'd have done things differently—knowing what she knew now, the violence, the death, the sorrow, the stains on her mind, the images of brutality that would never go away. "I won't try to stop you, Foley. But I do not consent. You've done enough. So has Dad. And I've given all I've got to this war that just keeps on taking. Now it wants my husband. I've earned my right to hold a grudge against this conflict."

Foley got up and resumed packing. "That's what war does. It takes and takes, and never cares about the feelings of those it deprives. Believe me, if the stakes were anything less than the freedom to worship my God and protect my family, I'd gladly stay on the bench for this one."

He looked up and gazed into her eyes. "But if we lose, if the Alliance falls, we won't have any semblance of a life together anyway. We'll be slaves. And I'd rather die than live in bondage."

"Where will your team go when it's time to leave?"

"We'll meet up with other militia members at the Tulsa Air National Guard Base. They'll give us a lift to wherever we're going."

"You'll send me a text every night to let me know you're still alive?"

"When I have service. Remember, Markovich will use every trick in the book to disrupt communications. So, if you don't hear from me for a few days, it doesn't mean anything is wrong."

She frowned. "It doesn't mean everything is okay either. Text me as often as you can."

"I will." He nodded. "I promise."

A gentle rap came to the bedroom door followed by Charity's soft voice. "Hey, guys. You wanted me to let you know when the Patriot News Network started their five o'clock evening broadcast. It's on."

"Thanks, we'll be right out," Ava replied.

Foley leaned his rucksack in the corner. "I'll finish packing later."

Ava stood up and led the way to the living room. "Come on, Buck."

Ulysses came in the back door through the kitchen to join the others for the nightly news program. He leaned heavily on his cane.

"You doing okay, Dad?" Ava watched him press against the walking stick.

"I'm fine. I might have overdone it in the garden. I think it's atrophy from not moving much since I was shot. Getting out there and digging around in the soil is probably the best thing for me."

Ava felt guilty for even thinking it, but she couldn't help but feel some sense of relief that Ulysses, in his present compromised state, wouldn't be running off to battle. She plopped down on the couch next to Foley. Charity sat on the loveseat by herself, while Ulysses took the easy chair, propping up his leg on the foot rest.

The reporter for the Patriot News Network had already begun the broadcast. "Regime forces out of Denver launched a three-pronged attack early this morning. Ground troops crossed the border into Utah, pushing local militias and Alliance border patrols back to Provo. Thirty-four citizens of the Alliance States were killed in the assault before regime forces were repelled by air support.

"A separate group of SJL fighters crossed into Wyoming, penetrating to just outside of Cheyenne where they fired a barrage of artillery shells into the city. Alliance ground troops stationed at Francis E. Warren Air Force Base were able to push the SJL fighters back with the help of combat helicopters from the airbase, but not before significant loss of life and property. Several large buildings were damaged beyond repair by the shelling and casualties are estimated to be in the hundreds from the attack.

"The third action was taken against Ogallala, Nebraska, where regime forces sent an overwhelming number of ground troops, armored vehicles, and military supplies. Regime forces have taken the town and are embedded amongst the surviving residents. Markovich appeared today on multiple mainstream media stations which have been complicit in his communist overthrow of the country from the beginning. In his interviews, he stated that Ogallala was the first step in reclaiming Nebraska and bringing the state under regime control.

"In actuality, Ogallala is a town of less than five thousand, so taking it by no means equates to taking the entire state of Nebraska. However, Nebraska is a critical state to the Alliance because it connects geographically Kansas and Oklahoma to the northern Alliance States. If Markovich were somehow able to take Nebraska, Kansas and Oklahoma would be prime targets."

Ava put her hand on Foley's knee. "Do you think this is it? The big attack that the militia has been talking about?"

He shook his head. "I don't think so. The regime didn't take any ground except Ogallala. This smells like a classic fake. I bet Markovich is going to try to draw the Alliance into Nebraska for a supposed ultimate contest, all the while, directing the majority of his forces somewhere else for the real battle.

"But the reporter is right. Blackwell can't sit back and do nothing about Ogallala. He has to engage the regime there."

Ulysses added, "I agree, this is a red herring. I'm sure Blackwell is smart enough to not fall into the trap."

The reporter continued his presentation. "Acting President Blackwell is making one last call to Alliance citizens to give whatever they can to help support the masses of Christians and conservatives who have flooded in to seek refuge. Alliance relief centers have not lost anyone to starvation yet, but many refugees are malnourished and living on a single meal a day. While the Alliance is positioned to produce massive amounts of excess crops in the coming season, this past winter has been rough.

"Supply lines have been shut down and the Alliance States are cut off from all available seaports. The country has been forced to survive with what we have on hand. Knowing that we need to be self-sufficient, the Alliance will be able to build sufficient reserves in the coming growing season, but obviously, very few of us understood the suddenness or severity of this conflict.

"Canada's claim to remain neutral in the conflict has come under question by Acting-President Blackwell since they have been unwilling to trade with the Alliance or even allow goods to be transported across the northern borders of Idaho, Montana, or North Dakota. Canada's Prime Minister has assured Acting-President Blackwell that the regime-controlled states are being treated the same, but since Markovich controls the east and west coasts, the consequences are not nearly so severe.

"The UN is recognizing Markovich as the legitimate president, despite undeniable evidence that the outcome of the election would have been in Ross' favor, had it not been for the intimidation tactics against Ross supporters by Antifa and the Social Justice Warriors League.

"The Alliance Press Secretary Jim Wright gave an interview to the Patriot Times this morning where he stated that the administration is not surprised that the UN is siding with Markovich since they essentially share the same far-left communist agenda. He went on to comment on how unfortunate it is that the EU and most of America's allies will follow the lead of the UN in failing to recognize the Alliance States. Thus far, Israel has been the only country to break ranks with the UN in formally acknowledging the Alliance States as a valid power, although they have not gone so far as to offer military nor humanitarian support.

"Thank you for joining us for this broadcast. The Patriot News Network reminds you to keep our service men and women in prayer. Since we are considered to be a pariah on the world stage, if we are to prevail in this conflict, it can only be through God's providence. Take care of yourselves and each other, America. Godspeed and God bless."

Ava clicked off the television. "We've still got an hour before sunset. What else needs to be done in the garden, Dad?"

"Not much. You could plant some more tomatoes, peppers, cabbage, and cucumbers in the starter trays. But they need to stay on the back porch. We're not out of the woods for frost just yet. By the time they need to be transplanted, we'll be in the clear."

"Okay, I'll take care of that. Foley, do you want to give me a hand?"

"Sure." He stood up with Ava.

"I'll get dinner started," Charity said.

"Thanks." Ava turned to the dog. "Buck, you make sure Dad stays off his bum leg. We'll be right back."

CHAPTER 7

Love suffers long and is kind; love does not envy; love does not parade itself, is not puffed up; does not behave rudely, does not seek its own, is not provoked, thinks no evil; does not rejoice in iniquity, but rejoices in the truth; bears all things, believes all things, hopes all things, endures all things. Love never fails.

1 Corinthians 13:4-8a

Before daybreak Friday morning, Ava awoke to the sound of knocking on her bedroom door.

"Foley?" Ulysses' voice called from the other side.

"Yeah," he replied groggily.

"Militia commander is on the Ham radio for you."

"Be right there." He slowly eased out of the bed.

"What do you think it is?" Ava knew it was most likely the dreaded call that would steal her husband away from her and into the arms of his fearsome mistress, war. Yet she hoped against hope the summons could have another interpretation.

Foley pulled on his jeans. "I don't know. I'll tell you after I speak with the commander."

He was being gentle. Ava knew that Foley saw no ambiguities in the purpose of the pre-dawn communiqué.

Ava sat upright in bed, awaiting his return. Minutes later, Foley came back and took a seat beside her. Ava's heart sank before he began speaking.

"We've gotta move out. Markovich invaded Liberty and Idaho. They think he used Seattle as a base to launch an attack against Liberty. Armored vehicles are outside of Spokane right now. The commander said it's a pretty heated battle. But the real problem is in Boise."

"That's Blackwell's base of operations!" Ava's forehead puckered. "What's happening there?"

"Supposedly, the administration has been evacuated. They've taken Blackwell to an undisclosed location, Montana probably. But Markovich hit Boise with an overwhelming force. The commander thinks he initiated that movement out of Portland. The regime would have had a large pool of new recruits considering Antifa's popularity in Portland. If he minimized his training and induction process for new soldiers, Markovich would have been able to keep a very small footprint for troop movements in preparation for the attack."

Ava twirled the edge of the sheet between her fingers. "I guess you were right about what you said yesterday. The attacks out of Denver, they were just a smoke screen."

"Yeah." Foley hugged her tightly. "But I need to get going. My ride will be here in fifteen minutes."

"Fifteen minutes? I won't even have time to say goodbye!"

"Then don't say it. Just say *see ya later*." He kissed her on the forehead. "I'll be back—soon."

Ava's eyes were still puffy from sleep. "I'm coming with you. I can have a bag packed by the time they get here."

"You said you're done with the war."

"I am, but I want to be with you. I don't care where, and the conditions don't matter." She threw off the sheet and began to get out of bed.

"No, Ava." He restrained her shoulders to keep her from getting up. "You can't come."

"Why?"

"You just can't. You haven't trained with us and . . ."

"And what?" she demanded.

"And I don't function as well on the battlefield when you're there. When you're around, you are my priority. The mission has to be the priority."

"I have to come. I have to be there—to protect you." She pushed him back and sprung from the bed.

"No! That's not how this is supposed to work."

He grabbed her tightly, pulling her back from the closet where she'd already managed to grab her assault pack. "I love you. I know how painful this is for you. It's excruciating for me. But I *will* come home. You have to trust me and you have to trust God!"

She let the pack drop to the floor. She turned and hugged him for what could be the last embrace with her husband on this earth. The two held each other for most of the fifteen minutes Foley had to get ready.

A horn honked out front.

"I've gotta go." He kissed her, slung his rifle over his shoulder, grabbed his rucksack, a shirt, and his boots, then hurried out the door barefooted and shirtless.

She grabbed her robe from the hook on the back of the door and followed after him. "I'll be praying for you. Take care. I love you!"

"I love you, too!" He waved as he got into the back of the pickup truck.

In the days that followed, Ava tried desperately to keep her mind occupied with tending the garden and doing chores around the house. She barely spoke to Charity and her father. She checked her phone every ten minutes to see if she'd gotten a new text from Foley. Faithfully, he let her know that he was alive, but he could not provide any additional details that might compromise his team if the messages were intercepted. Ava could only speculate where he might be and what actions he might be involved in. She watched the morning and evening editions of the Patriot News Network as well as broadcasts from the mainstream media outlets, which were sympathetic to the regime. She knew the information delivered by the mainstream media was little more than propaganda for Markovich, but she listened closely for the slightest detail that could have been missed by the Patriot News Network and might provide a clue about Foley's whereabouts.

Despite her diligence, all of the data she took in from her various sources only proved to give her more questions; questions with no answers about the location or state of peril concerning her beloved. Having exhausted all other options, she relented and begged God to give her sufficient faith to trust Him with Foley's life. Each morning before rising and each night before bed, she pleaded with God to bring Foley home—alive.

Three weeks passed since Foley's deployment. Ava finished her work in the garden and rushed to get cleaned up before the five o'clock news on Thursday evening.

Charity joined her and Buckley on the couch near the tail end of the broadcast. "Anything new?"

Ava looked up from her phone. "What?"

"The news, did they have anything new to report?"

"Oh, no. Same stuff. Markovich is holding the southwestern corner of Idaho. The panhandle is standing strong and the militia in Liberty have completely expelled the regime from eastern Washington."

"Still no word from Foley?"

Ava looked back at her phone. "No, but it hasn't even been forty-eight hours since his last text. It's been as long as three days before. Signals aren't reliable in a war zone."

"He'll be okay." Charity patted Ava's leg.

Ulysses came in and took his seat in the easy chair. He'd stopped using the cane, but he still babied his leg when he walked. He'd always walked with an almost undetectable limp from his previous surgeries, but it was more pronounced after the most recent injury. "How's the garden looking?"

Ava put her phone in her back pocket. "Green beans and lettuce are coming up. So is the corn. But we could use some rain. Charity and I try to water every day, but it's a lot of ground to cover."

Buckley jumped off the couch and walked to the window.

"What is it, Buck?" Ava watched him closely.

Buckley started with a low growl, which soon grew into a full-fledged fit of barking.

She got up from the couch and peered out the window. "Humvees, two of them!"

Ulysses stood quickly. "Charity, take Buckley to the bathroom, then get your rifle and take cover near your bedroom door. Ava, get my rifle and stash it behind the door. Get yours and take up a position in the kitchen. If you hear me say *I have no choice*, come out shooting."

"Yes, sir." Ava sprinted to get Ulysses' rifle and her own. She propped Ulysses' gun against the wall near the front door where he stood peeking out the peephole. Ava squatted behind the refrigerator with her AR-15 ready to engage.

Ulysses called out to the girls, "The Hummers have Alliance insignia on the doors, but that still doesn't explain why they'd be here with no invitation and no advanced warning. If they're aware of who we are, they should have known better than to come slipping up on us.

"Two people just got out. One has on a black suit. The other has on a full military dress uniform, highly decorated." He paused for a moment. "Gold oak leaves, he's a colonel."

Ava's heart sank. If they were being attacked, the hostiles would send more than two people. And they wouldn't be wearing dress uniforms. This was worse than an attack. The only possible reason for the visit was to inform her that Foley had been killed.

Seconds later, she heard the knock. Ulysses didn't open the door, rather he called out from inside, "What do you want?"

"We'd like to speak with Ava Wilson."

"It's Mitchem," she whispered under her breath. She was honored that the military had sent such a high-ranking officer to notify the widow, especially since Foley was in the militia and not the regular army, but she couldn't understand how they'd botched her name.

"Sorry, no one here by that name," Ulysses replied, still not opening the door.

"What about Ava Adams?" the voice inquired.

"Getting warmer, but still not right," she said under her breath.

"I'm sorry, you have the wrong address. Have a

nice day," Ulysses said.

The voice implored him yet again. "Am I speaking with First Sergeant Ulysses Adams?"

Ava had never heard anyone address her father by his rank.

The voice continued, "We have a message for Ava, First Sergeant. It's from the acting president."

"Condolences from Blackwell," she whispered to herself. Ava felt sure it was nothing more than a form letter that may or may not have Blackwell's actual signature. It would say something about the great debt of gratitude that the Alliance owed to Foley Mitchem for his faithful service and absolute sacrifice in the contest for freedom. To not take it would be dishonoring to her husband. She leaned her rifle against the refrigerator and stood up. Ava checked her pistol tucked in the back of her jeans and pulled her shirt down over it. With her head already hung in mourning, she made her way to the front door. "It's okay, Dad. It's about Foley."

Ulysses seemed to know the nature of the visit without her explanation. His lips pressed tightly together and his eyes looked pained. He nodded and stepped back from the door.

Ava swallowed hard, took a deep breath, straightened her arms to steel herself for the grim report. She unlocked the deadbolt and opened the door. "I'm Ava. Ava Mitchem."

The man in the dress uniform looked at the one in the black suit as if this reply had taken him by surprise.

The man in the dark suit nodded to his compatriot as if to indicate this was indeed the woman in question.

"Ms. Mitchem," said the colonel.

"Mrs." She was aghast at the colonel's lack of decorum, especially over such a sensitive matter.

The colonel said, "I'm sorry, Mrs. Mitchem, Acting-President Blackwell requests the honor of your presence for a private meeting."

"Excuse me?"

"The acting president would like to speak with you, in private."

She looked behind the door at her father, then at the two vehicles parked out front. Ava was totally confused. "Is he dead?"

"Pardon me?"

"Is he dead?"

"Are you asking me if the president is dead?" The colonel looked as if he'd just awoken from a strange and disturbing dream.

"No! My husband, Foley Mitchem. If he's dead, why can't you just tell me! What's all this business about Blackwell wanting to see me?"

Ulysses stepped forward. "What's going on? Why are you people here? State your business plainly. If you have some news about Foley, just spit it out. Can't you see that you're upsetting my daughter?"

The man in the black suit pulled out a business card and handed it to Ulysses. "Look, First Sergeant, I'm not sure why you think we're here, but I assure you, we have no other motive than the one Colonel Barr has already told you.

"But please, allow me to restate our assignment. I'm Agent John Schaub with the Secret Service.

Unfortunately, we do not have any information about Foley Mitchem. We do, however, have a request from the acting president for an informal meeting with Ava. You'd be welcomed to come along, First Sergeant, as the acting president may want to involve you in the conversation as well."

"Blackwell is here?" Ulysses looked out at the Humvees.

"No, but he's very close. We can take you to him," Schaub replied.

Filled with hesitant-relief, Ava looked at her father, then at the two men. "So, Foley is still alive?"

The colonel took a deep breath. "As Agent Schaub has said, we don't have information regarding your husband. Since he's fighting with the militia we don't have any means of finding out his status or location."

Ava's worry over Foley slowly faded. "But why does President Blackwell want to talk to me?"

"The subject matter is confidential." The colonel straightened his jacket.

"Can I refuse?"

"It's a free country—at least for a little while longer. But the acting president really hopes you'll speak with him, ma'am."

Ulysses crossed his arms tightly. "Hold on! How did you people find us? And how did you know Foley is in the militia?"

Agent Schaub answered. "We spoke with some people at Altus Air Force Base. We heard Ava had been there with her father and her wounded fiancé. Sorry, we didn't know the two of you had gotten married since you were at Altus."

"That doesn't answer either of my questions completely."

Schaub put his hands in the air. "Please, allow me to finish. The sergeant who we spoke with at Altus said he thought you might be heading in this direction. We passed out pictures to military outposts and border security teams to keep an eye out for you folks. We got a call from a militia commander two days ago saying that he'd recently deployed Foley Mitchem and knew where he'd been staying."

Ulysses' eyes showed that he still didn't totally trust the man. "If Blackwell wants a meeting, he can call us."

The Secret Service agent frowned. "Very well." He pulled a phone out of his pocket and dialed a number. "Mr. President, I'm afraid they need confirmation from you personally." Seconds later, he said, "Yes, sir. I'll put you on with Mrs. Ava Mitchem, now." He paused. "Yes, sir, she's recently been married."

Ava took the phone. "Hello?"

CHAPTER 8

And David said unto Saul, Thy servant kept his father's sheep, and there came a lion, and a bear, and took a lamb out of the flock: And I went out after him, and smote him, and delivered it out of his mouth: and when he arose against me, I caught him by his beard, and smote him, and slew him. Thy servant slew both the lion and the bear: and this uncircumcised Philistine shall be as one of them, seeing he hath defied the armies of the living God. David said moreover, The Lord that delivered me out of the paw of the lion, and out of the paw of the bear, he will deliver me out of the hand of this Philistine. And Saul said unto David, Go, and the Lord be with thee.

1 Samuel 17:34-37

"Mrs. Mitchem, I was hoping to have a word with you. I wanted to personally thank you for your efforts in supporting the Alliance, but I also have a request which is . . . rather confidential in nature. Do you think I could have a few minutes of your time? I assure you I'll get right to the point and won't tie you up any longer than necessary."

Blackwell had been Ava's first choice in the Republican primaries. She held him in higher regard than any other politician because of his staunch position on freedom and many other issues she held dear. She recognized his voice, yet she was dumbfounded to actually be speaking with him on the phone. Her mouth hung open but made no sound.

"Mrs. Mitchem, are you there?" Blackwell asked.

"Um, yes, yes, I'm here. Of course, yes, sure. I'll follow Agent Schaub."

"Great, but Agent Schaub will give you a lift. They're being a little persnickety about keeping my location under wraps, even amongst friends. Markovich would stop at nothing to find out where I'm at. I'm sure you understand."

"Absolutely, Mr. President." She wasn't sure what else to say. "I'll see you soon." She hung up and immediately began rethinking her word choice. *See you soon? That's what I'd say to Charity. What a klutz!* Ava handed the phone back to the agent.

"Thanks."

"Shall we proceed?" Colonel Barr held his hand out.

Ava looked at her father.

He asked, "What are we doing?"

"Going to meet the president, I guess."

Ulysses said to Agent Schaub, "We're both armed. I understand you people have protocols when it comes to the president. Is that going to be a problem?"

The agent began walking down the steps. "Normally, yes. But the acting president specifically requested that we not infringe upon your rights."

"I'll just let Charity know where we're going. Or why we're going, rather. I guess I can't tell her where if I don't know." Ava turned to go back in.

Charity was waiting in her bedroom, still holding her rifle. "I heard the whole thing! Are you sure it's Blackwell? Do you think it could be a trap? Like somebody impersonating his voice, a computer or something?"

"No. It's him. I'm sure of it. I'll see you when I see you," Ava said.

"Be safe. I'll let Buckley out after the vehicles leave the drive."

"Thanks, bye." Ava felt the excitement rising in her stomach over the opportunity to meet Blackwell.

They approached the first Humvee. Agent Schaub handed a black cloth head covering to Ava and Ulysses. "Sorry I have to ask this of you, but if you'll put these on, it will be better for everyone. If you know where the acting president is staying, it could make you a target."

Ava watched Ulysses get in the vehicle and put the bag over his head. She did the same.

Ava listened as the vehicle drove for about an hour with very little chit-chat between the driver, the colonel, Agent Schaub, and herself. Finally, they came to a stop.

Ava's door was opened for her, then she heard Agent Schaub's voice. "Please leave your coverings on until we're inside."

Someone, Agent Schaub she assumed, led her by the hand through a door.

"You can remove your covering," said Schaub.

Ava pulled the sack off her head. She was inside the foyer of an old farmhouse. It must have been a brilliant spectacle in its day, but the antique dwelling had been neglected and never restored.

"Follow me, please." Agent Schaub led Ava and Ulysses through a set of double doors to the formal parlor.

Inside were several men and women, most of whom were dressed like Agent Schaub. Ava's eyes went straight to Blackwell standing nearby.

"Mrs. Mitchem, Mr. Adams, thank you for joining me." Blackwell extended his hand and embraced Ava's.

She felt like a school girl meeting her favorite movie star. "Please, call me Ava. It's a pleasure and an honor to meet you, Mr. President."

Ulysses also shook hands with the man. "Thank you for having us, Mr. President."

"Please make yourselves comfortable." Blackwell led them to the sitting area where they all took a seat.

Ava told herself the whole trip over that she wouldn't mention it, but whether it was nerves or uncontrollable geekiness, the instant she sat down, she blurted out, "I voted for you in the primaries."

Blackwell smiled. "I'll confess. I may have trolled your old Facebook posts before I invited you. I saw what an avid supporter you were. Thank you."

"Oh, I deleted my Facebook page."

Blackwell smiled. "Facebook is sorta like Hotel California. You can check out but you can never leave."

Ava curled her lip in disgust. "I wish someone would have made that creepy analogy to me before I signed up for it."

"Don't we all." Blackwell chuckled but his smile faded quickly. "I wish the circumstances of the meeting were better."

Ava sat forward on the couch and gave Blackwell her full attention.

"As you know, Markovich has taken Boise. In fact, his forces are currently holding the entire southwest corner of the state, all the way to Twin Falls. Boise is a big loss. It was very disruptive for us to pack up shop and relocate our administrative offices. But in the battle for confidence, it's absolutely devastating."

"You'll retake the ground. You've got the troops and the equipment. Right?" Ava didn't like the tone of defeat she was hearing in Blackwell's voice.

He exhaled deeply before continuing. "We can and we will. But Markovich understands what this invasion has done to the spirit behind the Alliance States. For him, any sacrifice to keep us out of Boise is worth it. And if we announce another capital, say Helena or Bismarck, he'll target that city as well.

"At some point, it's a numbers game. Markovich has the population. He has masses of millennials who have been indoctrinated into a die-hard commitment to socialism through the public schools and colleges."

"You mean communism," Ulysses corrected the acting president.

Blackwell nodded. "Communism, but they've been taught that it's socialism, so that's what they think it is. It softened it up a little, kept their parents from doing anything radical like jerking them out of the public brainwashing camps and homeschooling them."

"Right." Ulysses nodded.

"In addition to the huge pool of potential soldiers, Markovich is demanding two years of military service when people graduate from level-two re-education camps. That's how folks atone for their sins of dissent and prove they are good comrades, loyal to the regime."

"I don't understand why you're sharing all of this with me. What could I possibly do?" Ava instantly regretted asking.

"I'm glad you asked, Ava." Blackwell crossed his hands and looked her in the eye. "Rumor has it that you took it upon yourself to rip off the Social Justice Legion for a couple cases of explosives."

"Is that so?"

He nodded. "Subsequently, similar types of explosives were used to take down firearm collection centers around your stomping grounds. As a matter of fact, the regime thinks C-4 was used in the NRG Stadium attack in Houston when Steve Woods was assassinated."

"Wait a minute! Woods was knocked off by Markovich because he didn't want to wait until January to ascend the throne," Ava protested.

Blackwell nodded pensively. "So you have first-hand knowledge of the Houston attack."

Ava shrugged her shoulders. "As you say—rumor has it."

Blackwell grinned as if he were enjoying her coyness. "Fair enough. But let's assume for a moment you were somehow involved in such a string of events. Ripping off the SJL, perhaps we could write that off as luck or providence. But then, taking out all the major firearm collection points in Austin, and getting away with it—that took planning, skills, and determination.

"Now, to the grand finale, the assault at NRG— that took all of the above: providence, skill, planning, determination. But to hit a public gathering that you, or whoever, knew would be swarming with security and regime Secret Service, that took—guts."

"Or stupidity." Ava looked at her folded hands. "I'm afraid you're inventing some superhero in your mind that doesn't exist, Mr. President. One thing you left out in your list of attributes for this mysterious heroine is a team. And don't assume because some of the people involved in those actions were never caught, that everyone escaped the wrath of Markovich. Some people paid the ultimate sacrifice for those actions."

She looked at the floor, remembering Dr. and Mrs. Hodge, James, and how perilously close to death Foley had come. "At least that's what I hear through the grapevine."

"I wish I could offer my condolences to the friends and family of those brave souls." Blackwell took a solemn tone.

Ava did not reply.

Blackwell paused a moment as if to let her remember her fallen friends before continuing. Then he said, "And what was this incident down at the Texas Oklahoma border? Some sort of prisoner exchange? I know without a doubt that you were involved in that one. Altus Air Force Base bailed you out. That's how I found you."

Ulysses interrupted, "Can you tell us what you've called us here for, Mr. President?"

"Okay." Blackwell's eyes shifted back and forth from Ava to Ulysses. "As I stated, this war is going to come down to a numbers game. And to put it quite simply, we don't have the numbers. Maybe we can hold out for a year, maybe even two, but at some point, the Alliance will be defeated. Millions of patriots are going to fight and die, and we're still going to lose. That's the brutal facts."

Ulysses snatched the bait Blackwell was dangling in front of their noses. "Unless?"

"Unless—we get the southern states." Blackwell ticked off the states on his fingers. "West Virginia, Kentucky, Tennessee, the Carolinas, Georgia,

Alabama, Mississippi, Louisiana, and Arkansas. The governors of every one of those states are just waiting for somebody else to go first. Arkansas shares a border with Oklahoma, so I've been working hardest on getting them to join. If they do, I'm praying it will start a chain reaction, and they'll all topple like dominoes—in our direction. If the southern states join the Alliance, we'll have a fighting chance. But without them, we're simply stretched too thin on soldiers and resources."

"And I suppose you're going to explain how we can miraculously convince them to join." Ava's curiosity was eating her alive.

Blackwell held up one finger. "Bear with me for one more minute. I've had meetings and conversations with every one of the governors from the southern states. The main thing that is keeping them from making the commitment to join is a significant population of far-left socialists in their respective states. Remember, the indoctrination by the education system, media, and Hollywood has been in full force in the south just the same as it has been in the rest of the country."

Ulysses shook his head. "You're talking about forty years of damage, rewriting history, expelling God from the classroom, removing critical thinking skills from students; you can't undo that in a day. There's no silver bullet."

Blackwell responded, "Maybe there is."

"Like what?" Ava asked.

"The militant leftists, they've been taught to believe contradiction after contradiction."

"You mean like communism and anarchy are

almost the same, be tolerant of everyone unless they disagree with you, and disincentivizing hard work is the best way to have a productive society?" Ava asked.

"I was thinking about how hard the left fought for equality so they could rate themselves between a one and a ten with the SVA program, but yeah—what you said." Blackwell smiled. "I should've had you writing my campaign speeches.

"Back to what I was saying. This constant state of contradiction leaves the leftist youth in a sort of unconscious mode of not really having any true convictions. They've been purposely taught not to think for themselves. They need a leader, sort of a Pied Piper to keep them marching to the beat of the revolutionary drum. Markovich isn't that person. He doesn't connect with them. He can't motivate them to actually get involved and get in the fight."

"Shane Lawrence. He's the Pied Piper!" Ava sat up straight.

Blackwell snapped his fingers. "Bingo!"

CHAPTER 9

For unto whomsoever much is given, of him shall be much required: and to whom men have committed much, of him they will ask the more.

Luke 12:48b

"So, what are you asking, Mr. President?" Ava felt sure she knew the answer.

Blackwell leaned back on the couch and crossed his legs. "Cut off the head of the snake. Give those governors a chance to do the right thing without having Lawrence put out a call to burn down their capital buildings."

"Don't you have clandestine services for this sort of thing? Why are you calling on us?" Ulysses asked.

Blackwell replied, "CIA, NSA, DIA, they're all in DC. And the top levels have long been infiltrated by the same people who are trying to pull off this revolution. Do you think people like Szabos would have ever been able to push the overthrow of America this far without those agencies being complicit in the scheme? Sure, we've had some good people from the intelligence community defect to the Alliance, but remember, they worked side by side with the enemy. And don't think for a minute that Markovich isn't watching their every move."

"You think he isn't watching me?" Ava asked. "My face was plastered all over the news after the explosives heist and the collection-point bombings."

"The news cycle is pretty short. People don't remember stuff from one week to the next. Besides, we could help you with a disguise, although I suspect you may know a thing or two about that already. Your face being on the news didn't seem to deter additional attacks," said Blackwell.

"What exactly would the mission entail?" she inquired.

"Slip into California, as a leftist refugee perhaps. Get close to Lawrence and take him out."

Ava threw her hands in the air. "Oh, is that all? Why didn't you just say so?" She got up from the couch. "Mr. President, it was an honor meeting you, but whatever role I had in the resistance, if any at all, I'm done. Could you please ask Agent Schaub to take us home?"

Blackwell said nothing for a long time. Ava stood, waiting for his response.

Finally, he looked up, staring deep into her eyes. "When the Alliance falls, best case scenario, you'll go to an education center. So will your father. So will I. And if your husband manages to live long enough, which is highly unlikely, so will he. If you have any other friends or people that you care about, so will they."

Ava swallowed the lump in her throat as she thought about Foley, her father, Charity, Megan, her neighbor from her apartment building in Austin, and Megan's little girl, Danielle.

Blackwell did not relent. "You know what Markovich has planned for the people who can't be rehabilitated, don't you?"

"What?"

"Euthanization."

Ava looked back up at him in animal terror as she thought about the people she knew and loved being put down like unwanted strays.

"Don't tell me you're shocked. These are the same people who fought to block a five-month abortion ban in the Senate years back. Anyone who doesn't encounter a moral dilemma with murdering an innocent child who could easily survive outside of the mother's womb really shouldn't see anything wrong with killing off unwanted members of society. And in the same way that Planned Parenthood sold off the body parts of those well-developed murdered children ripped from their mother's wombs, Markovich will be making the organs of those who can't be reintegrated with the revolutionary society available for sale on the world market.

"Just imagine, all those Christians who don't drink and don't smoke, that's a huge supply of healthy lungs and livers available to those who may have been just a little too excessive in their lust for life. Yes, I know gluttony is the Christian sin of choice. Obesity and cholesterol levels might be a little high, but that's not anything a re-education camp diet won't cure. In six months' time, the regime will also have a healthy supply of hearts ready for transplants!"

Ava gritted her teeth, clenched her fists, and would not look at Blackwell.

"But you've done your part. Thank you for hearing me out. I'll have Agent Schaub take you home so you can live out the next twelve to twenty-four months in relative comfort. Good evening, Mrs. Mitchem." Blackwell began to walk out of the room.

Her blood seethed in her veins. "Wait!"

Blackwell stopped but did not turn around.

"Suppose I agreed to take on this *impossible* task. What kind of support would I have from the Alliance?"

Blackwell rolled his head to the side. "Colonel Barr would discuss that with you. I could never have any official knowledge of any such activities. I'm sure you understand."

Ulysses cut in. "So, it's a black op, meaning that if Ava is captured, she'll be left to rot in one of Markovich's death camps."

"Which will be all of our fates if nothing happens to correct our present course." Blackwell returned to the couch and sat back down. "This mission can never be acknowledged as being condoned by the Alliance States. I have to think about the future. If the Alliance is able to survive, and that's a big if, we'll need to reach a peace agreement or at least a ceasefire with Markovich. As you said, Mr. Adams, forty years of communist indoctrination can't be undone in the blink of an eye. In the best possible outcome, we end up with two separate Americas that are able to coexist in relative proximity without killing each other. Admitting to officially sanctioning an assassination would severely hamper reconciliation efforts."

Ulysses shook his head. "No, Ava. You can't do it. You cannot fathom what it is like to be left behind by your country; to be abandoned to decay in a musty, dark hole; essentially buried alive." He gazed at the wall as if looking beyond it for several seconds without speaking.

Ava put her hand on his shoulder softly. "But, Dad, that will happen anyway."

He blinked several times as if trying to escape a trance. "I'm sorry, what were you saying?"

"Left to die in a hole, that's where we're headed anyway." She looked at him with compassion. "At least this way, we have a chance, even if it's a small one."

Ulysses took her hand. "No. We can get out of the country. Start over somewhere else."

"Where?" Blackwell asked. "America is the last bastion of freedom. The rest of the globe has been consumed by some variant of communism."

"Plenty of countries are better off than where we'll be after Markovich controls the entire country." Ulysses stood up "Come on, Ava."

Blackwell countered, "Ava thinks Markovich killed Woods just to get into office two months early. Does that sound like a man who will be content with one country or do you suppose he'll want to take over the world? I hate to be a wet blanket here, but I don't think there's anywhere left to run."

Ulysses retorted, "You've obviously seen my resume. I'm confident that I can find some remote corner where we'll be left alone."

Ava did not get up from the sofa. "I don't want to run. You don't have to help me, but I'm going to do this."

"I thought you said you were finished fighting." Ulysses' face looked unsettled.

"I was."

"Then you'll do it?" Blackwell asked.

Ulysses put his hand up. "Hang on. Like she said, all those actions you talked about took planning and teamwork. Many of the skills required to pull off what you're asking, she doesn't have. If I'm going to fill in those gaps, I need some assurances."

"I'm listening," Blackwell said.

"You don't have to acknowledge the mission. I understand what that means, probably better than anyone. But you do have to promise that if things go wrong and you have a chance to get her out, you'll take it."

Blackwell nodded. "Like you, First Sergeant, I served. I understand what it means to leave a brother behind. And I can give you my word, that if things do go wrong, leaving you, Ava, or anyone else behind will only happen after every other option has been exhausted. The good of the country has to come first, so I can't swear that I'll bring you home at all costs, but I'll utilize every covert means at my disposal to get you both back."

No one said anything for several moments.

Blackwell finally broke the silence. "Is that good enough for you, First Sergeant Adams?"

Ulysses looked at Ava who had a grin of determination growing on her face. His jaw tightened. "I guess it will have to be."

CHAPTER 10

A prudent man concealeth knowledge: but the heart of fools proclaimeth foolishness.

Proverbs 12:23

"You're watching TMZ?" Charity looked at Ava like she had three heads.

Ava continued petting Buckley who was curled up on the couch next to her. "Research."

"I can't even believe TMZ is still on with a civil war raging."

"It's part of the bread-and-circuses campaign the left uses to keep people from paying attention to what's really happening. Markovich will make sure it stays on the air, even if the regime has to foot the bill."

Charity put her hands on her hips. "And what,

pray tell, are you researching?"

"Not what. Who."

"You're gonna make me beg, aren't you?"

"Dad and I may be going on a little trip. We could be gone a while."

"This is about your little get-together with Blackwell, isn't it?"

Ava wished she could tell her friend more. "Can you keep an eye on Buck while we're gone?"

"Okay, I get it. It's for my own good to stay in the dark about what you're up to, but can you at least tell me when you're leaving?"

"I don't really know. Soon."

"How long will you be gone?"

"Not long, I hope."

"Is that less than a week, more than a week?"

"A week, maybe two. But I really don't know." Ava held up her hand. "Hold on, I need to hear this." Ava listened closely to the late-night tabloid gossip show as the people began discussing Shane Lawrence. Paparazzi photographs showed Lawrence dipping into a limousine with a scantily-clad young woman. The photos of the girl were not clear as the shot was from a distance and from a rear-side angle, so the gallery of commentators speculated on who the mystery starlet might be. The segment was short and soon over. Afterward, Ava turned off the television.

Charity watched quietly, but it was obvious that she was wondering why Ava had been so interested in Lawrence. "So, whenever whatever happens, will I know it was you?"

"Probably." Ava got up from the sofa. "I'm

going to turn in."

"Your dad still isn't home?"

"No. Late night for him, I guess." Ava let Buckley out to do his business before bed.

Charity waited by the door with Ava for the dog to return. "I know you're short on help with Foley gone—and James." Charity looked at the floor. "But if you need me for this, I'll do what I can."

"Thanks, but taking care of the house and Buck is what I need. With everything else I have to deal with, at least I don't have to worry about him, knowing that you're taking good care of my buddy."

Ava saw headlights turn into the long drive. "Buck! Get in the house, now."

She was pretty sure it was Ulysses' truck but couldn't be certain. Buckley came up to the porch but paused to look at the vehicle before coming inside. His tail wagged, which gave Ava confidence that it was indeed her father's vehicle.

"Where has Ulysses been all day anyway?" Charity watched him pull up to the house.

Ava smiled apologetically but didn't answer.

"Never mind." Charity rolled her eyes. "I'm going to hit the hay before I hear something that will get me killed."

"Goodnight." Ava hugged her friend.

"If you're not here when I wake up, I guess I'll see you later."

"I'll be here," Ava said.

Ulysses closed the truck door and walked up the stairs with a backpack slung over his shoulder.

Ava waited for him to come in, then locked the

door behind him and Buckley. "Did the colonel give you anything good?"

Ulysses listened for Charity's door to close all the way. "Let's go into the kitchen."

Ava followed him.

He unzipped his pack. "New identities and supporting documents for both of us." He handed her a Utah driver's license.

"Paul Whitmore, from St. George. What brings you to the sunny state of California, Paul?"

Ulysses looked too tired for role-playing games, but he went along with it. "I'm a registered Democrat. It's not safe for people like me in Utah."

"They have democrats in Utah?" Ava tilted her head as if she were suspicious of the answer.

"My town was 17 percent Democrats; before the war broke out, that is. We quickly became a persecuted minority."

Ava shook her head and made a tisking sound. "Too bad, too bad. But you're among friends now, in the utopic land of tomorrow, the People's Socialist Republic of California. Welcome, Comrade Whitmore." She handed him the ID. "Where's mine?"

He frowned. "Before they mock up your ID, you'll have to cut and dye your hair again. And put on those goofy glasses that you love so much."

She huffed. "Great."

"The colonel wants you to get some collagen treatments also."

"Are you serious? You mean big fat lips like Angelina Jolie?"

"Not necessarily. You have that very distinct

jawline. He thinks they can soften that up enough and do a few other key spots on your face to trick facial recognition software."

"It's supposed to be a disguise to help me blend in. I'm going to end up looking like a circus freak; like someone who got a botched facelift."

Ulysses crossed his arms. "You do realize we're going to LA, right?"

"Oh yeah, never mind. I'll fit right in." Ava took a seat at the kitchen table. "What else did you talk about with the colonel?"

"Our profiles are of people from St. George that have been killed since the war. He's got a guy from NSA that has a backdoor into Facebook. They'll photoshop us into their pictures and the posts will keep the original timestamps."

"Their friends will recognize that the photos have been changed."

Ulysses shook his head. "Being Democrats in Utah, both of them were loners. Didn't really have many real friends. Most of their Facebook friends are just people they've connected with online and in socialist Facebook groups. The few people who are real-world friends or relatives are being fed a static ghost feed that shows the original content. Everyone else navigating to the actual Facebook pages will see the doctored content."

"Sounds risky."

Ulysses nodded. "You signed us both up for risky."

"No," she protested. "I signed *me* up. You signed yourself up."

Ulysses cleared his throat. "Anyway, the NSA

guy also has backdoor access into most operating systems: iOS, OS X, Android, Windows."

"That could be helpful."

"Yeah. He's able to monitor all of Lawrence's emails and texts. The problem will be getting that information to us. Markovich has blocked out all phone calls and web traffic from outside the states he controls."

"A communist censoring the internet? Who'd have thought!"

Ulysses snickered. "Yeah. Colonel Barr has an email account set up for us inside the regime. We'll use it like a drop box. We'll never send or receive emails with the account."

"Then how will we get information?"

"The colonel will send an operative across the border, have him login to the email account and save our messages as an encrypted draft. We'll log in periodically and read the encrypted messages."

Ulysses took out a small bottle.

"Hand sanitizer?"

"Don't judge a book by its cover; or in this case, a bottle by its label."

"Poison?" Ava asked.

"VX nerve agent. It's what Kim Jong Un used to kill his big brother, Kim Jong Nam. He basically sent a woman carrying a towel laced with VX into Kuala Lumpur International Airport where Nam was waiting for a flight. She walked up behind the brother, wiped the rag across his face and ran off. You can watch the video on YouTube. Being the brother of such a notoriously nice guy, Nam immediately knew he'd been attacked. He informed authorities then headed for the airport clinic. By the time he'd crossed the terminal, he was already experiencing paralysis. You can see his legs getting stiff as he walks in the video. A few minutes later he was dead."

Ava held the bottle in her hand. "I guess you'd want to be wearing gloves when you open this."

"That wouldn't be a bad idea at all."

"So, is that what we're going to do?"

Ulysses nodded. "Getting the VX on his face will be the easy part. Getting away before we're caught will be the real challenge. The only way we'll be able to get close enough to him will be to do it in a public place. We'll have to think of ways to minimize our exposure to cameras and eyewitnesses."

"What about a bathroom? What if we set it up to look like an accident? You said the nerve agent didn't act instantaneously. If it looked like a casual mishap, maybe we could get out of the area by the time he started feeling the effects."

"It's possible. We'll have to see what opportunities present themselves." Ulysses seemed apprehensive about the operation.

Ava asked, "What's my refugee name?"

Ulysses pulled a manila envelope from his pack and handed it to Ava. "Tamara Jones. We'll work on your appearance tomorrow so the colonel can have your IDs made up. We'll need to head to California no later than Sunday. Once those Facebook profiles have been modified, we'll be up against the clock. We have to get in, eliminate our target, and get out before anyone discovers they've been tampered with."

Ava felt the intense pressure of the insane mess she'd volunteered herself for. That was bad enough, but she also had the weight of dragging her father into it. Although he'd volunteered, he never would have done so if she hadn't jumped head first into this muddle.

CHAPTER 11

And Joshua the son of Nun sent out of Shittim two men to spy secretly, saying, Go view the land, even Jericho. And they went, and came into an harlot's house, named Rahab, and lodged there.

Joshua 2:1

Ava handed her driver's license to the SJL soldier manning the checkpoint in Utah, adjusted her thick black fake glasses, and ran her fingers through her, once again, too short, too black hair.

"Why didn't you go to one of the refugee centers in Las Vegas? That would have been much closer for you."

"We have friends in Hollywood. We were forced

out of our homes by the fanatics in our town. I've always been against violence, so I wanted to come here."

The man puckered his forehead and returned Ava's ID. He stared at Ulysses' ID a little longer. "And how do you two know each other?"

"We worked together at Dixie State University. I was an economics professor."

"I taught literature." Ava smiled.

The guard passed Ulysses' ID back to him. "Isn't Dixie State a Mormon college?"

"Not anymore," Ulysses answered. "The Utah Board of Education took it over in 1935."

"You'll have to have your Social Value Audits before you can get passes to Los Angeles. The citizens of LA mostly scored well above five. So, we haven't had to send very many residents to education centers. We really don't have a need for citizens here. Have you considered settling in Texas? The leader is anticipating a high failure rate out of the Texans who required level-one and two education programs. That equates to lots of openings for favored citizens. The state will be allocating housing as well. Many of those people who won't be returning from their educational programs have left behind very nice homes."

Ava shook her head and tapped her index finger against her chest. "I supported the leader all the way through the primaries. And in an area where it was not a popular thing to do. I risked my life by being very vocal about my politics.

"I've been called a murderer for my stance on abortion, I've been threatened over my staunch arguments pushing for gun control in my community. And my job as a professor of literature. I shudder to think where the country would be today were it not for the literary contributions of like-minded Americans who challenged the antiquated notion of some mystical God who created the world and everything in it.

"I tell you, literature has done more to debunk the tyranny of absolute moral truth and replace it with personal subjectivity than Darwin and modern science ever could! I've made my sacrifices and I am entitled to a seat at the table!"

The guard nodded. "You can request an expedited SVA. If you score a nine, you can petition for placement in the service sector. If you score a ten, you'll automatically qualify for the service sector. Or you can apply to join the SJL as an auditor."

"What about me?" Ulysses put his thumb to his chest. "I almost lost my job because a handful of parents opposed me using Rules for Radicals as supplemental curriculum in my economics course. Thankfully, the board backed me up on the premise that the book deals with how low-income communities gain political power, despite not being from privileged families. The whole reason I went into economics was so I could teach our youth the evils of capitalism. I certainly deserve favored status."

The soldier nodded again. "Unfortunately, without a pass to get into the city, the closest SVA center for you is in Santa Clarita. Go there and apply for an expedited audit. I'm sure everything will work out for you both."

Ava dared not thank the man for the information. No bona fide snowflake would ever do a thing like that. Instead, she shrieked a loud cry of frustration like a spoiled two-year-old. She pulled her own hair and stomped off from the checkpoint in a tantrum.

Ulysses rushed after her like an enabling fellow revolutionary, hurrying to validate her adolescent outburst.

Once they were out of earshot, Ulysses said, "That was a disturbingly good performance."

She waved her hand. "Once you learn to control your gag reflex, the rest is easy. But you played your part well, also." She took out her burner phone. "I better get us an Uber so we can get to Santa Clarita and get a hotel for the night. We didn't count on the efficiencies of communism when we planned our trip."

Monday morning, Ava and Ulysses stood in line at the Social Value Audit office which had been erected pop-up style in a recently vacated church. Since church attendance immediately qualified citizens for residential educational programs, congregants either quit going or were relocated to a camp.

"$37.50 for an expedited audit?" Ava whined. "We're refugees of the war!"

The woman behind the desk replied curtly, "We can provide you with transportation to a relief center in Nevada. Unfortunately, since California isn't a border state, we don't have any relief centers set up here."

"You're aware that transporting us to a relief

center in Nevada will cost way more than $37.50, aren't you?"

Ulysses kicked her foot. She quickly realized that she'd just tried to use logic on an indoctrinated socialist. *What was I thinking? I could have blown the whole operation!*

The clerk stared at her blankly. Fortunately, Ava's comment hadn't seemed to interrupt the woman's zombie-like condition.

Ava dug through her purse and retrieved the credit card with the same name as her ID. She handed it to the woman.

"I'll need you to fill out this authorization form allowing me to research your social media history." The woman gave Ava a pen with the document.

Ava knew better than to point out the absolute hypocrisy in having her fill out an authorization form for an expedited audit when the government required no such permission to execute a regular audit on their own timeline. Like a compliant communist, she simply began filling out the paper. "About how long does the expedited audit usually take?"

"Three to five days," said the woman dryly.

"Will your office forward the audit to LA for us? We're trying to get passes into the city. We have friends there."

"The SVA office is federal. We don't have any connection with state or local jurisdictions. You'll have to handle that on your own."

"Oh. Okay." Ava completed her form quietly, then waited for Ulysses to finish filling out his authorization papers.

"How will we be notified when the audit is completed?"

"We'll send you an email. It will have a case number that you can reference when other government agencies are involved." The woman looked past Ava and Ulysses, signaling that their time with her had expired and there would be no other questions. "Next!"

Ava assumed expressions of gratitude were neither expected nor welcomed, so she stood up abruptly and headed for the door.

Once outside, she looked at her father. "We've got a couple of days to kill. Do you want to do some sightseeing?"

"No," he answered. "We need to stay in our hotel room, keep a low profile. Your disguise is good, but the more people who see you, the higher our chances of someone recognizing you. We'll order in as much as possible. If you start feeling claustrophobic, maybe we can step out for dinner tomorrow night, but for the most part, we'll stay out of sight and out of mind."

She opened the Uber app on her phone and requested a ride. "Okay. But sitting around twiddling my thumbs isn't going to help my nerves. I'll be obsessing over the operation."

"I'll get us some cards, maybe a puzzle or two. We'll keep our minds occupied."

"We passed a hobby store on Old Road. Maybe you could pick us up some board games."

Ulysses smiled warmly. "I missed out on buying you toys and things. I'd like that."

Ava fought to not get choked up over the

sentimentality of his statement. "Great. What are we having for lunch?"

"Looks like mostly fast food around the hotel. That sub shop might be the least-bad option."

"A sub is fine with me. Seems the regime states aren't as affected by the war. I haven't seen many restaurants or grocery stores closed down."

"They might be out of a few items here and there, but they've got all the seaports. Supply disruptions will be minimal." Ulysses waved at the Uber driver as he pulled up.

Ava didn't feel like putting on the pretense for the Uber driver so neither she nor Ulysses talked on the way to the hotel.

When they arrived back in their room, Ava reclined on the bed and turned on the television.

"I'll get those games and some lunch. I'm going to walk so I might be a while. I'll be back soon."

"Okay, be safe." Ava flipped through the channels knowing her only choices were filth or propaganda. She opted for propaganda. The news told a disparaging tale of regime victories in southern Idaho, claiming that Markovich's forces not only held the lower half of the state but that they'd also began a campaign to *liberate* surrounding states. Ava bit her nails as she listened to the reporter expound upon the regime's invasion into Salt Lake City, Utah and Jackson, Wyoming. Her heart ached from not being able to send or receive messages from Foley.

Thursday morning, Ava checked her email. Four days had passed since applying for an expedited audit. "I got it! Did you get yours?"

"Let me see your computer." Ulysses abandoned his microwaved sausage, cheese, and egg biscuit. He quickly logged into Paul Whitmore's account. "Nothing. Maybe I'll have it by the end of the day. What score did you get?"

"A nine. It's not a ten, but at least I won't have to go to a re-education camp."

"You'll never get a ten with an attitude like that."

"Ha, ha." She rolled her eyes.

"We should probably get your LA pass application started."

"What about you?"

"We'll start mine when I get my score, assuming it's high enough to earn me a pass in the first place." He handed the computer to her.

She navigated to the LA residential-and-visitor-pass website. "It's down."

"Imagine that. Why don't you try calling them and see if they have a walk-in office?" Ulysses went back to his highly-processed breakfast sandwich.

"I can't get the number with the site down. I'll try the DMV."

"Yeah, they're masters of efficiency, I'm sure they'll be able to help," Ulysses said sardonically.

Ava looked up the number and called. "Hi, I'm trying to get the telephone number for the office that issues entrance passes for LA."

"We don't have anything to do with that office." The person hung up.

"But . . ." Ava was too late.

Ulysses rinsed down his breakfast with a large single-serve chocolate milk. "Try City Hall, Clerk of Courts."

Ava looked up the number and dialed. She pressed several buttons to traverse her call through a seemingly-unending list of options. "I'm on hold."

Ulysses nodded and watched the morning news show on television.

Forty minutes later, a female voice said, "Clerk of Courts."

"Hi, I just need the number for the LA entrance pass issuing office."

"It's on their website."

"But the website is down!" Ava rejoined quickly before she was disconnected again.

The voice paused as if contemplating whether or not to just hang up on Ava. "Hold please."

"What's happening?" Ulysses asked.

"I'm on hold again." Ava gritted her teeth.

"Just think, once all this is done with, it can take up to a week for the request to be processed."

She shook her head. "Who would have ever thought that bureaucracy could be a form of defense."

"How do you mean?"

"It's actually these layers and layers of government red tape that are keeping us from our objective."

Ulysses nodded. "It makes a good deterrent, but we'll do what we came to do, one way or the other."

Ava understood that if her father got tired of playing nice, the gloves would come off and he'd do whatever was necessary.

Five minutes later, the voice came back on the line. "424-399-4114." Click. The woman hung up before confirming whether Ava had written down the number.

Ava quickly called the number. "Hi, I'm inquiring about getting a pass to visit my friends in LA."

"Sorry, our website is down," said a man with an effeminate voice.

"I know. But do you have a walk-in office where I can apply in person?"

"Yes, but it won't do you any good. The website is down and we can't work. Besides, we're inside the city limits, so you can't get to us without a pass."

"Then how do people get their pass when it's issued?"

"You don't get a physical pass, it's not like Willy Wonka's golden ticket that you carry around in your pocket." The explanation was condescending and impolite. "We simply use your social security number and it updates to your driver's license."

"I just spoke with DMV and they said you're not connected."

"We're not. It's in the federal database."

"But I'm a refugee, my driver's license is from Utah."

"Oh, good heavens!" The man sounded exacerbated from having to deal with an actual phone call, especially one from some refugee. "Then you'll have to get a license from a state that still wants to be part of the country." He hung up before Ava had a chance to pester him further.

She looked up at Ulysses. "Good news and bad news."

"What's the good news?"

"We get to go on a field trip, breathe a little fresh air."

"Let me guess the bad news." He pressed his lips together.

"Give it a shot."

"Our outing entails waiting in a long line at the DMV."

She pointed at him. "You're good. You should've been a spy."

He grunted. "It ain't all it's cracked up to be."

"Not even when it allows you to spend quality time with your favorite person?" She batted her eyelashes.

"Could have done that with a fishing pole by a lake if my favorite person wasn't so stubborn."

"Touché." She requested an Uber on her phone and grabbed her purse. "Come on. The sooner we go, the sooner we'll get back. We've still got that tiebreaker for Yahtzee."

Ulysses grabbed the second laptop. It was reserved strictly for communications with the colonel. The battery was kept separate from the laptop and only inserted long enough to check the dead-drop email account. "I'll see if we have any messages from Barr while we're out."

Ava instructed the driver to let them out at the coffee shop near the DMV.

They went inside. Ava ordered two coffees while Ulysses checked the drafts in the email account. Once she had the beverages, she brought them to the small table near the back of the shop. "Any news?"

Ulysses spun the computer to where she could see

it.

Ava read the draft which Ulysses had already decrypted. "Looks like Lawrence is having a big shindig at Lure on April 12th. He's renting out the entire nightclub for him and all his Hollywood minions. He wants them to volunteer for a public image campaign to help nurture a positive perception of the administration. Look at this guest list: writers, directors, actors, musicians. This is exactly what Blackwell was talking about."

"And it's exactly what we were sent here to stop," Ulysses added.

She whispered, "Just think of how involved the entertainment industry was in swaying cultural norms when its members were simply subjected to peer pressure. Now they risk having their Social Value ranks knocked down a notch if they don't play along. Nobody wants that."

"It's an added incentive, but I doubt very many people on that list needed much coercion. All these folks are true believers, revolutionaries through and through." Ulysses sipped his overpriced coffee.

"April 12th. That's only ten days away."

"Then we need to start coming up with some backup plans on how we're going to get into the city."

"That's just the beginning. We still need to figure out how we're going to get into the event. It will be crawling with security."

Ulysses nodded. "Yep. But by hook or by crook, we're going to be at that event!"

CHAPTER 12

Have not I commanded thee? Be strong and of a good courage; be not afraid, neither be thou dismayed: for the Lord thy God is with thee whithersoever thou goest.

Joshua 1:9

Tuesday morning marked nine days that Ava and Ulysses had been in California. She checked her email. "Finally! I've been honored with the privilege of visiting the human septic tank known as Los Angeles!"

Ulysses sat on the other bed of the hotel. "Congratulations . . . I guess."

"Check your email. Maybe you were approved as well."

He took the computer. "I doubt it. I didn't get my SVA score until the end of the day Friday. Then the website was down all weekend. I couldn't even apply until yesterday morning." He pecked away on the keyboard. "Nope."

"I couldn't fill out my application until Friday. I got mine in two business days. Yours could come soon."

"I hope so. We've only got four days until Lawrence has his big event."

"Maybe I should go into the city by myself."

"No. I'd rather sneak in together than risk you being alone."

"I actually think it would be safer for me if I'm playing by the rules. I could apply to get a job at Lure or I could try to get hired on with the catering company who is providing the food for the soirée."

Ulysses blew out hard to show his frustration over the predicament. "Why don't you try calling them to see if they're hiring first."

"I'm thinking to dress up kinda cute. Maybe if I can talk to the right manager, he'll find an opening for me."

Ulysses growled under his breath as if he liked that idea even less. "You don't have any experience in food service or nightclubs."

"We're talking about communism. I have a high score. It's all about loyalty to the party, getting a job has very little to do with one's ability."

Ulysses paused, as if he were trying to think of more excuses for Ava not to proceed with her latest plan. Finally, he said, "Map out your intended route and call in every half hour."

"I will, but you're limited on what you can do if I get in trouble. We couldn't bring guns on this trip."

"If you don't call in, I'll get a gun."

"Where?"

"I'll take it from one of those SJL punks at the checkpoint."

"I'm just going to fill out a job application." Ava grimaced. "I'll be fine. I'm going to get ready." She got up from the bed and went to the bathroom for a quick shower.

Two hours later, the Uber dropped her off at the catering company which, according to the message in her surreptitious dead-drop email, was to be the food provider at the upcoming affair. Ava pulled down her too-short skirt and checked her lipstick before entering the office.

Her heels clacked on the bare concrete floors of the catering company. "Hi, I'm here about a job."

The girl behind the desk looked her over with a snarl. "We're not hiring right now."

"Are you sure? Even part-time?"

The girl didn't look up but simply shook her head.

"Can I speak to your manager?"

The girl pressed a button on her desk phone.

"Yes?" came a woman's voice over the speakerphone.

"Some girl is looking for a job. I told her we're not hiring."

"Give her an application. Tell her we'll call if we have any openings." The woman hung up.

The receptionist held up a piece of paper for

Ava.

As bad as she wanted to tell the girl where to stick the form, Ava forced a smile and sat down to fill out the application. She placed it on the receptionist's desk and said, "Thank you."

The girl behind the desk did not reply. Ava walked out and requested another Uber.

The car arrived a few minutes later. Ava got in.

"Ma'am, you know Lure is not open at this time?"

"That's fine. I'm trying to get a job." She looked down at her phone to try to avoid further conversation with the driver as he drove across town to Sunset Boulevard.

Thirty minutes later, they arrived. "This is the club, ma'am."

She looked at a double-wide wooden door on a wall covered with ivy. "I don't see any signs. Are you sure?"

"Yes, ma'am."

"How do I get in?"

The driver looked at the rearview mirror. "I don't know. Maybe they have an entrance for deliveries in the back."

"Can you drive around to see?"

"Yes, ma'am." The driver took her around the block. A steel roll-up door was half open.

"Thanks!" She exited the vehicle and proceeded through the warehouse-style entrance. No one was around so she meandered through the club looking for a manager.

"Hi, can I help you?" A girl's voice came from behind.

Ava spun around. "Oh yeah, hey! I was wondering if you might be hiring?"

"What position?" the young slender girl asked.

"Cocktail waitress?"

"Probably not. Have you ever tended bar?"

"No," Ava replied.

"Sorry. Maybe try back another time." The girl offered a pleasant smile.

"Thank you. Could I fill out an application for you to keep on file—just in case something opens up?"

"Um, yeah, I guess that would be okay. You can have a seat at the bar. I'll be right back."

"Thanks." Ava had no intention of sitting at the bar. If this was to be her only opportunity to reconnoiter the premises she'd make the most of it. She walked around from the outside patio through the various spaces in the club. She made a mental note of all the exits, bars, and bathrooms.

A tall man in his late forties with a beard, short hair, and large-rimmed dark sunglasses walked in from outside. He wore dark jeans, a white shirt, and a dark vest. "Is someone helping you?" His accent was distinctly British.

"Yes, the young blonde girl from the office, she's getting me an application. Are you the manager?"

"I'm Roman, the owner." He looked at Ava's muscular thighs and calves.

She waited uncomfortably for his eyes to make their way back up to her face. "Nice to meet you."

"What position are you applying for?"

"Cocktail waitress, but I could be a hostess as

well."

Roman walked behind the bar and pulled down a bottle of tequila. He poured himself a shot. Even though no lights were on inside, he still did not remove his sunglasses. "What's your SVA score?"

"Nine."

"I don't have any full-time positions right now, but we have a special event this weekend. The host is . . . sort of picky. A lot of Hollywood's elite will be here and they don't want any staff with an SVA score below eight to be working. It's a political thing—kind of like a fundraiser but not really. I don't actually know what they're doing. But they're renting the club for the evening so they can do whatever they like as far as I'm concerned. I'm not going to start laying people off because they don't have a high enough SVA score, but this sort of thing may become a trend. If you'd be willing to help me out for this weekend's gala, it could become a full-time gig in the future."

He threw back the shot of tequila and looked Ava up and down once more. "You look like you'd fit in rather nicely around here."

"Oh! There you are!" The little blonde girl came by with the application. "I was looking all over for you!"

Ava hoped Roman wouldn't realize that she'd been snooping around. "Thank you." She took the application. "Sure. I can work this weekend. Do I still need to fill this out?"

Roman poured himself another shot. "No. Tiffany will have you fill out a W-4 form. She'll have to verify your SVA score. Come in Friday night. I'll have you follow Mercedes so you can get the lay of the land. Then you'll more or less know where things are for Saturday.

"Some of our clients can be a bit rude on occasion. You don't have to take any unwanted advances or anything, but we do expect you to be cordial, even with guests that may be less than pleasant. Is that going to be a problem?"

"No, sir." Under any other circumstances, Ava would never put herself in such a position, but this operation was for all the marbles.

"Good. Be here at nine on Friday night to start setting up. We open at eleven. Seven o'clock on Saturday. The event begins at ten, but they've given us an excruciating list of demands, so set up is going to be a bear."

"Thanks again."

"Come on, we'll get your paperwork knocked out," said Tiffany.

Two hours later, Ava walked into the hotel room. "I'm in! I got the job!"

"No kidding!" Ulysses looked up. "I would say thank God, but I'm waiting to see how this plays out."

"It's going to be alright." She kicked off her heels.

"Why don't you put on something a little more modest, and we'll go have dinner out of the room. We can eat at the steakhouse across the street."

"Okay." She smiled and went to the bathroom to change.

At dinner, Ava made a rough sketch of the club on the hotel notepad she'd brought for just such a purpose. "I'm training Friday night, so I'll be able to draw a better map before Saturday. I only saw one door on the front, then the delivery door and one fire exit."

Ulysses pointed at a box on the notepad. "You said this area is a courtyard, right?"

"Yeah, but it has barbed wire hidden under the vines."

"A jacket thrown over barbed wire can keep it from snagging you. But one exit is all I need anyway. We'll be long gone by the time Lawrence starts feeling the effects of the nerve agent."

"Now we have to figure out how we're going to get you in," she said.

"Check out that fire door when you go in to train. If we can disconnect the alarm, maybe you can bump it open and let me in."

"That should work. I won't have any trouble sneaking in the VX since it looks like hand sanitizer."

Ulysses shook his head. "No. I'll bring it when you let me in. Lawrence will have heavy security. They may search the staff regardless of their SVA scores."

"But if you can't get in for some reason, we'll miss our chance. If I have it, I can still make a play."

Ulysses said, "No, I'm not going to budge on this one. If I can't get in, we'll scrub the mission."

Ava was familiar with that determined look in Ulysses' eyes. She didn't bother arguing. "So, how are we going to get the VX on Lawrence?"

"I guess I'll bump him with it."

"What if he's in a VIP area where you don't have access?"

"Then you'll have to get me in."

Ava looked at the thick varnish on the wooden table. She wondered how well her father was going to fit in. His lazy eye and long scar down his mouth and neck didn't exactly make him look like someone who belonged in a posh nightclub. "We're going to have to get you an outfit. And maybe some sunglasses."

"It's at night."

"I know, but trust me on this one. I think you'll fit right in."

Ulysses grumbled under his breath but did not dismiss the plan.

Ava thought for a while and finished her ice tea. "What if you tripped, spilled a drink on Shane Lawrence? Then I could come to the rescue with a towel and dry him off."

"The VX would be on the towel." Ulysses considered the move. "And you'd have on clear plastic gloves. Because any contact with the VX on your skin will be lethal."

"Yes. I'll wear gloves."

Ulysses nodded. "Okay then. Let's put a pin in that."

"Great." Ava grinned big and pulled out her phone. "The mall in Valencia is still open. Let's go find you a disguise after dinner."

He sighed. "You look like you're enjoying this a little too much."

CHAPTER 13

Master, which is the great commandment in the law? Jesus said unto him, Thou shalt love the Lord thy God with all thy heart, and with all thy soul, and with all thy mind. This is the first and great commandment. And the second is like unto it, Thou shalt love thy neighbour as thyself. On these two commandments hang all the law and the prophets.

Matthew 22:36-40

Saturday evening, Ava stood in front of the mirror in the hotel bathroom putting on her makeup.

Ulysses walked up behind her. "Remember, if I get in trouble tonight, just get out of there. We'll rendezvous at Staybridge Suites in Vegas. It's off the beaten path and south of the main strip, so we'll pass by fewer surveillance cameras.

"Ditch all of your IDs and credit cards associated with Tamara Jones. You'll use your secondary alias to get back to the Alliance States. If I'm not at the Vegas hotel twenty-four hours after you arrive, head straight to Utah without me. I'll meet you back at the house."

Ava hated hearing contingencies for when things went wrong. It was a terrible reminder that things usually went wrong. She continued her liberal application of eyeshadow. "I'm sure you'll reciprocate."

"What do you mean?"

"If I get hemmed up at the club, you'll go on without me. Wait for me in Vegas for twenty-four hours, then head home?"

Ulysses cracked a nervous smile and put his hand on hers. "Ava, I have a different skill set than you. I'm better equipped to effect your rescue. If you stick around, I'll have to get *myself* out of a jam, then I'll still have you to worry about."

She couldn't think about any of that. Ava had to stay focused on the task at hand. Allowing her mind to venture into the territory of what-ifs would bring more harm than good. "Nothing is going to go wrong this time. It can't."

Ulysses nodded. "I wish it were as simple as that. But maybe you're right. Let's pray that we pull it off without a hitch. But just in case, stick to the backup plan."

"I really think you should reconsider letting me

carry the VX in my purse."

"Absolutely not," he replied precipitously. His tone softened. "I'm going to destroy the hard drives on the computers if you don't need them for anything else."

She transitioned to her eyeliner pencil. "I can't exactly send Foley an email, so I guess I'm done with them. I'll be glad when this is over with."

"Me, too." Ulysses walked away to dispose of their electronic footprints.

Ava continued to put on her makeup. She looked deep into her own eyes in the mirror. She wondered if she might catch a glimpse of her soul if she stared hard enough and long enough. And if she were to be successful in such an introspective venture, she pondered whether or not she'd like what she saw. "Who am I?" she whispered to the stranger in the mirror.

Ava thought back to the first life she'd taken, the hooligan on the bridge. No doubt, in that situation, it was him or her. Little did she know at the time, but he was to be the first of many. She'd felt no sense of moral dilemma whatsoever over the ruffian on the bridge. Likewise, the people she'd killed in various gun battles over the past months, it was self-preservation.

But the insurgency campaigns, they haunted her memories, and often her dreams. She'd felt remorse over her role in the gun collection point bombings, but there was one face she could never erase. "Delaney." The boy from the stadium bombing visited her often, both when she was asleep and when she was awake. She wondered what he might have become had he not been indoctrinated, poisoned by the culture, brainwashed into becoming a soldier for the regime. Unlike the other bombing victims, she'd seen his horrific demise up-close and personal.

Yet, with this next action, she would graduate to another level. She'd progressed from being someone willing to take a life in self-defense to someone who would kill with the most vulgar implements of death available to mankind. And on this night, she would dive into the very bowels of hell; she would become an assassin.

Ava thought about her father's warnings so many months ago. "War will change you, and there's no coming back from it," she whispered to the stranger in the mirror.

She meditated on the evening's program. She inquired of her innermost being, "Can I do this? Should I do this?"

She had not yet left the hotel, so backing out was still an option, albeit a bad one. Ava considered who she'd be letting down if she walked away. "Foley doesn't even know about it—if he's still alive, that is. Charity has no idea of the particulars. Dad never wanted to do it in the first place. He'd be thrilled if we simply packed up and went home."

"Blackwell, he'd be disappointed." She wisped mascara through her eyelashes. "But I don't owe him anything."

Ava's conscience wandered around inside her mind a while, looking for a space where the quandary over right and wrong didn't weigh on her like a dead elephant. No such place existed inside the confines of her personal gray matter. She did however, find a remote outpost of the predicament, one that was slightly removed, impersonalized.

"What if this were Hitler? Would I assassinate him?"

She considered every atrocity committed by the Nazis. "How was such unabated evil ever allowed to fester to such a point? Six million Jews were gassed, starved to death, worked to death in labor camps, or shot outright then burned in ovens."

"They were liberated of their right to bear arms," Ava told the woman in the mirror grimly. She'd found her first similarity in Hitler and Markovich. "The Nazis were unopposed, permitted to kill with impunity. Hitler would have succeeded in eradicating the earth of Jews. Then he'd have gotten rid of the handicapped, the blind, deaf, mentally challenged, and those born with birth defects. I'm sure he'd have proceeded to get rid of all people of color."

"But God would have never let him kill off all the Jews. He didn't. He didn't let him. How did God stop Hitler then?" she asked the unrecognizable person in the mirror.

The woman standing opposite Ava tightened her jaw, stiffened her back, then replied, "God stopped Hitler with a horrendous act of violence delivered via the tanks, guns, and planes of the Allied Forces. He smashed Hitler with the sacrifice of young American heroes—some who came home wounded, some who came home whole, and some who did not come home at all."

Ava considered the reasoning of the woman with

too much makeup. "Okay, so if I lived in the forties and had the chance to assassinate Hitler, I guess I would have done it. But Shane Lawrence is my own countryman. Does he deserve the same level of demonization as Hitler?"

The woman quickly retorted, "Six million Jews were killed under Hitler. To date, Shane Lawrence and the socialist policies he espouses have killed sixty million unborn Americans. And in their mothers' wombs, no less. At least those Jews had a chance to see a blue sky, laugh, feel the warmth of the sun. No such luxury was ever afforded to the murdered masses killed in the abortion mills of America.

"And that's just the beginning. If Blackwell is right, Christians will be euthanized if they don't renounce their faith, their organs sold off on the open market. You have a chance to throw sand in the gears of this hideous machine. Will you take it?"

Ava shook her head. "I don't know? What would God want me to do?"

"What are the greatest commandments?" she asked.

Ava remembered the words of Jesus. "To love God with all your heart, mind and soul. And the second is to love your neighbor as yourself. The golden rule. Do unto others as you'd have done unto you."

The woman in the mirror challenged, "If another person had the opportunity to put an end to this evil, to allow you to remain free, to read your Bible, worship in public, and live in peace with those you love, wouldn't you want that person to take that opportunity no matter what measures had to be taken?"

Ava nodded but did not reply.

"Then it is a sin, a godless transgression, a cowardly shame if you do not."

A deluge of resolve flooded into Ava's soul. Where hesitation and doubt had been, certainty and fortitude stood tall in their stead. She touched up her lipstick, placed the cap back on the tube, and walked out of the bathroom.

Ulysses came back in the room. "Are you ready?"

"Oh yeah!"

CHAPTER 14

For he is the minister of God to thee for good. But if thou do that which is evil, be afraid; for he beareth not the sword in vain: for he is the minister of God, a revenger to execute wrath upon him that doeth evil.

Romans 13:4

"Tamara, can you get us some more glassware? We need to have at least six champagne flutes on each of the VIP tables." Mercedes continued folding napkins on the corner of each table and placing a champagne ice bucket on top. "If you can't find any clean ones, you might have to run a couple racks through the dishwasher." Like all the girls working at Lure, Mercedes was young, thin, and beautiful.

And like all the girls at the club, she dressed provocatively.

"Sure. No problem." This was Ava's first chance to get away from Mercedes' watchful eye. She stopped by the back-service room and retrieved the tiny toolkit from her purse. She'd have to disable the fire alarm on the emergency exit before she was missed.

Ava first went to the dish room. She found several racks of clean flutes but sent a rack through the washer for an alibi. While they washed, she scurried to the exit door. She quickly removed the housing over the alarm, cut the wires to the alarm, and began replacing the housing.

"Tamara?" Mercedes called out from around the corner.

Ava's heart skipped a beat, she quickly secured the push bar and tossed her tools in the trash can by the emergency exit. "Yes?"

"Don't go out that door. The alarm will sound." Mercedes looked at her curiously. "We can take a smoke break after we get set up. But let's finish. How's it coming with those glasses?"

"I ran some through the dishwasher." Ava walked toward the machine which had just finished.

Mercedes grabbed a rack of the champagne flutes. "These are already clean."

"Yeah, but they had spots all over them." Ava pulled the rack from the dish machine.

"The spots wipe off with a napkin. Now we're going to have to dry those that came out of the machine, which will take much longer." Mercedes led the way with her rack of glassware.

Ava followed with the dripping rack. "Sorry, I didn't know."

"That's okay. Is this your first service job?"

"Yeah."

"What did you do before?" Mercedes began shining the dry champagne flutes with a cloth napkin.

"I was a professor at a school in Utah. I taught literature." Ava dried her glasses.

"Utah? I'd kill myself. Well, welcome to LA. Literature, huh?"

"Yeah."

"I read. Magazines, mostly." Mercedes laughed. "Who am I kidding? I don't read. Who has time?"

"But you must be a forward thinker," Ava said. "After all, your SVA score was high enough for you to work the party tonight."

"We only had a few people score too low to work tonight. I mean, unless you believe in some cosmic spaghetti monster that created the universe out of nothing, you're automatically in good standing. And all the social policies, well that's just common sense. It's what everybody thinks. Unless you live somewhere like Utah. You poor thing, I can't imagine."

Ava smiled and continued to help set up.

Two hours later, the guests began to arrive. Ava kept an eye out for her target. Mercedes was very helpful in pointing out some of the lesser-known celebrities that a hayseed from Utah probably wouldn't recognize.

"So you keep up with all of these people?"

"It's part of the job. At least that's what I tell myself." Mercedes giggled at her own shallowness.

"I saw on TMZ that Shane Lawrence has a new girlfriend, but nobody knows who she is. Is she from Hollywood?"

"No. She's some rising star on the political stage. But I won't even bother memorizing her name. Shane goes through girlfriends like I go through cigarettes. I guess you have a crush on him like everyone else?"

"He's cute." Ava shrugged.

"Yeah, well, he'll be surrounded by starlets tonight who are fighting to be his next fling."

Ava feigned a looked of disappointment. "At least I'll get to say I was in the same room with him tonight."

"You'll do better than that, little Ms. Tamara from Utah; he'll be in our section tonight."

"Oh, really!" Ava's delighted expression was genuine, just not for the reason she'd implied.

Roman walked up to the two girls. "Tamara, Mercedes, the catering company didn't get the memo about the SVA score requirements until they showed up. They had to send three of their servers home. I told the woman that it's not our problem, but they don't have enough help to pass hors d'oeuvres. Give them a hand if you can, but don't let it interfere with your drink service."

Mercedes sighed. "Let's go."

Ava followed her to the service room and grabbed a tray filled with cocktail shrimp and tempura vegetables.

The woman making up the appetizer trays said,

"Thanks for bailing us out. They're going a little too far with this new social-pecking-order thing if you ask me."

Mercedes picked up a tray filled with smoked salmon and cream cheese on bagel chips. "You better watch that attitude, or you'll get a demerit and be sent home too. Then who will make up the hors-d'oeuvres trays?"

The woman quickly looked down at her work and humbled her tone. "You're right. I shouldn't have said anything."

"I'm kidding! Don't be so serious!" Mercedes headed out to the club to pass around the food.

Ava followed her without making any comments.

"Can you believe that woman?" Mercedes chuckled once they'd left the back room. "She acted like she thinks we're in the KGB or something."

"Yeah, right?" Ava played along, wondering how long it would take Mercedes to understand the ramifications of Markovich's new leadership style.

The guests made short work of the appetizers and Mercedes led Ava back for another round. They picked up two more trays, one with bacon wrapped scallops and the other with king crab legs already removed from the shell. The club began erupting with applause as they left the service room.

"What's going on?" Ava asked.

Mercedes looked toward the entrance. "Shane is here."

Ava stood on her tippy toes to see. Shane Lawrence was coming in, shaking hands with all of the famous guests who'd arrived before him. In his wake was an entourage of big security guards and tiny girls wearing tinier dresses. Ava saw a red-head, a blonde, a brunette, and the one on his arm had short jet-black hair. Ava scanned the crowd coming in with Lawrence, then did a double take of the girl with the black hair. *No! It can't be!*

"I've got to run to the restroom. I'll be right back," she said to Mercedes.

Mercedes seemed to be enamored with Lawrence and all the pomp surrounding his grand entrance. "Take your time. We can't pass out appetizers or get drinks until all of this has settled down."

Ava quickly retrieved her phone from the back-service area and hurried to the women's room. She sent her father a text. Bad news. *The new girlfriend is someone that knows us both.*

Ava waited for his reply. Seconds later, she read silently. *Then we need to move up the timeline to limit the odds of you being noticed. Meet me at door in 30.*

Ava tucked her phone in the back of her skirt so she could keep track of the time, then rushed back to find Mercedes.

"Hey! There you are." Mercedes placed a stack of cocktail napkins on her tray. "I'm going to start taking drink orders. You can help Skylar serve champagne. But don't take that cheap garbage around our section. Shane bought a case of PJ for his guests. It's chilling in that big cooler by the ice machine."

"Sure." Ava was happy to be assigned to help out in another area. She'd have to avoid Shane Lawrence and his entourage until it was time. Ava assisted Skylar with pouring the house champagne for the various guests over the next twenty minutes.

"I guess that's it for now. Why don't you go back to helping Mercedes?" Skylar chucked three empty champagne bottles in the trash.

"Okay." Ava quickly ducked into the ladies' room once more. She sent Ulysses another text. *I've got a few seconds. If you could come now, that would be great.*

Right away he replied. *Five minutes out.*

Ava gritted her teeth, hoping she could steal away again without arousing suspicion. She wasted no time finding Mercedes. "We're done with the champagne service. What else do you need?"

"I've got like a gazillion Cosmos to run. The bartender is making them by the pitcher. Just start loading up a tray and running them out."

"How will I know who ordered them?"

"Number one, only girls drink Cosmos, so that slims down your odds. The girls who really want theirs will be waving you down when they see you coming. If someone takes one that didn't order it, it doesn't matter. Shane is picking up the tab and the bartender is making extra."

"Okay. I'll get right on it." Ava swiftly made her way to the bar and began loading her tray with tall martini glasses filled with a light pink concoction. She expeditiously ran the drinks out to the floor and auctioned them off. She estimated that it had taken her less than two minutes. "I should have time for one more delivery."

Ava headed back to the bar and reloaded. Once that tray was emptied, she checked her phone. "One minute left." She didn't want Ulysses to be caught loitering around the emergency exit by security, so she headed to the fire door.

She listened for the sound of her father walking up and kept an eye on the time with her phone. Exactly five minutes after the last text, she heard the faint sound of footsteps. She pushed the door open.

Ulysses quickly stepped through and handed her the bottle of VX nerve agent. "The girlfriend, is it who I think it is?"

"Yep," Ava said.

"Tamara! Where have you been? I need you on the floor!"

Ava spun around to see Mercedes glaring at her.

"And who is this?" Mercedes lowered her brows as she stared Ulysses down.

"He's my friend. He brought me my hand sanitizer." Ava held up the bottle to show Mercedes. "I'm sort of a germ freak. Sorry."

Mercedes' head began to shake back and forth, slowly at first, but it gradually picked up speed. "Oh, no! I know exactly what's going on here!"

"No, really!" Ava insisted.

"I hope he's paying you a lot and I hope you got the money up front, because when I tell Roman that you sneaked a paparazzi into Shane's party, you'll be fired on the spot." Mercedes began to turn around but paused to issue a warning to Ulysses. "And you better be gone before security finds you. If they have to escort you out, it could get a little rough. I've known people to get black eyes, split lips, all kinds of stuff from tripping on their way out the door, especially paparazzi."

Ulysses acted without hesitation. He grabbed

Mercedes by the arm, spun her around and put her in a chokehold. He squeezed his opposite bicep with the hand that was around her throat. Mercedes struggled for several seconds, then she went limp.

"Is she dead?" Ava looked on in horror.

"Just sleeping. She'll wake up soon, so we have to act fast. Help me tie her hands and feet with trash bags." Ulysses grabbed the industrial sized box of fifty-gallon can liners and tore one off. He handed it to Ava, then tore off another. He twisted it into a rope and secured Mercedes' hands behind her back.

Ava was less proficient than her father but eventually got Mercedes' feet bound. Ulysses already had a third trash bag tied around her mouth for a gag.

"Open the door to the walk-in cooler."

Ava complied with his request and Ulysses dragged Mercedes inside. Afterward, he slammed the door shut and pulled the padlock hanging on the door handle. He inserted it into the opening and locked it shut. "Someone will have the key. They'll find her soon enough, but we need her out of the way for the next few minutes."

"We need longer than that. We have to worry about not being seen by our friend."

"We may not have the luxury. The girl in the cooler just shortened our available time window. Whatever we're going to do, we need to do it now!"

Ava sighed wishing things could go as planned just once. She took out her protective gloves and the towel she would use to apply the nerve agent on Shane Lawrence's skin. "I left an extra glass of champagne behind the ice bin. You can use that to spill on Lawrence. Hopefully, we'll get an opportunity when our little friend isn't looking."

"Either way, it's now or never." Ulysses found the glass and headed out onto the floor of the nightclub.

Ava waited a few moments, then followed him out. She bumped right into Roman.

"Have you seen Mercedes?"

"She's up in the VIP section."

"She's not in the VIP section. That's why I'm looking for her. Shane Lawrence's trick du jour is barking at me like a menacing little chihuahua wanting to know where her Perrier Jouet is at—as if she'd know the difference between that and Freixenet." He rolled his eyes. "What's all this with the gloves? What are you doing?"

"A girl got sick on the sink in the women's restroom. I was asked to clean it up."

"By who?"

"The red-headed girl with Shane Lawrence."

Roman ran his hands over his face in exasperation. "What a fiasco. Go, go; clean it up and hurry back. Whether I find Mercedes or not, I need you up in the VIP as soon as possible."

"Yes, sir." Ava circled around by the bathrooms before heading to the upper level where Shane Lawrence was standing amidst his suite of adoring companions.

She saw the girlfriend walk away to talk to Matt Damon whose table was nearby. *This is it. This is our chance!* Ava felt sure her father would seize the moment, so she began making her way to Lawrence's table.

She watched, as if in slow motion, while Ulysses seemed to trip over his own feet and send the contents of his champagne flute hurtling through the air. Ava watched the slow, fluid arc of the substance float effortlessly over the table and splash Shane Lawrence right on the lapel of his designer shirt.

A sense of glee bubbled up inside her like the champagne which had been flowing so freely for the past hour. Urgency seemed to push her from behind and she darted into action with the towel.

Lawrence stood with his mouth open wide in shock. Ava pushed the towel to his neck and wiped it across his face. "Mr. Lawrence, let me help you with that. I'm so sorry."

"Stop it! Just stop it! You're making it worse!" He snatched the towel from her hand. He pointed at his largest security guard. "Harold! Grab that oaf! Bring him here!"

The red-headed girl took the contaminated towel containing the VX nerve agent from Lawrence and scowled at Ava. "What's wrong with you! It's like you're attacking him!" She snapped her head back toward Shane Lawrence and began gingerly blotting his face and forehead with the deadly towel.

Ava thought of a million snarky replies but knew the girl would be suffering the same fate as Lawrence in a matter of minutes. She began walking away but kept an eye on what was happening with her father.

The giant bodyguard, Harold she figured, had Ulysses by the collar of his jacket. He held him like a dog with his prey before his master.

Lawrence pushed the red-headed girl away.

"Who are you here with?"

"Clooney," Ulysses replied.

"We'll see about that. Gretchen!" He snapped his fingers at the young brunette. "Go ask George if he knows this character."

The brunette hurried off like a faithful slave.

Lawrence frowned at Ulysses. "For your sake, I hope you're not a paparazzi. This is a private party, and if you're here without an invitation, you will be spending the evening in jail for trespassing."

At that, Ulysses quickly peeled out of his jacket and made a run for it. Harold and two other bodyguards tackled him before he got out of the VIP section. Ava watched in horror. This was the time she was supposed to leave. Yet in her mind, she knew she could never leave her father behind. She looked on while the young brunette returned and spoke to Lawrence.

Ava couldn't hear her but understood the gist of the conversation. Of course, Clooney had no idea who Ulysses was. Ava shucked off the protective gloves and walked back toward Lawrence's table hoping to get an idea of how she could get Ulysses out.

Her father looked at her with scolding eyes that reminded her she was supposed to leave and leave now. She returned his gaze with an apologetic expression hoping he'd understand that she couldn't do that.

Lawrence pulled out his phone. "I'm calling the police."

Before he dialed the number, his neck twitched. He lowered his phone and grabbed the back of his neck. He looked concerned for a moment but seemed to dismiss it. Once again, he raised his phone to dial the number. When he did, he shivered violently and yelped out in pain. "Ouch! I'm having a muscle spasm in my back!" The blonde rushed to his side, grasping at the opportunity to rub his shoulders.

Ava wondered if the residual contact would be enough to kill her, also.

The red-headed girl squealed out. "My hand! My hand! It's cramping!"

Lawrence looked at the redhead, then at Ulysses. "What did you throw on me? That wasn't champagne."

Ava made a beeline for the fire alarm. Her only hope for getting Ulysses out was to create a commotion. Ava pulled the lever and the loud buzzing alarm pierced the air. Instantly, chaos ensued. Guests and staff looked at each other wondering if they should leave the building or not. Soon, they all began rushing toward the few exits, pushing and clawing past one another like ravenous animals.

Ava rushed back to Lawrence's table. Shane Lawrence and the red-head were lying on the floor. She looked up at her father who was still being held by the bodyguards.

His lips mouthed a single word. *GO*!

She saw no way to get him free without a gun, and maybe an army. Disappointed, she nodded and mouthed three words. *I love you.*

His face was pained as he nodded to show he understood.

Ava swallowed hard as she headed for the crowded exits. Suddenly, the fire alarm halted, and the bright lights came on, replacing the hypnotic low colored lights, which panned around the floor and up the walls. Roman's English voice came over the speakers.

"Ladies and gentlemen, please calm down. There is no fire. We believe we had an assault on this evening's host, Shane Lawrence. EMS is en route. I'm sure Shane will be fine if we just keep thinking positive thoughts on his behalf.

"Unfortunately, Lure security staff will be manning the exits until the police arrive. This was a hostile attack and the police will want to get statements from everyone before you are allowed to leave. Thank you in advance for your cooperation."

Ava shook her head. "No, no, no!" She had to get out of the building before anyone discovered Mercedes.

She headed for the back door where she'd let her father in. Two bouncers stood guard.

"Please, I'm having an anxiety attack. I need to get some fresh air. You can watch me. I work here, I'm just freaking out right now."

The larger of the two looked at the smaller, who wasn't all that small. "What do you think?"

"Sorry, ma'am. We can't let anyone out the door. The police will be here in a few minutes, then they'll start letting people leave."

"This is false imprisonment. That's a felony! Both of you can go to prison for this!"

The bigger guy again looked at the more moderately sized bouncer. He seemed to take her claim seriously.

But once again, the comparatively-smaller guy shook his head. "No one is going to leave until the police get here! Go get some water or something!"

Ava stormed off to try the same tactic on the remaining exits.

"Ava?" said a female voice from behind.

Particularly since everyone in the club knew her as Tamara, that was not a name she wanted to hear. She squinted and clenched her fists, knowing exactly who was behind her.

"I like what you've done with your hair. And the outfit! If I didn't know better, I'd say you were trying to look like me. What's wrong? Did you get tired of your prude life? Well, I've got news for you! If Shane doesn't pull out of this fit, you'll be in for some excitement alright. I'll make sure you die the most horrific death you can imagine. You've already killed one of my boyfriends. If this one dies, I'm going to take it as a personal insult."

"I had every intention of upholding my end of that bargain. You double-crossed me. Chip's death is on you." Ava looked at the empty champagne bottle on the bar. She wondered if she could break the bottom out of it and cut Raquel's throat before security grabbed her.

"Restrain her, guys. Whatever happened to Shane, you can bet that she's in on it."

Ava turned to see that Raquel was flanked by four Lure security guards. She glared at her nemesis. "You've slept your way to the top, Raquel. Who says you don't have ambition?"

Ava had no choice but to let the guards put the

zip-tie restraints on her wrists.

Raquel snarled. "Your dad missed all those father-daughter dances when you were a little girl. But now you'll both get a chance to make up for it. I know some people around town. I'm sure we can arrange a father-daughter execution."

Reality began to set in. Ava felt sick at her stomach. She could think of no possible way out of this mess.

CHAPTER 15

Thou art my hiding place and my shield: I hope in thy word. Depart from me, ye evildoers: for I will keep the commandments of my God. Uphold me according unto thy word, that I may live: and let me not be ashamed of my hope.

Psalm 119:114-116

Sunday afternoon, Ava was brought into the small concrete interrogation room wearing an orange prison uniform with her hands cuffed and her feet shackled together.

"Wait here." The guard slammed the heavy metal door shut before Ava could reply.

"Do I have a choice?" she asked of the empty

room in which she sat. Ava took a seat at the metal table which was bolted to the floor.

Minutes later, a heavy-set woman in a grey pinstriped skirt suit came in with a worn leather briefcase. She put the case on the table and opened it. She pulled out a folder and passed a form to Ava. "My name is Vanessa Cooper. I'll be your advocate for the tribunal."

"Advocate? You mean like a court-appointed lawyer?"

The woman tapped her finger on the form. "Not exactly. Your status as an enemy combatant doesn't afford you any rights under the constitution. This form clarifies my role. Look it over and sign it."

"Not that the constitution has proved to be much of a deterrent for the regime anyways." Ava read the paper. "So, no attorney-client privilege." She continued scanning the text. "Wait, you're from the Social Justice Law Center?" Ava looked up at the woman. "Can I request an advocate from another organization?"

"Let me be clear, Ms. Wilson . . ."

Ava cut her off. "It's Mrs. Mitchem."

Vanessa replied sharply, "Wilson is what is on your most recent government documents. We will not be recognizing any of your aliases. And no, you can't request another advocate. My advocacy is for justice, not necessarily for you. My role is simply to inform you of what you can expect from the tribunal. So you can prepare yourself."

"You don't represent me?"

"My fiduciary duties in the tribunal are to justice. Not either party."

"Forgive me if I'm hesitant to believe that you'll be impartial, being from the SJLC. After all, the person I'm accused of killing was close with Mark Polpot and other top-level people at SJLC."

"I won't pretend to be impartial. Shane Lawrence has long been a champion of progress in America. His death marks a tragic day for this country. He can never be replaced." Vanessa glared at Ava. "However, the SJLC is tasked with overseeing the tribunal, and I've been granted the pleasure of preparing you for the process."

Ava sensed that Vanessa was sincere about it being a pleasure. It would be her opportunity to watch Ava squirm while she detailed the horrible path that lay ahead. "Okay, what's next?"

"The tribunal will be held one week from tomorrow. It will be televised." Vanessa looked up from her briefcase. "The execution will also be broadcast via the internet and cable news networks. Lethal injection is the only available form of execution in California."

The blood drained from Ava's face. "Execution? You mean if I'm found guilty?"

"Ms. Wilson, multiple eyewitnesses saw you apply the nerve agent on Shane Lawrence. We have the towel, the bottle, as well as the gloves which have trace amounts of the nerve agent on the outside, and your fingerprints on the inside."

"So, I'm already condemned. What's the point of the tribunal?"

"The public at large has been wronged, Ms. Wilson. This coming week, they'll have the opportunity to mourn Shane's death. Then the tribunal and execution will grant them some small amount of closure."

"Can't I appeal?"

"Like I said, you are an enemy combatant and aren't afforded any rights under the Constitution." Vanessa seemed to be suppressing a grin of enjoyment.

Ava looked at the metal table. "What about the other man that was incarcerated with me? If I agree to confess on television that I killed Lawrence, will they let him go?"

"Your father is being held in a separate facility. As you can imagine, the administration has some questions for him. For one, VX nerve agent isn't readily available on the black market nor is it easy to produce. President Markovich is curious about the role that the Alliance, and more importantly, Turner Blackwell had in the assassination. The CIA will be seeking those answers from your father."

Ava understood that Vanessa was referring to torture. "I can tell you everything you need to know if you'll let him go."

"That won't be necessary. The president has determined that your father will be the one to provide the information, and you'll be the person who will go before the tribunal. Your trial will be very public, for the good of the people. We wouldn't want you to look like you've had an intense interrogation."

"Of course not!" Ava interjected. "We wouldn't want people to think this is a communist dictatorial regime that executes people without a trial!"

Vanessa placed a pen on the form. "I understand

that you're upset. If you'll just sign the form, stating that you understand our relationship, I'll let you get back to your cell where you can process all of this. I'm sure it's difficult."

Ava grabbed the pen and lunged at Vanessa who jumped out of her seat.

"Guard!"

The door flew open and a giant correctional officer stormed in, shooting Ava with a Taser. She was restrained hand and foot, then dragged back to her cell.

Tuesday morning, a guard came to Ava's cell. "Stand up and face the wall."

She lay on her bunk. "Why should I?"

He drew his Taser.

"Okay! Okay!" Ava held her hands up and complied.

She heard the door open behind her, then close again. Ava turned around to see a woman wearing an orange uniform in her mid-forties standing inside the door.

"Hi." Since Sunday, she'd not seen another person other than the orderlies who brought her food.

"Hello." The woman's face was downcast.

The LA County facility Ava was being held in was known as Death Row, so if the woman was in Ava's cell, she wasn't long for this world. "I'm Ava."

"Maggie. Nice to meet you." She took a seat on the floor with her back against the bars of the entrance.

"What are you here for?"

Maggie glanced up, but not for long. "I've got a healthy liver, and I'm the right blood type. Someone with a high SVA score wants it. So . . . tomorrow, it will be theirs."

"Oh." Ava felt terrible for the woman. "But I meant why are you locked up in the first place?"

"I was sent to a level-one education facility in San Francisco. I continued to pray openly while I was incarcerated, so I was expelled. I can't be rehabilitated. Organs are harvested and transplanted in LA. That's why I was brought down here."

"Sorry."

"Don't be. I've wanted to get out of California for years. Now I'm getting out. And I'll be going to heaven. It's a good trade." She smiled for a brief moment and nodded confidently. "A really good trade."

Ava sat beside the woman and took her hand. "Me, too."

The woman's smile quivered and she began to cry. "But it's tough. They took my husband to another camp. I can't get any information about him. He's strong." She dried her eyes with the tail of her shirt. "My kids, they're the ones I worry most about. My son, Daniel, he's twelve. We taught him about God, I think he'll hang on to his faith. But my daughter, Diana, she's only seven." The woman's voice cracked and she quit talking for a while. Finally, she dried her eyes again and said, "I'm afraid they'll turn her, convince her that there is no God."

She hated to hear the woman say such a thing.

147

What could be more terrible? Ava thought. Yet it solidified in her mind that she'd done the right thing and that her sacrifice was worthwhile, even though she had less than a week to live. No price was too high to put an end to this wicked regime.

"What's your story?"

Ava didn't admit to pulling off the assassination, but briefly described what she'd been accused of.

Maggie smiled. "Lawrence was effective at delivering propaganda. For my children's sake, I'm glad he's gone. Not that the administration won't be able to brainwash the children they've taken away from conservatives without Shane Lawrence, but every time they lose a major player on the board, America has a better shot at survival.

"My kids, they're wards of the state. California has taken over a million children from parents who have been assigned to re-education camps. I'm sure a lot of parents will go along with the re-education program to get their kids back. California has nowhere to house them. For now, the kids live in tent cities, refugee camps basically. No one knows how long the administration will attempt to re-educate minors before they're classified as unable to be rehabilitated and euthanized.

"The ones who are successfully brainwashed will go into the Social Justice Legion's security force when they're eighteen. The ones who aren't . . ." She looked down at her hands. "They'll be organ donors.

"I begged my husband to get out of California when the riots started, but he didn't want to leave his job. He said things wouldn't get this bad. I wanted to believe him, so I didn't keep pushing.

"We'd hear people from time to time talking about a second American civil war or a communist revolution, but I thought it was hyperbole or political rhetoric. Our pastor at church felt the same way. He said to just ignore that kind of talk—focus on Jesus and not get caught up in politics."

The woman sighed. "Of course, now I think it was the Holy Spirit that we were ignoring."

Ava clenched the woman's hand. "But you know where you're going. It still works out in the end."

Maggie nodded. "For me, and for my husband— I'm confident. But my kids, Markovich is going to use every tactic in his satanic arsenal to get them to turn from the faith. Retrospectively, I realize how successful this agenda has been in keeping the American Church in a blissful state of complacency. I have no illusions about how powerful the state is when it comes to convincing children there is no God. Unless you have little kids, you can't possibly know how that weighs on a mother's heart."

Ava said the only thing she could think of that might possibly lift Maggie's spirit. "Then let's spend the time we have left asking Jesus to protect the souls of your children. Let's ask him to guard their hearts and minds and to put the right people in their lives who will get them home to heaven."

"I'd like that." Maggie looked up into Ava's eyes, then the two took turns praying for Daniel and Diana.

Ava awoke on Wednesday morning to the sound of the cell door buzzing. Soon after, she heard the guard's voice. "Maggie Sloan, it's time."

Ava's heart sank for the woman she'd known only a few hours.

Maggie crawled down from the top bunk. Her lip quivered, and she looked at Ava. "Thank you."

Ava forced a smile. "See you soon."

Maggie bit her lip. "Yeah, see you soon."

The guard slammed the cell door and escorted Maggie away.

Ava prayed for Maggie and her children. She prayed for Ulysses and for Foley. She wanted to see her father and her husband once more before departing this world. She missed them both so badly it made her sick.

Wednesday afternoon, Ava was served lunch in her cell by another inmate at the prison. "Thank you," she said to the trustee.

The woman wore a prison uniform like Ava's, but it was blue. She did not reply to Ava's expression of gratitude but looked at her with sympathetic eyes.

Ava dissected the meal on the plastic tray. She had a fistful of shredded iceberg lettuce, two pieces of stale white bread, and a square-shaped item that smelled remotely like fish. Ava broke it in half. Inside the square, it was grainy, more like cornbread than fish. But, it was all she had, so she ate it anyway.

The meal acted as a temporary distraction, but it was soon over and Ava's mind returned to contemplating what her death would be like. Lethal injection was designed to not be painful, but how would she feel in the moments before, while she watched the needle being inserted into her vein? Would she panic? She felt afraid at this particular moment, just thinking about it.

Ava called out, "God! I'm so frightened! I know I'm coming home to you, but this is the scariest thing I've ever faced in my life. Please, God, send me an angel to comfort me or take away my fear. Please, Lord." Ava cried out for several minutes longer.

Soon, the terror of death faded and she felt peace welling up inside. It was slow at first, but her sense that everything was going to be okay grew and grew.

"Thank you, God. Thank you for your peace and for your Holy Spirit." Ava lay down on her bunk and fell fast asleep.

On Friday, Ava heard the door to the cell block being opened and a new prisoner being brought in. The woman entered the block singing a familiar hymn; her voice filled the block. The woman was still singing when the guard brought her to Ava's cell.

"Keep it down," the guard instructed as he slammed the door.

"What are you going to do? Kill me?" The young woman looked to be about Ava's age.

"Just keep it down!" the guard replied smugly and began walking away.

"Maybe you're going to beat me up. Oh, you can't do that. I'm donating both lungs and a kidney on Monday. Can't risk damaging the merchandise."

Ava liked the woman's spunky attitude. She was

glad to have company in the cell but hated that the two wouldn't have long to get to know each other; at least not in this world. "Hi, I'm Ava. Welcome to my humble abode—temporary, humble abode that is."

The young woman turned to her. "It's all temporary isn't it?"

"Yeah, I guess so."

"Anyway, thanks. I'm Yolanda."

"Nice to meet you. So, you're here for the weekend."

"Yep. Checking out Monday." Yolanda's face showed that she didn't feel as lightly about the matter as her words implied. "You?"

Ava swallowed hard. "Same. Checking out Monday." Ava proceeded to explain her situation, telling Yolanda how much she wished she could see her father and husband one last time.

"You'll see them. And you'll get to spend eternity together with them. No more war, no more pain, no more misery or heartache. It really is going to be wonderful."

Ava nodded. "I know. I'm just not particularly excited about the actual crossing over process."

Yolanda's smile was strained. "Yeah, tell me about it. Everyone wants beautiful white teeth, but nobody likes going to the dentist."

Ava chuckled.

"What?" Yolanda asked.

"Your analogy—I was a dental hygienist before all of this."

"Seriously?"

"Yeah. People would come in looking all fretful,

especially if they knew they needed a cavity drilled. But, half an hour later, it was over, and they were on their way with a big shiny smile." Ava grinned and took a deep breath. "That's all it is. A few seconds of discomfort, then we'll wake up in the arms of Jesus!"

Yolanda sat on Ava's bunk beside her and took her hand. "And we'll be wondering why we made such a big fuss over it, just like a trip to the dentist."

"Do you mind if I ask the particulars of you getting sent here?" Ava took a serious tone.

"I was first sent to a level-two camp. I worked at a church as a receptionist, so I was at the top of the list for being rehabilitated. I tried to play along. I thought maybe if I just did my time and kept my head down, that maybe I could get released. If I had gotten out of the camp, I was going to try to get to the border of Utah. But that didn't work out."

"What happened?" Ava asked.

"Most of the people in my camp were Christians. We had pens and paper in level-two, so we started trying to write down all the Bible verses we could remember. Some people knew four or five verses, others had memorized entire chapters. The idea was to write down as much of the Bible as we could and start memorizing those verses. That way, if we never got out, we'd at least have a few good verses memorized.

"I wished I'd spent more time memorizing the Bible when it was legal, but then again, I wish I'd done a lot of things differently when I was free.

"Nevertheless, we got caught and were all scheduled to be put down."

"I'm so sorry." Ava squeezed Yolanda's hand. "How did you get caught?"

"The SJL had informants planted in our camp. The informants were level-three and level-four people who had a chance to fast track their way to level six by proving their loyalty. One of them even knew a couple Bible verses." Yolanda looked at Ava and smiled with a nod.

"What are you looking at?" Ava asked curiously.

"You were a hero amongst my little group in level-two. We heard about Shane Lawrence. I mean, if it was actually you who pulled it off."

"You had a television in level-two?"

"Are you kidding? Of course! That's their primary source of propaganda and re-education." Yolanda rolled her eyes. "It has been for years, most of us just didn't see it. No point in reinventing the wheel, I guess."

"When was the last day you saw the news?"

"Yesterday morning. My group was pulled out of our camp in Oceanside right after lunch. They had my tests results back and matched me up with organ recipients before dinner. I've never seen the government be so efficient about anything in my life. But when it comes to collecting taxes or killing people, they can get things done."

Ava grimaced and changed the subject. "Any news about the Alliance States since Shane Lawrence died?"

"No. We only get regime propaganda news, you know, mainstream media. If Lawrence's death provided any advantage to the Alliance, we'd never hear about it."

"Oh." Ava still felt convinced that she'd done the right thing and that her sacrifice was not in vain, yet the smallest inkling that the mission made an impact would help her to feel better about the unbearable experience Ulysses was having.

Yolanda seemed to think about things for a moment. Finally, she looked up. "I will say that on Saturday morning before Lawrence was killed, the news was hyping up the imminent pledge of allegiance from the LAAM states."

"LAAM states?"

"Louisiana, Arkansas, Alabama, and Mississippi. Their governors were supposedly going to deliver a signed document to Markovich pledging their support and allegiance. I don't know if Lawrence's assassination was just too big of a headline that the news channels quit reporting on the LAAM pledge or if his death affected their resolve in some way. But whatever it was, I haven't heard a peep about it since Shane Lawrence was sent to meet his maker."

Ava considered the news, hoping the governors would hold off.

Yolanda continued, "The news was covering it like it was a pretty big deal. The LAAM states would have prevented the current Alliance States from being geographically contiguous with the rest of the southern states if they were to join. I think Markovich was counting on the LAAMs to keep the rest from seeing the Alliance as a viable option.

"Who knows? Maybe you . . . or whoever it was that offed Lawrence just changed the course of the war."

Ava sighed. That was what she needed to hear.

Her sacrifice was high, it cost her the chance to say goodbye to her husband, it cost her relationship with her father, and it would cost her life, but if it preserved the hope of freedom, it would be worth it. "So how many of those Bible verses were you able to memorize before they took you away?"

"I knew about ten and I memorized another thirty or so. Do you want to learn some?"

"I can't think of a better way to spend my last few hours on this planet. I'd love to." Ava smiled.

The rest of the weekend, Ava and Yolanda sang worship songs in their cell. Yolanda recited the Bible verses she knew to Ava so she could learn them as well. The two women kept their thoughts on the glory to come and ignored the dark cloud looming above their heads.

CHAPTER 16

We are confident, I say, and willing rather to be absent from the body, and to be present with the Lord.

2 Corinthians 5:8

Ava's blood ran cold as she heard the guard summon her cellmate on Monday morning.

"Yolanda Collins, it's time."

Yolanda climbed down from the top bunk, her face perplexed.

Ava's voice was not nearly as pleasant as Yolanda's, yet she began singing the same familiar hymn in an effort to inspire her new friend to take courage and hope.

Yolanda smiled and joined in with Ava. Their voices grew in tandem while Yolanda was taken from the cell block. Ava continued the song after her friend could no longer be heard. Her voice weakened, trailing off as her solo portion concluded.

Once again, Ava was alone. "But you're here with me Jesus," she whispered aloud. "Stay near me today, please. This is going to be a tough one." Ava spent the next two hours in silent prayer.

The door opened to the block. Ava looked out to see who it was. "Vanessa. Great." She watched as two guards escorted the woman to Ava's cell.

"Ms. Wilson," Vanessa said.

"I answer to Mrs. Mitchem." Ava lay back on her bunk.

"I can see that you've decided to make this day difficult. I understand that this is not a pleasant experience for you, but if you cooperate, I can assure you that it will go better."

"Oh yeah? How are you going to make my mock trial and my summary execution more enjoyable?" Ava sat up. "Do you think about the words coming out of your mouth, or are you so zombified from your liberal indoctrination that you don't even know what you're saying anymore?"

Vanessa sighed and looked at the guard as if she were pleading for his pity. "Ms. Wilson, if you cooperate, you'll be allowed to live out your final hours with dignity. You'll be allowed to dress in regular clothing and given a final courtesy meal of your choosing."

"Oh, so the regime won't look like the animals they are if they cart me into this dog-and-pony show shackled in an orange jumpsuit? No thanks. I'm not really hungry, and I have no desire to participate in your propaganda charade by getting all dressed up."

Vanessa looked at the guard. "You guys may need to call in some backup. It looks like you're going to have to hit her with the Taser and then do a forced extraction."

"What? I didn't say I wasn't coming out of the cell!" Ava had no desire to make the day any worse. She did not want to be Tasered again.

Vanessa gave a saccharine smile. "Now that's better. Another thing for you to remember, when executionees are prepped for termination, they are typically given a mild sedative which goes a long way in making those final moments more palatable. But a common mistake that has been known to happen with less compliant individuals is for them to receive a stimulant which, instead of relaxing them, causes heart palpitations and amplifies the general feeling of anxiety associated with impending death. I'm sure you wouldn't want anything like that to happen."

Ava had no illusions about how frightened she'd be in those last remaining seconds. She certainly didn't need to be injected with an amphetamine to make it worse. She lowered her head like a beaten animal. "No, ma'am."

"Good!" Vanessa's voice pepped up considerably. "Now that we understand each other, I think this day will go rather smoothly."

The heavy-set woman turned to one of the guards. "They have a suit for her in the intake area. Get her cleaned up and ready for transport."

"Aren't we walking her over to the courthouse?" the guard inquired.

"No. A prisoner transport van is taking her offsite. One of the professional television studios will be hosting the tribunal. This will be broadcast nationwide, so we need good sound and light. You simply can't get that in a real courtroom."

Ava hated being used for the regime's agenda, but she could do little about it. The guards ushered her out of the cell that had been her home for the past eight days. She watched as Vanessa hurried toward the sally port door.

"Pardon me, ma'am," Ava called to the woman.

"What is it?" Vanessa scowled.

"If the offer is still open, could I request a steak and baked potato for my last meal?"

The heavy security door buzzed open and Vanessa walked through it. "Fine."

Ava had told the truth when she stated that she wasn't hungry, but on the off chance that her steak dinner included a steak knife, it might give her some options. Surely, she didn't dare think that she'd be able to escape with a steak knife, but it might allow her the possibility of ending her life on her own terms. If she was to die anyway, perhaps she could deprive the sadistic state of the right to parade her on national television while they made a mockery of justice.

Ava walked between the guards through a series of thick stockade doors. She finally arrived in a small secure room. The door was shut and locked behind her. She found a skirt suit draped over the steel bench which was bolted to the concrete floor.

Reluctantly, Ava changed into the suit. No other shoes were provided other than the cheap plastic flip flops she'd been given upon arrival. "Obviously they don't intend on the camera getting any shots of my feet."

Once she'd changed, Ava sat on the simple bench and waited. Time dragged on and she filled it by praying silently for courage, strength, and comfort from the Holy Spirit. Her life on earth would soon come to an end and her life on the other side of the veil would begin.

Forty minutes later, the door opened. "Ms. Wilson, it's time." Vanessa, flanked by two guards, stood holding her leather satchel.

"Could you at least call me Ava?" She stood up from the bench.

Vanessa looked at the brown suit which Ava had put on. "I think I can make that small accommodation."

"Thank you." Ava's shoulders slumped as she began the procession to her death.

She held out her hands while the guards placed shackles on her before loading her into the back of the transport van.

"I'll meet you at the studio." Vanessa waved.

The guard slammed the van door shut.

Ava let herself be pulled out of her seat by the same guard who'd put her in the van. She looked up at the stark white, windowless wall of the television studio. She'd never seen one from the outside except on TV or in a movie. She never dreamed she'd see one in person, and certainly not under such bizarre circumstances.

"Take her inside. There's a small green room on the right. Lock her in there until the tribunal begins." Vanessa issued orders to the guards. Next, she addressed Ava. "Your steak is on the table in the green room. I'm going out on a limb here by having the guards remove your shackles. Don't make me regret it."

"Of course not. Thank you." Ava walked obediently to the green room. Once inside, she held out her hands for the guards to remove her cuffs and then stood still for them to take off her ankle irons. They closed the door on their way out.

Ava stood in the studio waiting room. A small sofa was against one wall. In front of it was a simple coffee table and on it, a Styrofoam container. "I guess that's my steak. I had to be silly to expect a fancy covered dish." Ava walked over and sat on the couch.

She exhaled deeply, wondering if she'd find a steak knife inside, asking herself if she'd be able to take her own life if the utensil was there. Her fingers trembled as she reached for the box and pressed the tab to open the top. Ava closed her eyes, not wanting to know if the knife was in the container. She felt her mouth go dry. She took a long, heavy breath, held it, and opened one eye. Her mouth frowned at what she saw.

The to-go container held a baked potato with the foil and a single pat of butter. The butter had long since melted. Beside it was a tortured bit of meat, burnt beyond recognition, and cut up into small bite-sized cubes, but no knife. Instead, a clear plastic bag held a flimsy white plastic fork and a small folded napkin. "I suppose I should have been more specific when I said *steak*. I wasn't expecting Ruth's Chris, but I didn't think they'd go to Denny's either."

Disappointed, Ava was in no mood to eat. But then, a thought struck her. "What if Dad was able to get free? What if he's staging some kind of rescue operation right now? I'd need my strength to escape."

With this desperate thought, Ava peeled the plastic off the disposable fork and pushed herself to consume the tepid potato and the leathery cubes of poorly seasoned meat. She washed it down with a bottle of lukewarm water left on the coffee table.

Soon, the door opened. "Ava, let's go." Vanessa waved for her to hurry.

"Okay." Ava saw no point in dragging it out. Either she would be rescued or she'd be going home to Jesus. Both options entailed a highly stressful event in the near future followed by a period of bliss and happiness. "Best get on with it then." She followed Vanessa on to the set.

CHAPTER 17

O Lord God, to whom vengeance belongeth; O God, to whom vengeance belongeth, shew thyself. Lift up thyself, thou judge of the earth: render a reward to the proud. Lord, how long shall the wicked, how long shall the wicked triumph? How long shall they utter and speak hard things? and all the workers of iniquity boast themselves? They break in pieces thy people, O Lord, and afflict thine heritage. They slay the widow and the stranger, and murder the fatherless. Yet they say, The Lord shall not see, neither shall the God of Jacob regard it. Understand, ye brutish among the people: and ye fools, when will ye be wise? He that planted the ear, shall he not hear? he that formed the eye, shall he not see? He that chastiseth the heathen, shall not he correct? he that teacheth man knowledge, shall not he know? The Lord knoweth the thoughts of man, that they are vanity.

Psalm 94:1-11

Bright studio light shone down on a courtroom movie scene.

Ava wondered what she'd missed in the media coverage which described the proceedings to the public. Vanessa whispered as they approached the defendant's table at the front of the courtroom, "We're on a five-minute delay, so any last-minute speech intended to rally your rebel friends in the Alliance States will be cut out. However, any such outburst will definitely earn you that special treatment at the execution that we talked about."

Ava nodded that she understood. Despite Scripture's call to love her enemies, Ava couldn't help but hope that if her father were to stage a rescue, Vanessa might catch a stray bullet.

"All rise for the tribunal," said a woman in uniform acting as a bailiff.

Ava recognized the man who came out and took the judge's seat. It was none other than the Social Justice Law Center's own Mark Polpot.

"This tribunal is to determine the guilt and punishment of Ava Wilson for her crimes against the United States and civilized society. I will be presiding over this hearing under the federal authority of the Social Justice Legion." Polpot slammed the gavel. "The tribunal is now in session. The tribunal calls the first witness, Raquel Kohut."

Ava shuddered with anger. Of all the people who might possibly be qualified to be her accuser, Raquel was the least. Raquel wore a sleek black pencil dress and a black hat with the slimmest band of black tulle, as if she were in mourning. She made her way to the stand.

Ava rolled her eyes. The only reason Raquel was still considered Lawrence's girlfriend at the time of his death was that Ava had killed him before he'd had ample opportunity to replace her with the next little Hollywood starlet in waiting. But Raquel would milk this production for all it was worth. She'd use it to propel herself even higher into the SJL politburo.

"Ms. Kohut, I understand that this most recent run-in with the defendant is not the first encounter you've had with her," Polpot said.

"No. Unfortunately, fate has brought our paths together far too many times. And with each crossing, she has rained down misery and sorrow, not only upon me and those I care about, but on the heads of the collective, diminishing the lives of everyone who believes in social justice, equality, and fairness."

For the next half hour, Ava had to listen without being allowed to respond while Raquel dragged her name through the mud and painted a heavily-slanted version of the events where she and Raquel had both been involved.

Raquel told of how Ava had robbed Chip, a valid munitions officer in the SJL, of the material necessary to murder hundreds of peaceful people looking only to turn in their guns and seek a world without bloodshed.

She explained how Ava had kidnapped Chip in the middle of the night, then tortured him for information before executing him with the very explosives she'd stolen from this fine upstanding member of society. Raquel spoke of her time of sorrow and mourning. She told how she'd fought to find purpose and contemplated ending it all in her darkest hours.

Then she explained how, like an angel from above, Shane Lawrence had called her personally to express his condolences for her loss and to extend his gratitude for her diligent role in the revolution. Raquel choked up when she described the conversation where Shane Lawrence had invited her out to Hollywood, to get her mind off of things for a while. Her eyes glazed over, dripping the occasional contrived tear while she gave the account of her friendship with Shane and told how it had grown into something deeper, reviving in her the feelings of love she thought she'd never experience again.

Ava regretted eating the harsh meal of room-temperature potato and sinewy flesh. It felt heavy and sour in her stomach and became more so while she listened to this skewed rendition of the facts salted with outright lies.

Next up, Secretary of Homeland Security Alexander Douglas took the stand. He proceeded to give a drier, less emotional account of Ava's supposed crimes. He evaluated the evidence against her citing multiple eyewitness accounts that Ava knew to be false. Douglas painted a picture for the television audience that made Ava sound like a one-woman terrorist organization who, besides assassinating Shane Lawrence, had single-handedly destroyed the Austin firearms collection points, triggered the explosions at NRG Stadium and killed the former regime president, Steve Woods.

No other witnesses were called. Ava was not afforded an opportunity to cross-examine nor to give her version of the events. Rather, Mark Polpot slammed the gavel and delivered his verdict. "The tribunal finds the defendant, Ava Wilson, guilty of treason, murder, and the assassination of a sitting president as well as one of the country's most treasured gifts, Shane Lawrence. Her execution is scheduled for tonight at midnight Pacific Time and will be broadcast live on all the major news stations. For those of you on the east coast, the execution video will be available on the White House website as well as the SJL's, and my website, SJLC.com. I hope it will, in some small way, provide the closure that our hurting nation so desperately needs."

Ava looked at Vanessa. "That's it? I don't even get to defend myself or address the court?"

"I'm sorry. That's it. Let's get you back."

Ava stood. "Where will they. .?"

Vanessa replied coldly, "The execution will be at the prison."

"But they said it would be televised. They don't want to do it in a studio?" Ava knew if Ulysses were somehow able to rescue her, it would have to be outside of the prison. He simply wouldn't have the means to get her out of such a high-security facility.

"No. That won't be staged. It will be the same execution chamber that the SJL has been using for enemy combatants since you people started this." Vanessa compressed her lips. "I realize this is a tough thing to take, but you brought it on yourself, and now it's time to take your punishment."

Ava felt ill inside. She anxiously allowed the guards to escort her back to the van. Once inside, she knew the window for a rescue was closing fast.

Ava looked out the back window of the transport van looking for any clue that something might be up. If the van were to be struck by another vehicle in the rescue operation she'd need to brace for the impact. She remained vigilant, ready to participate in her own liberation, should an opportunity arise.

No such occasion came to be. The van pulled into the enclosed bay of the prison and the back door swung open. Two guards helped her out of the van and into the facility. She was taken to a room to change back into her orange uniform. Once dressed, she was handcuffed, shackled, and taken to a holding cell in the basement of the prison.

Ava's mind raced frantically. *No one is coming for me. I felt so sure Dad, or Foley, or President Blackwell would try to get me out of here. I guess I've been in denial all along. Maybe that was my brain trying to cope with the situation.*

Reality sank in. *I'm really going to die.*

Ava guessed it was after six when she'd left the studio. *In less than five hours, I'll be dead.*

She had no clock and no one was around to ask the time. For Ava, there was nothing left to do but to prepare herself for the inevitable. She recalled the 23rd Psalm, which she'd memorized over the weekend with Yolanda.

Ava whispered it to herself. "The Lord is my shepherd; I shall not want. He maketh me to lie down in green pastures: he leadeth me beside the still waters. He restoreth my soul: he leadeth me in the paths of righteousness for his name's sake. Yea, though I walk through the valley of the shadow of death, I will fear no evil: for thou art with me; thy rod and thy staff they comfort me. Thou preparest a table before me in the presence of mine enemies: thou anointest my head with oil; my cup runneth over. Surely goodness and mercy shall follow me all the days of my life: and I will dwell in the house of the Lord forever."

The hours ticked by like months while Ava remained in her cell, waiting for the final call. She occupied her mind by reciting the verses she'd learned with Yolanda and praying. She tried to sing a time or two, but her soul was simply too downcast to pull it off.

Then, she heard footsteps coming down the hall.

Her heart pounded and her face burned hot with anxiety. She knew she should be at perfect peace, but she was not. Fear had a grip on her, and she could not get the horrifying thought of death out of her mind.

The door opened. Two guards glared down at her. "Ms. Wilson, it's time."

Too frightened to put up a fight about them

getting her name wrong, Ava nodded and stood to her feet.

They escorted her down a long sterile hallway. The unpleasant glow of fluorescent lights reflected off the high-gloss paint on the cement-block walls. The sound of her cheap jail-house flip flops echoed off the bare concrete floors. The heels of the guards' boots clicked in lock-step, haunting the otherwise-silent corridor.

"What time is it?" she asked.

"11:40."

Ava walked by a door and looked through the small window. "Is that the mortuary?"

"Yes, ma'am," one of the guards replied.

"What do they do . . ." She swallowed hard. ". . . with the bodies?"

The guard's answer was more awkward than her question. "They—are taken to the county crematorium."

Ava nodded.

One of the guards stepped forward and opened the final door. Ava walked into the execution chamber. Inside stood the warden and a man in a medical coat. Ava looked around at the surroundings. *This is it. The last place I'll visit on this earth.*

The cinder-block walls were painted with the same high-gloss, sky-blue paint that was in the hallway. The room was stark. It contained only a hospital bed with a series of leather straps and buckles. A single clock hung on the wall, ticking off the final minutes until her fate was to be sealed. Across from the bed was a window. On the other side was a viewing room where more than forty chairs surrounded a large television camera mounted on a tripod. All the chairs were filled. In the front row sat Raquel, her eyes seething with hatred and a smirk of victory across her mouth.

Suddenly, a feeling of serenity washed over Ava. Soon, she'd be home. All the terrors and pain of this world would be done. She'd endured the worst this realm had to offer: heartache and violence, abandonment and loss. There'd be no more of that where she was going. But for Raquel, the handful of years she had left on this planet was as good as it would get for her, unless she repented, of course. And over the years that Ava had known the wild, bitter girl, she'd never seen any hope of that happening. Despite her position and the fact that Raquel was responsible for putting her there, she couldn't help but feel sorry for the misguided and deceived young woman on the other side of the glass.

Ava calmly let the guards take off her handcuffs and strap her arms to the hospital bed. They secured her legs then removed the irons of the shackles. She looked up at the clock. *Ten more minutes.*

Ava looked around the room, wondering if there were angels waiting for her, escorts from the heavenly realm who would walk her through the gates of Glory. *I can't wait to see Mom again. I wonder if she knows I'm coming? I wonder if Dad is already there? I wonder if I'll recognize my birth mother? I don't think Foley is there yet. He's a fighter. God, please don't let him grieve for me too long. Let him meet someone else, move on, and enjoy life—but not too soon. And watch over Charity and Buck.*

She'd never felt the presence of God so strongly before. She felt as if she could almost touch Him.

The minutes ticked away, then the man in the lab coat approached the side of the bed. "I'll administer a mild sedative first, then I'll give you the injection."

Ava had no say in the matter. She turned her head away from the needle and felt the light prick. Seconds later, her body felt soft and limber, her thinking slowed. She didn't quite understand why they bothered with the sedative other than to make themselves feel better.

The warden said with a mirthless voice, "It's twelve o'clock, midnight. Please administer the injection."

Despite Ava's state, she still felt the icy coldness of the second needle as it plunged into her vein to deliver the terminal dose.

Instantly, she felt the substance dragging her away from consciousness. Then, everything went dark.

CHAPTER 18

Blessed is the man whom thou chastenest, O
Lord, and teachest him out of thy law; That
thou mayest give him rest from the days of
adversity, until the pit be digged for the
wicked. For the Lord will not cast off his
people, neither will he forsake his
inheritance. But judgment shall return unto
righteousness: and all the upright in heart
shall follow it. Who will rise up for me
against the evildoers? or who will stand up
for me against the workers of iniquity?
Unless the Lord had been my help, my soul
had almost dwelt in silence.

Psalm 94:12-17

Ava opened her eyes and saw only white. A soft glow filtered through. She felt blissful and at perfect peace. She heard a light hum. "Wings of the cherubim?" she murmured softly. She turned her head and felt the gentleness of the milky air. She tried to focus but saw only white. Quickly, her thoughts grasped for an explanation. This was not at all what she'd expected. *Where's Mom? And where's Jesus?*

She turned her head back and finally began to recognize what she was seeing. "A sheet," she whispered. She wiggled her fingers and her toes. "I'm alive!"

"That hum, it's tires on a highway." She started to rip off the sheet but promptly thought about the ramifications of such an action. *I'm headed to the crematorium! They somehow mixed up the doses. He probably gave me two injections of the sedative. They think I'm dead.*

"She's starting to wake up," said a voice.

Ava realized she wasn't restrained. She still wore the same orange uniform but had no handcuffs or leg irons. *Why wouldn't they secure my hands and feet if they knew I was alive?*

"Ms. Wilson?" Someone pulled the sheet down from her face.

She closed her eyes and pretended to be unconscious.

"Ms. Wilson, it's me, Warden Mahoney."

She recognized the voice but did not respond.

"I'm sure you've got some questions. They'll all

be answered in due time. What I can tell you is that you are indeed very much alive and being transported to the desert. We're meeting a stealth Blackhawk helicopter from the Alliance States. I'm not sure what your people will tell you when you get where you're going, but I have a message from the governor of California. Your death was broadcast across America and the public believes you to be dead. It would be best for all parties involved if you do your part to keep it that way. Otherwise, it will embarrass the governor, and he'll see to it that you are called to account."

Curiosity got the better of her. She opened her eyes then her mouth. "Why? Why is he letting me go?"

"I'm not at liberty to discuss the details. But let me reiterate, don't go public about this. It's best to let sleeping dogs lie. Where ever you go, we can get to you."

Ava understood this was not a gesture of mercy and goodwill. Whatever was happening, they were being coerced into doing it. She was alive, and that was good enough for now.

Within minutes of Ava regaining consciousness, the van stopped and the warden opened the back door. He helped Ava up from the mortuary stretcher she'd been lying on.

Outside of the van stood four soldiers holding M-4 rifles, fully kitted out with tactical vests, helmets, and drop-leg holsters for their side arms. Behind the soldiers was a helicopter which looked to Ava more like a spaceship. The top rotor was spinning but made much less noise than she ever thought possible by a helicopter.

"Mrs. Mitchem, come with us," said one of the soldiers succinctly.

Ava ducked her head low as she hurried to the completely blacked out aircraft visible only by the ambient light from the headlights of the van which had brought her to this stretch of otherwise-desolate wasteland. Whoever these people were, they'd addressed her by the correct name. In addition to not being dead, she felt things were moving in the right direction.

Seconds later, Ava and the soldiers were inside the chopper. The ground fell away into the darkness below. The inside of the helicopter was pitch black. Ava couldn't see any of the soldiers' faces. None spoke to her so she did not try to engage them in conversation. She was unsure of how much time had passed when the craft landed, but she estimated roughly one hour.

The side door opened, and she was escorted out. Ava looked around. She was at a small regional airport. "Where am I?"

"Cedar City, Utah, ma'am," the soldier on her left answered.

"Where are we going?"

He pointed to the small commuter jet ahead. "To that plane, then to Oklahoma."

The light was better than it had been in the desert or inside the helicopter. Ava saw the Alliance States insignia on the uniforms of her escorts.

"Can you tell me if my father was taken out of California?"

The soldier gently put his hand on her back to

signal for her to hurry alongside him to the jet. "I'm sorry, I don't have any information for you. Someone will be able to answer all of your questions when we get to Oklahoma. This isn't the most secure section of Utah, so we need to get off the ground as soon as possible."

She nodded and jogged to the plane.

Once inside, she was met by the pilot who had a friendly smile. He pointed to a cardboard box and a small cooler in the first row of seats. "We've got some chips and water for you. Sorry we didn't get you a change of clothes. We were in a rush to get here. I'm sure they'll have the red carpet rolled out for you when we get to Oklahoma."

"Thank you, the water and snacks will be great. I'm fine with what I'm wearing. I'm just happy to be alive."

The pilot nodded. "We're happy to have you with us, Mrs. Mitchem. If everyone will get seated and buckle up, we'll be on our way." He waved and disappeared into the cockpit.

Ava took two bottles of water and a bag of pretzels, then buckled in next to the window. Barely giving herself a moment to appreciate her own second chance at life, she immediately began to be heavy-hearted for her loved ones. Her mind raced wondering if Ulysses had made it out alive. She desperately hoped Foley was okay. She even said a short prayer for Charity and Buckley.

Ava relaxed during the flight and despite her anxious mind, she drifted off to sleep.

She was awakened when the wheels struck the

runway. Ava looked out the window. She saw rows of military cargo planes and fighter jets on the tarmac. The surrounding buildings looked vaguely familiar. "Altus?"

The jet taxied to an ambulance, which was waiting with its light on. The clamshell door of the plane opened and Ava walked down the airstair.

"Fancy meeting you here." A man in a doctor's coat stood behind a wheelchair at the bottom of the stairs. "Need a lift?"

It took Ava a moment to remember his name. "Captain Murphy?"

"At your service." He bowed his head.

"I think I can manage to walk." She smiled.

"Very well, but I would like you to get in the back of the ambulance. I need to take you to the medical center and check you out."

"Okay, for what?"

"Just a precaution. We want to make sure Governor Quincy isn't trying to pull a fast one on us." The doctor joined her in the back of the ambulance and closed the door.

"How could he do that?"

Murphy lifted his shoulders. "I don't want to worry you, but he could have had you injected with any number of compounds that won't take effect for days."

"You mean like a poison or a virus? Why would he do that?"

Captain Murphy took her hand. "I doubt he would. But we need to be sure. I assume you haven't been brought up to speed on what's going on."

"No, enlighten me, please."

"Governor Quincy's daughter was abducted from UC Berkeley by actors who demanded your release in exchange for her safe return."

"Actors?"

"Militia."

"Anyone I'd know?"

"One of them may be a former patient of mine."

"Foley? Is he okay? Where is he?"

"He's okay, but his location is undisclosed until the operation is completed. I'm sure you understand."

The ambulance stopped at the medical center and the back doors of the ambulance opened.

"Mrs. Mitchem, it's nice to see you again."

Ava turned to look at who was holding the door for her. "Sergeant Griffith! Thank you. Good to see you, also."

He smiled. "I understand you've been busy. You'll need some time to recuperate. I've tried to set up the guest house to your liking, but if you have any special requests, I'll do everything I can to accommodate your needs."

"Thank you, Sergeant." Ava smiled and followed Captain Murphy into the medical center.

"What about my father? Did he make it out?" she asked.

"We don't have any information about him right now. Colonel Barr is coordinating with Foley on the operation, and they're doing everything they can to bring Ulysses home as well. Let's get you checked out, and hopefully the colonel will have some good news for you when we're done."

"Sure." She entered the exam room.

The doctor drew blood and ran a series of tests over the next half hour.

"How does it look?" Ava asked.

"I don't see any signs of contamination. I'm going to take these samples down to the lab. I've got a change of clothes for you hanging on the back of the door. I've got an entire team waiting in the lab for your blood samples. But it will be at least an hour before they can give me any results. And even if they're clear, I want to keep you under observation for a minimum of forty-eight hours."

"Under observation?"

He nodded and smiled. "On the base—at the guest house. But I need you to promise you'll tell me if you notice anything unusual."

"Like what?"

"Anything: dizziness, headache, loss of appetite, rash, heart palpitations, blurry vision. If it's out of the ordinary, call me right away. I'll be back soon." He pulled the door closed behind him.

"Okay." Ava found a pair of sweatpants and a tee-shirt hanging on the door and changed out of her prison clothes.

Moments later, a knock came to the door.

"Come in." She sat on the exam table and swung her legs.

"Hey, there's our hero!" Colonel Barr walked in with an ear-to-ear grin.

She quickly cut him off before he could say anything else. "Captain Murphy said you were trying to get my dad out of California."

His exuberant expression faded. "We're doing

everything we know to do."

"What is that supposed to mean?"

"It means, the militia group who abducted the governor's daughter from UC Berkeley released her at the same time you were handed over. But shortly thereafter, they informed Governor Quincy that his daughter had been injected with an undisclosed synthetic toxin. They told him she had forty-eight hours to get the antidote or she'd die. The team leader is demanding the release of your father in exchange for the antidote."

Ava nodded. "That's why Captain Murphy wants to keep me under observation. He thinks the regime may have used this same tactic."

"The US has quite an arsenal of such compounds, but to my knowledge, they are all housed at Dugway Army Base in Utah, which we control. I can't completely rule out the possibility of the regime having bought some similar toxin from Russia or China, but the odds are very remote given the time they had to react to the demands.

"So far, Governor Quincy has kept the exchange from Markovich. At least that's what he's telling us. He didn't feel confident that Markovich would be willing to trade you for the life of his daughter."

"Where are we at with my dad?"

"That's the tricky part. Your dad is in the custody of the Social Justice Legion, which is considered federal."

"Are they under the DOJ?"

Barr shook his head. "They're autonomous. They're not under anyone except Markovich. That includes the Supreme Court and Congress. The

Constitution has been subjected to death by a thousand cuts. I'd say it has officially bled out; at least in the regime-held part of the country."

"What's Quincy doing to get my dad out?"

"He's limited on what he can do. I've listened to the negotiation communications. I genuinely believe he has no idea where your father is. Quincy's voice is one of a desperate father."

"So, his daughter is going to die?"

"The team leader who was holding the daughter injected her with a saline solution. It was just a ruse. She isn't going to die, but Governor Quincy doesn't know that."

Ava felt relieved that the girl wasn't at risk but hated the fact that they were no further along in getting her father back. "This team leader, is it Foley?"

Barr nodded. "He'll be here after the time has expired, but he's still hoping the governor will get creative and locate Ulysses."

"And if he doesn't?"

The colonel took her hand. "You and your father knew the risks of this operation when you accepted the job. We'll keep trying, but you have to realize that once the SJL thinks they've got all the information they can out of him . . ."

"Yeah." Ava knew all too well what would happen. She didn't need anyone to spell it out for her.

The colonel changed the subject. "But anyway, good job. What you and Ulysses did may have changed the direction of the war. I'm sure you already know all of that."

"No. I heard that Louisiana, Alabama, Arkansas, and Mississippi may have backed out of a deal to pledge support to Markovich, but that's it."

"That's it? Don't you realize how huge that is? The LAAMs backing out changes everything. Not only will their decision influence the other southern states, but if they join the Alliance States, it will give us seaports. Access to international trade provides us with the lifeline we need to survive."

Ava crossed her arms. "But they haven't joined the Alliance. And even if they do, what makes you think the international community will still want to do business with us? We've been labeled a pariah by the UN."

"So has North Korea and Iran, but plenty of countries are willing to trade with them. Heck, international companies even buy and sell with Somalia, knowing the goods they buy and the money they receive for goods sold likely comes from piracy. World leaders may be quick to condemn us for not getting on board the socialist bandwagon, but when it comes to money, they'll quickly turn a blind eye.

"And we're working on the LAAM governors. I think they're coming around. President Blackwell has a verbal commitment from Kentucky and Tennessee to join the Alliance if the LAAMs unite with us."

"All of this has developed since Lawrence died?"

"Every bit of it. You should be proud."

Yet she was not proud. She could only think of her father. If she had not dragged him into this mess, he'd still be alive. As it stood, despite Foley's best efforts at getting him back, Ulysses was either dead already or quickly approaching his demise. Still, if his sacrifice meant the Alliance had a chance at surviving the war, she could be proud of her father.

Colonel Barr's phone rang. "Hello?" He paused. "Yes, sir." He passed her the phone. "It's the president."

Ava took the phone. "Hello?"

"Ava, on behalf of a grateful nation, I can't thank you enough for what you've done. Your country owes you a debt that can never be repaid."

"Thank you, Mr. President."

"Acting President," Blackwell corrected. "Your bravery and valor will not be forgotten. Neither will your father's."

"If you can get him back, we'll call it even; that debt which can never be repaid, I mean."

"I'll spare no resource in trying to make that happen."

"Thank you, and thanks for bringing me home."

"Don't thank me. Your rescue was the work of that tenacious husband of yours. He loves you very much."

"I love him as well. But I doubt he'd have been able to locate the governor's daughter without a little assistance from one intelligence service or the other."

"Yes, well, I have no official knowledge of any such help. Obviously, I could never condone an action like that, particularly by any members of the Alliance government. But these militia types, you know how they are—it's a bit like herding cats. Or perhaps in Foley's case, herding pumas, big dangerous cats that slip around in the night and can never be caught."

"I hope you're right, Mr. President. Thanks again, and please keep up the search for my dad. Any information that might trickle down to me about his whereabouts or possible ways to retrieve him would be appreciated. I'm sure I'd never remember the source of any such help if someone were to ask."

"You've proved that, Ava—in spades. Once more, thank you for what you've done. Goodbye."

"Goodbye." Ava handed the phone back to the colonel.

"I'll give you a lift over to the guest house if you like," offered Barr. "Once you're done here, that is."

"I think I'll walk. I could use the fresh air. I've been cooped up for the past week and a half."

"That's understandable." The colonel nodded. "Let me know if I can do anything else for you, anything at all."

Ava jumped down from the exam table. "Could you get word back to my dad's farm that I'm still alive? My friend, Charity, she would have seen the execution on television. She's been through a lot."

Barr smiled. "It's the least we can do. I've got some back channels to the local militia guarding the border around there. I can send an encrypted message and have them stop by and let her know that you're okay."

Captain Murphy returned. "Good news, no apparent toxins that we were able to identify. We're not out of the woods yet, but it's a good start."

"Thanks." Ava turned to Colonel Barr before he left. "When will I be able to leave?"

Barr looked at the doctor. "Captain Murphy wants to keep an eye on you for two days. In the meantime, I'll be monitoring our intelligence reports. As long as Markovich doesn't catch wind that you're still alive in the next forty-eight hours, you should be safe to return home then.

"If news of you being among the living leaks out after you go home, I'll send a team to scoop you up and take you somewhere safe."

"Could you let Charity know that I should be back in a couple days?"

"Sure," the colonel said. "Sleep well. You've earned it."

"Thank you," she said. "Thank you both for everything."

CHAPTER 19

For He bruises, but He binds up; He wounds, but His hands make whole. He shall deliver you in six troubles, yes, in seven no evil shall touch you. In famine He shall redeem you from death, and in war from the power of the sword. You shall be hidden from the scourge of the tongue, and you shall not be afraid of destruction when it comes. You shall laugh at destruction and famine, and you shall not be afraid of the beasts of the earth. For you shall have a covenant with the stones of the field, and the beasts of the field shall be at peace with you. You shall know that your tent is in peace; you shall visit your dwelling and find nothing amiss.

Job 5:18-24 NKJV

Ava slept late again on Wednesday. She'd been at the guest house on Altus Air Force Base since before dawn on Tuesday. Provided she didn't become symptomatic in the next twenty-four hours, she'd be headed home the next day. Ava made herself a cup of coffee and some frozen waffles since the dining facility had quit serving breakfast hours earlier.

Despite her love-hate relationship with sweets, Ava soaked the waffles with syrup and took her sugary treat to the living room to eat on the couch. She turned on the television and watched the latest coverage of the ongoing civil war. The Patriot News Network showed footage of desperate clashes between the two sides in the Pacific Northwest. The city of Idaho Falls was ground zero for the fighting.

What had once been a bustling, thriving town, was now a ruinous ash heap. The camera panned around the town and Ava couldn't spot a single building which was free from mortar, tank shell, or RPG damage. The reporter explained how the Alliance forces had been pushed back in southern Idaho to the Wyoming border. He explained how Blackwell's forces had rallied there, regained ground in Idaho, and was on the verge of retaking Idaho Falls.

"We've got a long fight ahead of us in this battle, but what the Alliance lacks in support from the global community, we make up for in military experience. Roughly 60 percent of persons who were active military when the war broke out sided with the Alliance States. We also estimate that 80 percent of military veterans who are engaged in the civil conflict are backing President Blackwell.

"I'm getting a breaking news alert from my producer right now who is telling me that Arkansas and Louisiana have just officially joined the Alliance. Pundits have been predicting this move since the sudden death of Shane Lawrence who played an active role in the Markovich Administration.

"Lawrence was seen as a sort of arbitrator between America's disassociated youth who feel left out by the political process and the Markovich Administration. Many of these youths have joined the SJL and backed Markovich fully, but large swaths of them who were still not fully integrated are falling away since the death of the man they saw as their spokesman.

"Raquel Kohut, the woman Lawrence was dating at the time of his demise is attempting to carry the torch left behind by her deceased lover, but she appears ill-prepared and ill-connected among the Hollywood elite to sustain the momentum of the movement."

Ava felt a flicker of accomplishment, but the smoldering wick of fulfillment was swiftly extinguished by the knowledge that the mission had likely cost her father his life.

Her heart jumped when she heard a key hit the

lock of the guest house door. She quickly placed her coffee cup on the end table and stood up. She scurried to the kitchen to retrieve a knife, the only nearby weapon she could think of.

The door opened. "Ava?"

"Foley?" She let her arm drop to her side, the kitchen knife dangling at her side.

He dropped his duffle bag inside and closed the door behind him. Foley walked briskly toward her. "Can I have a hug?"

A shiver of emotion raced up her back and down her arms. "Yeah!"

He stared hesitantly. "Do you want to put the knife down first?"

Her mouth hung open in surprise. She glanced down at the weapon. "Yeah!"

She placed it on the counter and embraced Foley. With one hand around his waist and the other around his neck, she pulled him so tightly against her that their very molecules could have fused together.

After more than two minutes of the elongated embrace, he pulled his head back from her shoulder to look her in the eyes. "I missed you."

"Me, too." She was simply too overwhelmed to elaborate.

He kissed her long, and deeply, and passionately. Then, the newlyweds made their way toward the bedroom.

The next evening, Ava was in the shower. She heard the landline at the guest house ring.

"I'll get it," Foley called out from the living

room.

Ava hurried to finish rinsing and cut the water off. She grabbed a towel, briskly dried off, then wrapped it around her. She took another towel to wrap around her head and scurried out to the living room. "Who was on the phone?"

"It was Captain Murphy. You're officially cleared, as long as you haven't become symptomatic in the last hour, that is."

"Oh." Her excitement faded.

"Ava? Are you hiding something from me? How are you feeling?"

"No, no. I'm fine." She plopped down on the couch and crossed her hands. "But every time the phone rings I'm hoping it's news about Dad. Every time that it's not, I realize the odds of him being found grow increasingly slim."

Foley took a seat beside her. "But you're okay?"

"Physically, I feel fine." She looked up at him. "But I can't stop thinking about my dad."

"Why don't we go over to the bowling alley? It's on the base. Maybe they'll have a pool table. It might help to get your mind off of things for a while."

She shook her head. "No. I wouldn't feel right. You go ahead if you want."

"No. I'm not going if you're not. I guess I'll start getting my things packed. You still want to head back to the farm first thing tomorrow morning, right?"

"Yeah. Seeing Buckley and Charity will help me more than anything. Besides, I'm sure she has her hands full between the garden and the chickens.

Maybe getting out and working the soil will distract me."

"Maybe so." He pulled her in close for a long hug.

"You're staying, right?" She ran her hand along his beard. "At the farm, I mean."

"For a while."

"A while? Foley, you can't leave me; not until I find out something about Dad."

"I'll stay around for a couple of weeks, but the other soldiers are still engaged in battle. What you did gave us a fighting chance, but the war isn't over. The Alliance needs every able-bodied soldier to keep pressing in until we see this thing through."

"Maybe I'll go with you—when you return to the battlefield."

"We'll see."

She understood his tone to mean *no, but I don't want to fight about it right now.*

"Whatever." She put her head on his shoulder, happy to have him by her side—for now.

CHAPTER 20

Cast thy burden upon the Lord, and he shall sustain thee: he shall never suffer the righteous to be moved.

Psalm 55:22

Days later, Charity opened the door to Ava's bedroom, letting Buckley in the room. "Hey, what's wrong? Why are you crying?"

Ava sobbed and passed the note she'd found on Foley's pillow to Charity.

Charity sat on the edge of the bed and read the hand-written letter. She sighed and hugged Ava. "I'm sorry, but I guess I'm not surprised."

Double breathing from her distraught emotional state, Ava struggled to speak between breaths. "He . . . he said . . . he'd stay for two weeks!"

Charity put the note down and comforted her friend with both hands. "But you know his heart has been on the front lines for the past few days."

"Why? Why can't he be content to stay here? Am I not enough?"

"Ava." Charity looked at her compassionately. "You know better than anyone how a sense of duty can overrule every other argument. Don't blame Foley for his conviction." She offered a firmer expression. "That would be downright hypocritical."

Ava would have none of it. She continued to lay out her case against the man. "But a note?" Ava crumpled the paper in her hand angrily. "I get a Dear Jane letter? Am I not even entitled to the courtesy of a proper farewell? What the heck is that about?"

Charity took the letter from her hand and placed it on the nightstand. "Would you have let him go if he'd told you he was leaving today?"

"Obviously, I'm powerless to stop him."

"No, but I've heard you talk about going with him on more than one occasion since the two of you came back last week."

"But a letter? What if he never comes home? What if I never get to say goodbye?" Her anger quickly melted back into pure heartache and sorrow.

"He'll be back, Ava. Foley is the best of the best."

She sighed. "So was Dad. And no one has heard from him since we took out Shane Lawrence. Need I remind you that next Monday will mark a month since that operation went so terribly wrong?"

Charity calmly held her friend. "This war has been tough on all of us."

Ava remembered the sacrifice that Charity had paid in this conflict. She felt selfish for only thinking of herself. She hushed her crying and embraced the girl who'd been like a sister to her over the past few months.

"What do you say I make us some breakfast?" Charity offered.

"I'd like that," Ava replied.

The weeks passed and Ava kept busy around the house. News from Foley was sporadic. From his coded messages, Ava speculated that his team was engaged in the battle to retake Idaho. She watched all the news like a hawk perched above a rabbit hole, but she paid particular attention to the coverage of the battles in the northwest.

One evening in late May, after the garden had been tended, dinner finished, and the dishes put away, Ava and Charity sat down in the living room to play their nightly game of Gin while watching the evening news. Buckley lay on the floor nearby and watched as if he'd been invited to play but wasn't up for it on this particular evening.

Ava dealt out the cards. "You saw that Georgia, West Virginia, and the Carolinas joined the Alliance, right?"

Charity picked up her cards. "Yeah, that makes nineteen states now."

"Twenty counting Alaska."

"Yeah, but they're up there all alone. I doubt they'll be exposed to any fighting unless the

Alliance fails. At that point, I expect they'll make a stand. Although, I'm not sure Markovich would even bother with them."

Ava drew a new card and discarded. "Alaska has lots of resources: timber, oil, fish."

"Lots of guns, too. Plus, if Markovich sends troops up there, his forces will be fighting against people who are accustomed to the harsh environment. I think he'll let them be. Maybe we can head that way if all else fails." Charity picked up a new card.

"If the Alliance fails, do you really think Markovich will allow Alaska to remain free? It will be a thorn in his side. The UN will see them the same way. I think they'd nuke Alaska before they allowed them to be an island of liberty on an otherwise socialist globe."

Charity nodded. "You may be right about that."

"Gin!" Ava put down her cards.

"Ugh!" Charity tossed hers on the table.

Ava added up her score and jotted it down on the pad of paper. "What do you think about Florida? They're completely cut off from the rest of the Markovich states since Georgia and the Carolinas joined the Alliance."

"I don't know. I think they'll come into the fold."

"No way. All the liberals fleeing the new southern Alliance States are pouring into south Florida. It's becoming like another left coast."

Charity shuffled and began dealing the next round of cards. "You've got a point."

Ava held up her hand. "The reporter is talking about Idaho. Can we take a break from the cards for a moment?"

"Sure." Charity placed her cards face down on the coffee table.

The young male reporter on the Patriot News Network continued speaking. "Alliance forces have officially taken control of Boise after a prolonged ground war against the Markovich regime. All regime troops in and around Idaho's capital city have either retreated, been killed in combat, or been taken prisoner by the Alliance. The news comes exactly one week since the Alliance States regained control of the nearby Mountain Home Air Force Base.

"The Alliance States border patrol forces are still engaging with rogue bands of hostiles along the Oregon and Nevada borders with Idaho, but the state is expected to be fully secured in the next few days.

"President Blackwell made an impromptu visit to Mountain Home Air Force Base today to address Alliance States troops and their militia counterparts returning from the conflict in Boise. The president thanked the soldiers for their perseverance and sacrifice but reminded them that the war is far from over.

"No word has been given as of yet to say when or if Blackwell's administration will return to Boise. The city has suffered severe devastation from the fighting, but pundits believe Blackwell will want to reestablish his operations there, even if only as a show of defiance to the Markovich regime."

"That's great news! Do you think Foley will be able to take a break, come home for a visit?" Charity asked.

Ava shook her head. "I don't know. I'm not even sure he was involved in the battle for Boise."

"If he was in the Pacific Northwest, he was in Boise. Both sides had their troops concentrated there."

Buckley jumped up suddenly and began barking at the door.

Ava turned off the television, grabbed her rifle and flipped off the lights. "You know the drill."

"Yep, I'll be at the back door. If there's trouble, I'll come around the side and flank them. Do you want me to put Buckley in the bathroom?"

"No." Ava watched the headlights coming down the long drive. "His barking will keep the aggressors' attention so they don't hear you coming around the side of the house."

Ava peered out the peephole as the vehicle came closer. "It looks like an official Humvee. And it's only one. Possible friendlies."

"That's good, but I'll stay out of sight until we know for sure," Charity called from the back of the house.

"On second thought, why don't you go ahead and take Buck? It's just a driver and guy in dress uniform." Ava's heart sank, hoping the visitor wasn't a bearer of bad news, come to tell her of Foley's demise.

Charity called the dog. "Buckley, come here boy."

He looked at Ava and gave two more quick

barks.

"It's okay, Buck. Go with Charity. I've got this." Ava patted his head.

Buckley obeyed and Ava watched carefully as the two men from the Hummer crossed the yard to the house. She placed the rifle by the door jamb and checked the butt of the pistol in the back of her waistband for ease of accessibility.

When the men walked onto the porch, she could make out their faces by the ambient light of the vehicle's headlights. "Colonel Barr?"

She unlocked the deadbolt and flipped on the porch light. Her mind shuffled through possible reasons for his visit. The one which stayed at the top of the deck was Foley's death. She opened the door. "Colonel, good to see you again."

"Mrs. Mitchem, it's always a pleasure."

She opened the door, "Please, come in." She let the visitors in and turned the lights back on.

"Did we wake you?"

"No. Sound and light discipline. I guess I'm a little paranoid."

"Not at all. You're a prudent woman." The colonel wiped his feet before coming in.

The driver who'd come with the colonel looked at the rifle near the door, then at the colonel.

Barr smiled. "Like I said, Corporal, she's a prudent woman."

Ava crossed her arms tightly. If he'd brought bad tidings, she wanted to get on with it. The terror of Foley's doom had haunted her day and night since he'd left more than three weeks prior. "With it being after dark, I doubt you're dropping by for a friendly visit. Do you have some news for me?"

His face was neither sad nor joyous, giving Ava no clue of what he was about to say. "Prudent and perceptive. Do you mind if we sit down?"

Ava felt sure he was going to tell her the thing she feared most. "Sure. Please join me on the couch."

Barr took a seat, as did the corporal.

"Colonel, tell me, is Foley okay?"

"I don't have any news about Foley. I'm not sure."

"Then what is this about?" She sat forward on the easy chair.

"It's your father, Ava. We've found him."

Her mouth went dry. "Is he . . . alive?"

Barr nodded, but shallowly. "He is alive . . ."

She cut him off. "Oh, thank God!"

The colonel held up his hand. "But you should temper your expectations. He's . . . not in good shape."

"He's injured?" Her face contorted from a surge of emotional distress.

"Physically, he's not so bad off. He was severely dehydrated and malnourished. He's lost some weight. But we got him cleaned up, he's being fed intravenously and the doctor expects to start reintroducing him to solid foods tomorrow."

"Where is he? Can you take me to him? How did you find him?" She unleashed a barrage of inquiries as quickly as they came into her mind.

"Take it easy; you'll get all of your questions answered, I promise. But let me take those one at a time. For starters, he's at Altus. Captain Murphy is personally handling the physical side of his recovery."

"Physical side? Why? What other side is there?"

The colonel took her hand. "Ulysses is dealing with some psychological issues as well. I flew in a behavioral health expert, formerly of the National Center for PTSD. He specializes in dissociative disorders."

Ava crossed her hands and stared at her fingers. "Dissociative disorders—how bad is it?"

Barr compressed his lips. "You're familiar with your father's history, I assume."

"Yes."

"I'm not sure how many of the details he told you, but when he was brought back from China, he didn't know what year it was, not even close. After he came home, it took him a while to understand that he wasn't in China. It also took a while for him to completely remember exactly who he was. He could give his name, rank, and serial number, but he couldn't really provide many details about his life.

"Markovich's people must have treated him pretty badly while trying to get information out of him. He's regressed to a mental state similar to when he first came home. He's displaying the same dissociative amnesia."

Ava felt horrible. She wanted to break down and cry. While she was relieved that her father was still alive, she couldn't stand the thought of him being in such an awful condition. But she wouldn't cry just yet. For now, she'd hold it in. Ava tightened her jaw. "Are you returning to Altus? Can I go back with you?"

The colonel looked at the corporal. "We're not going to Altus, but I can arrange for someone to pick you up tomorrow or the day after. I don't think Captain Murphy and the psychologist want Ulysses to have any visitors until they've at least got his vitals back to normal. Besides, I believe they're keeping him sedated for the time being."

"I don't care if he even knows I'm there. I just need to see him. I'll drive there myself."

"It would make me feel better if you'd let me send someone to pick you up. As far as we know, Markovich still thinks you're dead, but he has spies in every relief center and probably every small town in the Alliance States. If you can give me until tomorrow, I promise I'll have someone here before lunch."

"I guess that would be okay."

"Good," replied Colonel Barr. "Now, about the details of how we got him. It was a trade. Blackwell gave up ten spies we'd pulled out of various refugee centers."

"Won't they divulge the information they collected to Markovich's camp once they're back?"

"Yep, but your dad is a hero—just like you. The information that can be obtained in a refugee center is minimal anyway."

"The expert from the PTSD center, what does he think? Will my dad get better?"

Barr raised his eyebrows. "The fact that your father has already been down this road before speaks to his resilience. His mind already has a path for him to come back to us. He'll just need some gentle direction to help him find it."

"He told me it took a long time before. Two years later, he was still having issues with reality."

Barr nodded. "His emotional trauma was compounded by the severe injuries he'd sustained while in the Chinese prison. Additionally, he'd been in that filthy communist hole for decades. Perhaps his recovery will be quicker this time around."

Ava hoped the colonel was right and that her father had not slipped too far over the edge. "I don't suppose you'd venture to guess when I might be able to bring him home?"

"Ava, I'm sorry. It's too soon to tell." Barr cleared his throat. "If you don't have any more questions for me, we'll get out of your way."

"None that I can think of right now." Ava stood up to walk Barr and the corporal to the door. "Thank you for making a priority out of letting me know about my dad. I really appreciate it."

Barr let the corporal exit first, then followed behind him. "It was my pleasure, Ava. Anything I can do for you, let me know."

"If you have any way of finding out about Foley, that would be fantastic. I haven't heard from him since Mountain Home Air Force Base was retaken."

"I wish I could help you out with that one, but as you know, the president doesn't want us keeping tabs on the militia. They get handed lots of stuff we want to maintain plausible deniability on. But I'll reach out to my militia contacts, send a message for him to let you know he's still alive as soon as he can."

"Thanks again." Ava watched the two men return to their vehicle, then locked the door.

"Did you catch all of that?" she asked.

Charity emerged from the back room. "Yeah, I didn't want to be a total lurker, eavesdropping from the back room, but I didn't really feel like there was a good time for me to come in. It sounded pretty personal."

"No problem." Ava's mind was preoccupied with her father's condition.

"So, you're heading out again tomorrow?"

"Oh, yeah. I'm leaving you here to mind the farm all by yourself again. Sorry."

"Don't worry about that. You go see your dad. Buckley helps out quite a bit. I haven't taught him to weed yet, but he's really good company."

Ava smiled to show her appreciation of Charity's attempt to lighten the mood. "Thank you. I'll be glad when we're all back here together. I suppose I should pack a bag. I'm not sure how long I'll be gone."

"Okay. I'm going to bed. I'll see you before you leave in the morning."

Ava hugged her friend. "Good night."

CHAPTER 21

Surely oppression maketh a wise man mad.

Ecclesiastes 7:7

Ava held tightly to Captain Murphy's hand as he escorted her to her father's recovery room at the Altus Air Force Base Medical Center.

"He may not recognize you." The doctor gave her an empathetic look. "I want you to be prepared for whatever."

"I know." She frowned. "Is he eating solid food?"

"Soft foods. I'm not confident that his digestive system is ready for anything too hard to process. Mac and cheese, mashed potatoes and gravy, soup, pudding, that sort of thing. We'll be serving dinner soon. You can eat with him if you like."

"That would be nice," she said. "But he's not sedated?"

"No. After dinner, I'll give him something to help him rest through the night. But he's awake."

"Seeing me won't upset him, will it?"

"I can't imagine that it would. If he gets anxious, I can give him a shot. I'll be in the room with you."

Ava nodded and took a deep breath before walking into the room.

Murphy opened the door. Inside was a hospital bed, a television, which was turned off, a window with the blinds open looking out at the tennis courts, and two chairs. In one of the chairs was a thin frail man who resembled her father.

Her first thought was that this was not her dad. Despite the best intentions of Colonel Barr, they'd somehow been given the wrong prisoner. Yet when the man looked up at her with his confused eyes, she quickly recognized him as Ulysses Adams. He was clean-shaven, dressed in comfortable clothes, but he appeared to have lost nearly twenty pounds in the forty-six days since she'd last seen him. She couldn't imagine what that time period had been like for him. She felt the knot forming in her throat but through determination, pushed it down. She would not break down in front of him. She had to be strong for her father and for herself.

The emaciated figure in the chair looked up at her. "Kimberly?" He reached out for her hand.

She took his hand. "No, Dad. It's me, Ava. Kimberly is dead. She died giving birth to me— thirty years ago."

He put his hand on her stomach. "The baby!" His

eyes looked up at her face with an expression of pain and bewilderment. "Where's the baby?"

Ava's lips quivered and she lost her fight against the tears. "Daddy, I'm the baby. I'm Ava, don't you remember me?"

He stared at her silently for a long while. After several minutes he spoke, his voice telling that he did not fully comprehend what she was saying. "You're—the baby?"

She sat in the chair next to his. She gripped his hand tightly. Ava dried her eyes and nodded. "I'm Ava. I'm your daughter."

He looked at her again for a good long while, saying nothing. Finally, he said it again, but with slightly more conviction. "You're—the baby."

She nodded, feeling so sorry for this poor tortured soul in front of her.

Ulysses looked up at the doctor. "Why did you bring her here?"

Ava felt confused, wondering if for some reason her father didn't want to see her.

"She's your daughter, Ulysses. I thought you'd like her company," said Murphy.

Ulysses shook his head. He began speaking in a language Ava only recognized as oriental.

Murphy pulled out his phone and dialed a number. "Hi, it's Captain Murphy. Can you send Sergeant Chen to the medical center, room 107? He'll know what it's about."

"What's he saying?" Ava pleaded.

"I've got a translator on the way," the captain replied.

Ava held her father's hand as he continued to

speak in an unknown tongue. Distressed, she asked, "What language is that?"

"Mandarin."

"Like Chinese? I didn't know he spoke it."

"I'm sure he picked it up over the course of nearly three decades. He would've had to. He may not even remember it when he's not in this dissociative state."

Ava hated seeing her father like this. The man who'd had all the answers, the person who'd been stronger than anyone she'd ever met, her hero; to see him so vulnerable was more than she could handle. Yet handle it she did. She clenched her jaw, fought back the tears and held his hand as he babbled on about something she couldn't understand.

Sergeant Chen knocked before entering.

"Come on in," Murphy said. "You remember First Sergeant Adams."

"Of course, the man who may have turned the course of the war." Chen looked at Ava as if he recognized her. "You're not Ava Mitchem, are you?"

"Yes, sir."

Chen straightened his back. "It's an honor to meet you."

"Thank you, and thank you for your service, as well. My dad, he keeps saying something in Chinese, can you tell me what it is?"

Ulysses looked at Murphy again and repeated the phrase.

Chen sighed. He looked at Ava with solicitude.

"What is it?" she asked. "I just want to know."

Chen replied, "He's saying to the doctor, you shouldn't have brought her here, to China. They'll hurt her. You have to get her out of the country before they find out."

Ava's gaze fell to her father's hand, which was still in hers. She looked up at Chen. "Tell him he's not in China. Tell him he's in Oklahoma. Tell him he's home."

Chen nodded and relayed the message.

Ulysses listened and shook his head with distrust. He glared at Chen, then turned to Murphy with a look of disappointment.

Ava tugged on his hand and peered into his eyes. "You're home, Daddy. You're with me. And wherever we are together, that's home."

She pointed out the window, beyond the tennis courts. "Look, Dad. An American flag. You're in America—with me."

Ulysses furrowed his brow and closed his eyes. His lips pressed together as if he were grasping at some distant memory, at a dream he'd had long ago and had forgotten until this very moment.

Eventually, he opened his eyes and stared at the shine from the heavy wax on the linoleum floor. Minutes later he looked up at Ava once more, his eyes more certain this time. "You're the baby."

She nodded and leaned in to hug him. "Yeah, Dad. I'm the baby."

The days passed and Ava spent as much time as possible with Ulysses who slowly seemed to regain his grasp of reality. The psychiatric specialist left, leaving Captain Murphy in charge of Ulysses' mental health care. Adhering to the advice given by the psychologist, Murphy asked Ava to limit her visits to three hours a day in order to give Ulysses time to process and rest.

Ava had been at the base for one week when her father got cleared to leave his room in the medical center. She met him at his room, and the two of them walked across the base to the dining facility for lunch.

Ulysses was quiet as usual. Ava talked about the farm, about Charity, and about Buckley, but she never mentioned the war.

The two approached the dining facility known as Hangar 97. Ulysses paused to look around before entering the building. "Where is Foley?"

Since Ava had avoided speaking of the civil conflict, she'd necessarily had to steer clear of discussing Foley. Ulysses had recalled Foley from his own memory. To Ava, it was the most favorable sign of Ulysses' recovery yet. She smiled happily. "He's in Idaho. His militia team is backing up the border patrol there until things settle down. After that, he'll be coming home for two weeks of R&R."

"Idaho." Ulysses looked northwest as if he might be able to spot the state from Oklahoma. "Which border?"

Ava shrugged. "Either Oregon or Nevada. Colonel Barr told me. He couldn't get more specific. They don't have to guard the Washington border. The new state of Liberty, which was the eastern half of Washington, is secure. Do you remember any of that?"

Ulysses seemed to think for a while, still

standing outside the DFAC. "Liberty. Yeah, I remember that."

Ava held the door open and Ulysses walked through, seeming to be still pensive about the memories she'd just stirred. Once inside, four soldiers sitting at the table nearest the door noticed Ava and Ulysses come in. They stood up and saluted them. The men and women sitting at the tables around them soon became aware of their presence, and also stood up. Soon, everyone in the dining facility left their seats with the tips of their fingers on their foreheads.

Ulysses looked confused. "Why are they looking at us?"

"Because you're a hero. You should salute them."

He seemed anxious to get the attention off of himself, so Ulysses did as Ava had suggested.

The two made their way to the cafeteria line where three other soldiers insisted that they go in front of them. Ava thanked them and accepted the gesture. Once they'd filled their trays, Ava and Ulysses took a table near the back.

Ulysses stared at his food for a while, then looked up. "What did I do?"

"Do you remember us taking a trip to California?"

Ulysses took a deep breath and his eyes opened wide as if he'd just seen a ghost. "California! That was real?"

"I'm not a hundred percent sure what you're thinking of, but if it's about a secret mission to take down Shane Lawrence, yes, that was real."

"There was a nightclub." He looked at her with anguished eyes. "You were supposed to leave right away, but you didn't." He began to cry. "Why didn't you leave?"

Ava joined him with her sobs. She slid her tray out of the way and grabbed his hands. "I couldn't leave you. You'd have never left me behind like that. I just couldn't. But it's okay. We both made it out alive. And what we did—what you did, changed the course of the war."

"Is this seat taken?" Captain Murphy stood with his tray of food from the cafeteria line.

"No, please. Sit down." Ava dried her eyes and offered the doctor a friendly smile.

Murphy looked at the two of them. His face showed a sudden look of concern. "If it's a bad time, I can come back."

Ulysses shook his head. "Not at all, we were just catching up on some memories. We'd love to have you join us."

"If you're sure I'm not imposing." Murphy slowly placed his tray on the table and pulled out his chair.

"Some things just came back to Dad." Ava took Ulysses' hand. "We had sort of an emotional moment there."

The doctor nodded. "That's to be expected. You never know what's going to trigger a memory or an emotion. But it's good news. It shows you're progressing. In fact, Ulysses, you can move into the guest house with Ava. I'd like to keep you around the base for a couple more weeks at least before we send you home."

Ulysses looked at Ava, then back at Captain Murphy. "Are you sure? Am I—safe?"

"Yes, absolutely," he replied.

Ulysses clinched Ava's hand. "What if I have another episode? What if I forget where I'm at and who Ava is again? I don't want to do anything to hurt her. I couldn't live with myself if something like that happened."

Murphy nodded as he finished chewing. He took a sip of his tea and replied, "I understand your concern, but I looked over your records from when you first came home from China. Even then, you never displayed any violent or hostile behavior."

"But that doesn't mean it couldn't happen." Ulysses looked sternly at the doctor.

Captain Murphy shook his head. "At this stage of your recovery, it won't happen. Not unless you had some new trauma to cause a complete relapse. I would never put you in that situation if I thought there was even the most remote chance you might become dangerous to Ava or yourself."

"That's great news!" Ava exclaimed. "We'll get to spend more quality time together."

The doctor added, "But let's avoid the news and war movies for the next week. If you feel like you have to know what's going on, read the paper. It's not as likely to trigger an episode as the television with all the sights and sounds of battle."

"I think I can handle that," Ulysses turned to Ava. "If I remember correctly, that guest house has some cards and board games."

Ava grinned. "I've been playing a lot of Gin with Charity. I'll show you how it's done."

The doctor took another drink from his glass. "And get out of the house at least once a day. The base has a pool, bowling alley, tennis, plenty of activities to get you both outside."

"Sounds like a great idea. We'll take your advice. Thanks," said Ava.

The three of them enjoyed their meals, then Ava helped get her father settled into the guest house.

On the following Saturday, Ava and her father sat on the over-stuffed couches reading the morning paper.

Ava had taken the first section containing the front page. "Wow! Mexican gangs are chewing up Shreveport, Louisiana, and Oklahoma City. It says they are gushing into the Alliance States from the porous borders with Texas."

"Can I see that?" Ulysses placed his section of the paper on the coffee table and held out his hand.

"Sure. The article is right at the top." She passed him the paper and got up. "Will you have another cup of coffee if I make another pot?"

"Yes, please." Ulysses opened the newspaper and sat back on the couch.

Ava made her way to the kitchen, filled the coffee maker with grounds and water, then clicked the start button.

A knock came to the door.

"I wonder who that could be."

Ulysses jumped up from his seat. "Don't open it!"

"Relax, Dad. I have my pistol. Besides, we're on an Air Force Base. I think we're pretty safe. You know I'll check to see who it is before I open the door." Ava wanted to wait for her father to calm down before checking the peephole. "Remember your breathing exercises. Count to four and breathe in, hold it for four seconds, then count to four as you breathe out."

Ulysses nodded as if he understood his reaction to the knock at the door was not normal.

She watched him begin his breathing exercise and slowly made her way to the door. She looked out the peephole. Ava covered her mouth in shock and gasped for air.

Ulysses suspended his breathing exercise and hurried to the door. His voice was frantic. "Who is it?"

She shook her head and quickly flipped the latch to the deadbolt. She opened the door.

Foley dropped his duffle on the porch and embraced Ava.

Seconds later, she pulled back. "I had no idea you were coming!"

Foley grinned. "I stopped by the farm first. Charity told me you were here." He turned to Ulysses. "I was glad to hear that you were okay."

Ulysses hugged him. "*Okay* might be a stretch, but I'm alive and doing better than I was . . . thanks to my special girl."

"You're home for two weeks?" Ava asked hopefully.

Foley held her hands. "One week, but we'll make the most of it."

"One week? Why? What happened?"

"It's this business with the gangs. Markovich is

using them to harass the Alliance. By sending them flooding across the borders, the Alliance States have to dedicate more men to border security. Plus, the militia is having to back up the local law enforcement in the larger cities, particularly the ones near Texas borders."

"We were just reading about that in the paper." Ava picked up his bag and brought it inside. "But come in and take your boots off. I'll get you some coffee. I just started a fresh pot."

Foley leaned his rifle near the door and took off his utility belt. He sat on the couch where Ava had been sitting and removed his boots. "We've thinned out Markovich's forces. His soldiers are mostly undisciplined new recruits. A much larger percentage of the experienced military personnel sided with the Alliance. In combat, our experience acts as a force multiplier. Markovich had us far outnumbered, but we're beginning to even things up, little by little.

"Now that his military is getting thinned out, he's resorted to utilizing the Mexican gangs. They provide him with a not-so-well-trained yet excessively-violent pool of warriors. And they work for cheap. What's more, I can't see an end in sight to his potential supply of ruffians."

"But you've taken back Idaho and Liberty. The southern Alliance States are secure. Why can't we get a definitive victory?" Ava felt frustrated over the deadlock.

Foley leaned back. "It's a catch 22. If we push Markovich too hard, he'll take this war to the next level."

"You're talking nuclear," Ulysses said.

Foley nodded.

"So what?" Ava sat down on the couch by her husband. "We've got nukes, too."

Foley shook his head adamantly. "If we start popping off nukes in our own backyard, no one will survive. There will be nothing left of America but the cockroaches."

"Markovich knows that. He'd never attack a city in the Alliance States with a nuclear missile." Ava held Foley's hand.

Foley pulled her hand close to his body. "The leaders of the various state militias aren't so sure about that. They think if Markovich feels like he's losing the war, that whole mutually-assured-destruction thing will go out the window. That's what I mean by a catch 22. It's like we can't lose, but we can't win either."

Ulysses sat pensively for a while. "The Alliance needs a definitive victory. Something that will tip the balance of power just enough for Markovich to want to take his toys and go home. We can never be a single country again anyways. The liberals are so far to the left that we'll never be able to coexist with them. We each need our own country."

Ava saw the conundrum but felt happy to see her father's analytical mind beginning to function like it used to. "I could be content with that. We've been two Americas for decades anyway. Perhaps a good strong geographical separation between the two is just what we need."

"I'd take it," Foley said. "Otherwise we'll keep massacring each other until no one is left who can hold a gun. Basically, mutually assured destruction, but the slow-motion version."

The three of them spent the rest of the morning catching up with each other, then headed to Hangar 97 for lunch.

CHAPTER 22

Seest thou a man diligent in his business? he shall stand before kings; he shall not stand before mean men.

Proverbs 22:29

Ava had enjoyed Foley's company for the better part of a week. She knew their time together was coming to a close and made the most of every moment. Ulysses continued to show signs of improvement. He had fewer episodes of anxiety, no flare-ups of the dissociative amnesia disorder, and his nightmares came less frequently.

Thursday afternoon, the landline phone in the guest house rang. "I'll get it." Ava hurried to the kitchen.

"Hello?"

"Ava, hi. It's Colonel Barr."

"Good afternoon."

"To you, as well. Listen, I won't keep you but I was wondering if you, your father, and Foley would honor me with your company. Will you have dinner at my home this evening? I'm at Altus often enough to justify keeping one of the guest homes. It's just a couple of blocks over from where you're staying."

"Wow, that's a fantastic offer. Let me just check with the guys."

"Sure."

Ava placed her hand over the receiver. "Dad, Foley, it's the colonel. He's inviting us to have dinner at his place tonight. It would be great if we could go. Is it okay with you both?"

Foley looked over from his seat on the couch. "Yeah, sure."

"Tell him, thank you. I'd love to come," Ulysses said from the other couch.

Ava put the phone back to her ear. "We'll be there. What time?"

"Is six o'clock alright?"

"That will be great. See you then." Ava hung up the phone.

"I wonder what this is all about?" Ulysses asked.

Ava walked into the living room and sat next to Foley. "It's just dinner. Tomorrow is Foley's last night here. I'm sure he figured we'd want to be alone, so tonight was the best choice."

Ulysses turned the page of his paper. "If you say so."

Ava got up and sat by her father. "Why, what do you think it's about?"

"You got me, but it's not just dinner."

"Dad, everything isn't a clandestine operation. Sometimes people just want to be people."

He peeked over the top of the paper at her. "Okay."

Ava moved to the arm of the sofa where she could see her father's face rather than the back of the newspaper. "Okay? You said that like you're trying to get rid of me."

"Not at all. But I'm not going to debate the matter."

She crossed her arms playfully. "Insinuating that you think I'm wrong and you're right."

"I don't think anyone is right or wrong, but I can tell you this isn't just dinner."

Ava wasn't successful in getting him to acknowledge that she was right, nor was she able to draw him into a deeper squabble over the issue. "Fine. I'm going to go see if I have anything besides jeans and tee-shirts to wear to this exquisite social engagement."

"I hope it's not a black-tie affair because I'm limited when it comes to clothing options also," said Foley as she walked to the bedroom.

Later that evening, Ava heard a knock on the bathroom door. "Just a second. I'm putting the finishing touches on my makeup."

"Sure, baby. I don't mean to rush you, but it's five till six. I know in your world there is such a thing as fashionably late. But, for your father and I, being military men, fashionably late equates to KP duty, push-ups, and ten-mile midnight runs in the rain; that's if the commanding officer is in a good mood."

Disgusted with the cheap makeup she'd bought from the on-base exchange, she tossed the compact in the sink. "Okay. Maybe the colonel will excuse my appearance on account of there's a civil war going on." She opened the door to find her adoring husband waiting outside.

"You look beautiful." He leaned in for a kiss.

Ulysses called out from the living room. "Our ride is here."

"Thanks." She checked her teeth for lipstick in the mirror, then quickly followed Foley out the door.

"Hey, Sergeant Griffith, are you coming to dinner?" Ava asked the driver as she got into the back seat of the waiting car.

"Not this evening ma'am." Griffith smiled at her in the mirror.

The ride was a short one. Colonel Barr's on-base accommodations were only a few streets over. Sergeant Griffith stopped the vehicle, got out, and opened the door for Ava. "Have a nice evening."

"Thank you, Sergeant." Ava held Foley's hand as they proceeded up the walk to the colonel's porch.

Ulysses trailed close behind them. "I told you this wasn't just dinner."

"Why?" Ava asked.

Ulysses looked left, then right. "You don't see those guys hanging around?"

Ava hoped he wasn't having an episode. She looked at the house to the left to see a man with dark sunglasses and a light jacket sitting on the front porch. She looked next door on the right and noticed two men, also with jackets and dark glasses standing near the garage. "So?"

Ulysses replied, "It's six o'clock. You might need sunglasses if you're driving, but not to loiter around your own property. And it's June in Oklahoma, you certainly don't need a jacket."

Ava puckered her forehead. No doubt about it, something curious was afoot.

The front door opened and the colonel stepped out. "Ava, Ulysses, Foley, it's so good to have you. Please, come in."

Ava walked in cautiously. The first thing she noticed was that the table was set for six. It was obviously intended to be less intimate than she'd supposed.

From the rear den, appeared another guest.

"Agent Shaub, what a surprise to see you here," she said. "This is my husband, Foley Mitchem. I believe you remember my father. Foley, this is Secret Service Agent Shaub."

"Please, call me Mike." Shaub shook hands with Foley.

The colonel held out his hand toward the table. "Why don't you three go ahead and take a seat. We're still waiting on one other guest."

As they sat down, Ulysses whispered with a smile and a wink, "I hate to say I told you so, but—I told you so."

Foley leaned in and spoke low. "Secret Service? Why would Secret Service be here?"

Ava nodded at the extra chair. "Typically, they investigate credit card fraud and protect the life of the president. So, unless you've been placing card skimmers on ATMs and gas pumps in your spare time, I'd say we just narrowed down the possibilities of who the other guest is."

Foley shook his head. "No way."

"I realize this is your first time meeting the man but try not to act like a hayseed and embarrass Dad and me," Ava whispered with a wink.

Shaub spoke into the cuff of his jacket and nodded to the colonel as he went to the door.

Instinctively, Ava stood up. Foley and Ulysses did likewise.

"Ava! So good to see you again." Blackwell came in and walked straight to the table. "Ulysses, I'm so glad to see you are doing well. We were praying for you."

"Thank you, Mr. President." Ulysses shook his hand.

"And this must be the man I've heard so much about." Blackwell grabbed Foley's hand and shook it vigorously.

"Yes, sir," said Ava. "This is Foley Mitchem, my husband."

Foley said, "It's an honor to meet you, Mr. President. Thank you for your help in getting Ava home."

Blackwell threw his hands in the air with a chuckle. "Whoa, hey! I don't know anything about that. All that kidnapping the governor's daughter stuff, wow, that's way outside of my wheelhouse. But, I'm glad you were able to get her back."

"Yes, sir." Foley seemed to not understand why Blackwell would deny his involvement but didn't press the issue.

Blackwell patted the colonel on the back. "Smells good in here, Tom. What are we having?"

"Seafood linguini. I'm half Italian."

"Barr? That sounds Scottish or something." The president took the chair at the head of the table, next to Ava.

"On my mother's side. Her maiden name was Rossi. My grandparents came over from the old country. Mom was born here."

"Can I help you with something, Colonel?" Ava offered.

"Mike is giving me a hand," Barr replied.

Agent Shaub brought several plates in and set them at each chair before taking a seat himself.

Barr brought in the last of the plates along with a basket of bread. He took the last seat and said, "Mr. President, will you ask the blessing?"

They all bowed their heads while President Blackwell prayed.

Afterward, Barr said, "Please, everyone enjoy and let me know if you need anything at all."

Ava took her first bite. "Mmm! Colonel, this is spectacular!" She finished chewing and looked at the president. "I feel so honored to see you again, but you'll have to pardon my suspicious nature. Are we here for some purpose other than appreciating the colonel's culinary wizardry?"

Blackwell took a long drink of water and dried the corners of his mouth with his napkin. "I honestly did want to have dinner with you and Ulysses, to thank you for what you did. But I'm afraid I am having to multitask here."

Everyone listened as the president spoke.

"Did you happen to hear about our little operation down in Amarillo?"

"No, I've been following the news and didn't see anything about Amarillo." Ava broke off a piece of bread and dipped it in her linguini.

"We were—testing the fence, for lack of a better term. Last week, I sent in two battalions, to see if we could take and hold Amarillo. The obvious objective was to establish a foothold in Texas. My strategists have looked at this thing from every angle imaginable. The consensus is that we'll never end this war without taking back Texas."

Ava looked at her father. "The decisive victory you were talking about the other day when Foley came home. You said we needed something that will tip the balance of power enough for Markovich to want to take his toys and go home. Taking back Texas would be just the thing."

Blackwell nodded. "That's almost verbatim what my strategists are telling me."

"So, what's stopping us?" Ava asked.

"The reason no one is talking about Amarillo is that it was essentially a loss for both sides. We went in hard and fast. We took the city, but . . ." Blackwell let his fork rest on his plate and his expression grew grim.

"What?" Ava begged.

The president swallowed hard. "Markovich gassed three education camps located in Potter County, outside the city."

"Gassed? You mean like Nazis?" She let go of her bread and wiped her hands.

"The Nazis used Zyklon B. Markovich used Cyanide gas, but yes, the same concept," the president answered bleakly.

Everyone was silent for a while. Finally, Blackwell spoke. "I wanted to wait until after dinner to discuss this, but you obviously knew we had an important issue to cover." He looked at Ava with apologizing eyes.

"I guess my curiosity ruined dinner." She turned to the colonel. "Sorry about that."

"Don't mention it." Barr smiled kindly.

Blackwell continued, "Anyway, when we took the city, the administrators of the three education camps already had the gas hooked up to the ventilation systems. Two of the facilities were level-one. One was a men's facility, the other a women's facility. The third camp was level-two. It was mixed, families. He had fathers, mothers, and kids all staying together in that one. It was supposed to be an incentive for them to not get kicked down to level one."

Ava listened to the story. "Why? Why didn't anyone want to report it?"

"Markovich told us if we didn't pull out of Texas, he'd start gassing more education centers. His side doesn't want to announce the brutality, and we don't need to broadcast the fact that we tried to take Texas and got our tails handed to us." The president looked around the table.

Ava shook her head. "That's all very tragic, but what can we do about it?"

Blackwell's demeanor improved. "I'm glad you asked."

CHAPTER 23

And Jonathan said to the young man that bare his armour, Come, and let us go over unto the garrison of these uncircumcised: it may be that the Lord will work for us: for there is no restraint to the Lord to save by many or by few. And his armourbearer said unto him, Do all that is in thine heart: turn thee; behold, I am with thee according to thy heart.

1 Samuel 14:6-7

Ava listened closely to Blackwell's next words.

The president's eyes darted from Foley, to Ava, to Ulysses. "The bottom line is, we have to take back Texas. The resources, the borders, the people, and even what the state symbolizes to America are all critical to sustaining the Alliance States."

Ava interjected, "But you can't invade because Markovich will execute hundreds of thousands of people."

"Try millions." Blackwell's eyes showed his grief over the situation.

Foley looked at Ava then back at the president. "So, you're asking us to liberate the education centers first?"

Ava shook her head. "That's impossible! Markovich must have re-education camps all over the state."

"Actually, not that many. And they're all located close to other camps. Lubbock has two. Two in Odessa. Only one in Abilene. Fort Worth and Dallas have four between them. Houston has four. Austin and San Antonio each have three." The president paused to take a bite of his pasta.

Ava sighed. "Nineteen. You need nineteen teams to simultaneously secure and hold one camp each. Not only that, but you need each team to get across the border, armed to the teeth, without being spotted by the SJL or the regime's regular military.

"And what are they supposed to do while they're waiting for the cavalry to arrive? Austin and San Antonio are at least three hundred miles from the nearest border. You'd still have to fight your way through Houston to get to them."

"Not if we come up from the coast." Colonel Barr entered the conversation.

Ava turned to the colonel. "You don't think Markovich will be watching for an invasion from the Gulf? Besides, why are you telling us all of this? We're three people, and my dad isn't even supposed to be watching coverage of the war on television."

"You are three very resourceful people." Blackwell wiped his mouth with his napkin. "Ulysses would be very helpful to us, working in a planning capacity."

"Ava's role would also have to be restricted to planning and advising. She's finished getting her hands dirty." Foley resumed eating.

Ava held her hand up. "Hold on, now. I assume you'd want us to assist in the effort to secure the re-education centers in Austin, since we're familiar with the area." She likewise took another forkful of her food, which had turned cold since her last bite.

Blackwell nodded. "That's correct. Foley, you'd be in charge of putting together a militia force large enough to take and hold all three facilities in Austin. I know you fought side-by-side with the best militia fighters in this country when you were in Boise. Should you accept the mission, you could hand-pick as many or as few soldiers as you need. I completely trust your judgment. Ava's role is . . . open to discussion."

"No, it's not. If you want me to lead this raid on Austin, I have to know she's staying here." Foley's eyes burned with resolution.

"I'm not sitting on the sidelines for this!" She faced her husband with an equally determined scowl.

"You said you were done with the war. And that was before you tromped off to California and *literally* got yourself killed on a mission I didn't hear about until I saw you on television." He glared at her harshly.

"I had no idea where you were or how to get a hold of you. But I assure you, if I had, I certainly would have given you the courtesy of a proper goodbye before leaving." She crossed her arms and looked away.

Ulysses held up his hand. "We can discuss all of this when we get back to the house. The president has seven other cities to consider and plan for besides Austin. Let's decide if the three of us are willing to dedicate ourselves to this challenge so we can give him an answer. I think that's the least we can do."

Ava looked at her father, then at Foley. "It's Texas, it's Austin, it's my home. Of course I'm in."

Foley pressed his lips together, staring at his wife, obviously wanting to make sure Ava understood she would not have a combat role. "I'll put together a team of the best guys I know."

Ulysses nodded to the president. "Whatever you need from me. I'll do my best."

The president took a long drink from his water glass. "Good. Thank you very much. Colonel Barr will make sure you have all of the logistical support you need. If he can't get something and you require it for this mission, contact Agent Shaub directly, and he'll make sure I get the message.

"Keep your plans close to your chest. Markovich still has sympathizers embedded amongst the Alliance States' military ranks."

Ulysses said, "Any information you could get about the gas system used in Amarillo would be helpful. Anything at all, who the administrators were that triggered the executions, what the activation mechanisms looked like, every little bit helps."

Foley nodded. "I need all the data you have about security for the camps as well as an estimation of armed troops in and around Austin. We'll be limited on how many people we can bring in without drawing attention to ourselves, but once we take out the guards at the camps, every SJL in the vicinity will answer the call for backup."

Blackwell turned to Shaub. "I'll make sure Mike gets you everything we have on Austin."

The guests of the dinner party attempted to lighten up the conversation and enjoy the remainder of the evening. However, like a boomerang, the topic of the upcoming invasion kept coming back around.

Later that night, Ava and Foley got ready for bed.

She stood outside the bathroom door while he brushed his teeth. "I guess this means you won't be leaving to go back to Idaho."

"I'll still be going, but not to fight or guard the border. I have to put together a team." He rinsed his toothbrush in the sink. "Or more like an entire company of soldiers."

Ava made sure he couldn't see her grin in the mirror. She knew the discussion about her involvement in Texas would be heated, but that was okay. Foley wouldn't be running off to fight without her, at least not just yet.

"Before we go to sleep, I want to get one thing settled." Foley dried his face and turned around.

"Oh yeah? What's that?"

"You're not going to Texas."

She decided on a subtler approach than she'd used at dinner. Ava put her hands around his waist. "Let's talk about that in the morning."

He smiled and leaned in for a kiss. "Okay, but just so you know, there's nothing to talk about."

Ava, Foley, and Ulysses spent most of the day Friday, brainstorming and spitballing ideas for the mission. By Friday night, they'd received hard numbers on how many regime fighters they'd be up against, if Foley's team actually made it to Austin before being killed or captured.

On Saturday morning, Ava rode across the base with Foley to the runway where he'd be catching a ride on a supply run back to Idaho. "When will you be back?" She pulled his bag out of the trunk.

He positioned his rifle on one side, then slipped the shoulder strap for his duffle bag over the other. "Less than a week, I hope. The soldiers I fought with are spread out up and down the border, so I've got my work cut out for me in rounding them all up."

He pulled her close. "We never did get to have that talk."

"Nothing to talk about, right?"

He pulled back and looked her in the eye. "Yeah, as long as we're on the same page."

"Texas is my home. You can't deny me the right

to fight for it." She held his hand in her own and tenderly rubbed her thumb across the top of his hand. "If you love me, if you understand who I am at all, then you'll know this means as much to me as it does to you. I don't like you running off to war, but I know how you feel. If I asked you to stay home, I'd be killing a small part of who you are. And I love you too much to do that, even if it costs me everything."

She looked up into his eyes. "Are we on the same page?"

Foley turned at the sound of the jet engines starting up. The back ramp to the colossal C-17 was being retracted. "I've gotta go." He kissed her, turned, and sprinted toward the giant cargo plane.

CHAPTER 24

And when Abram heard that his brother was taken captive, he armed his trained servants, born in his own house, three hundred and eighteen, and pursued them unto Dan. And he divided himself against them, he and his servants, by night, and smote them, and pursued them unto Hobah, which is on the left hand of Damascus. And he brought back all the goods, and also brought again his brother Lot, and his goods, and the women also, and the people.

Genesis 14:14-16

On the morning of July 2nd, Ava sat in the front

row of the briefing room at Altus Air Force Base. Some 120 men and women sat in the chairs beside and behind her. Colonel Barr, Foley, and Ulysses sat next to one another at a long table facing Ava and the other soldiers. Three weeks had passed since the dinner with Turner Blackwell. The troops had been selected, the plans had been drawn, three platoons of forty soldiers each had been formed. Each platoon was assigned to one of the three re-education camps in Austin.

Ava thought about how many other covert teams were sitting in briefing rooms similar to this. The only difference was their targets. Rather than Austin, they would soon be deployed to Dallas, Fort Worth, Houston, Odessa, Abilene, and San Antonio. Every assault had to be flawless. The timing had to be perfect. Once the operation commenced, Markovich would know that the camps were all under a coordinated attack.

Austin Company, the soldiers who would be responsible for liberating the camps in Ava's hometown, were primarily from the Alliance militia. They'd trained hard over the past ten days with each platoon drilling over and over in mocked-up shoot houses designed to look as much like the camp administration buildings as possible.

Despite Foley's objections, Ava had trained alongside of him and Platoon Alpha in the shoot house, which was erected to mimic the layout of Austin's level-two camp known as the Sanders Education Facility. Sanders, like many level-two camps, housed families. If Ava's team failed, men, women, and children would be gassed instantly.

Colonel Barr addressed the room with a speech intended to reinforce the dire importance of precision in this operation. Ava's mind drifted back to the training she'd undergone over the last ten days. She recalled watching her father on the second day of training, his mind seeming to disconnect from his body as he relapsed into the worst dissociative state she'd seen him in since arriving at Altus six weeks earlier. When he recovered the following day, Ulysses had been ordered by Captain Murphy to stick to the planning-and-oversight side of the mission. Nevertheless, four days later, Ulysses had arrived at the shoot house at 7:00 AM with the rest of the platoon, geared up for training. No one dared tell him that he couldn't participate, not until he had yet another episode. At that point, Foley had to put in the call to Colonel Barr, explaining that Ulysses simply wasn't in any condition to be an operator.

She looked at her father and husband sitting side by side at the long table in front of her. She could still see the tension between them. But, unlike the two days prior, they were at least talking to each other.

Colonel Barr finished his discourse and took his seat, yielding the room to Ulysses.

Ava's father stood and walked to the whiteboard at the front of the room. "When you leave the briefing room, Austin Company will fly to Biloxi where you'll board several fishing vessels, which are flying Mexican flags. The boats will insert you at the harbor in Brownsville, Texas. Coast Guard patrols will let you pass without question as they'll assume you are just another wave of militants being sent up by the gangs and cartels who are working with the regime to harass cities in the Alliance States.

"We tried to distribute the Hispanic troops evenly between the three platoons, but it will be up to you to make sure you have someone fluent in Spanish on each of the fishing boats in case the Coast Guards double check. We've briefed all of our Spanish speakers on the cover story they're supposed to give if questioned. Obviously, everyone's Spanish doesn't sound like the native Mexican dialect, so try to have a Hispanic from Texas or Mexico on each boat."

Ava smiled at Octavio Hernandez who was sitting on her left. "I'm riding with you," she whispered.

Octavio, who'd been born in Juarez, Mexico, grinned and replied sarcastically, "I'll lend you my sombrero. You'll fit right in."

Ava rolled her eyes and turned back to the lecture.

Captain Murphy, who'd be going along as one of the medics, sat in the chair to Ava's right. He whispered to her, "You walked right into that one."

Ulysses continued, "Provided all goes well, you should be at the safe house before sunset the day after tomorrow. The safe house is a large warehouse in Bastrop, about thirty miles outside of Austin. You'll stay there and rest up for the operation. Everyone will need to be in position to commence their respective attacks at exactly 4:00 on the morning of July 5th. The 4th is a big drinking holiday for the SJLs as well as the soldiers in Markovich's regular army, so hopefully many of them will still be inebriated when you strike.

"The local resistance will be providing meals and support for you while you're at the safe house. Also, if you get in trouble, they're all you've got in the way of backup until the cavalry arrives. And keep in mind, it could be up to 24 hours for Alliance forces to penetrate all the way into Austin. They'll be coming in from Fort Polk or up from the Gulf. Either way, it's a long haul through very hostile territory.

"Keep in mind, you're not in Texas alone. Blackwell is sending seven other companies. You won't know anything about them, and they don't know anything about you. Obviously, the less everyone knows about the other companies, the fewer details they can share if they're caught. The downside to that is no company can help out the others in case of a jam."

Ulysses looked at Barr and took his seat. "I'll give the floor back to the colonel."

"Thank you." Barr stood. "Any questions?" He pointed to the raised hand in the third row.

A militia member asked, "How are we getting from Brownsville to the safe house?"

"Good question," Barr replied. "We've got transportation lined up for you. Some will be traveling in migrant-worker buses, others will be riding in the back of box trucks."

Another militia fighter raised his hand. "If those box trucks aren't air-conditioned, we'll be in bad shape. The high temperature today will be flirting with 100 degrees. A box truck with no windows and no AC could easily hit 200."

"They'll be climate controlled. But still, dress comfortably, and look poor so not to trip any alarms." Barr looked around the room. "Any other questions?"

No one else raised their hand.

"You're dismissed. Load up your gear. The plane will be leaving to Biloxi in half an hour." Barr walked out of the room.

Ava approached the table where her father and husband were gathering their notes. She put her arms around Ulysses. "I love you, Dad. I know how much you wanted to come, but you'll be helping out so much by staying here with Colonel Barr. All the various teams will need your expertise, especially if something goes wrong, and stuff always goes wrong."

He nodded and hugged her tightly. "I'll do what I can, but none of the teams will be able to break radio silence until the operation has begun."

She kissed him and gave his hand a squeeze. "Yeah, but nothing is going to go wrong until the op starts."

"Let's hope not." Ulysses smiled.

Foley put his hand on her arm. "We need to get going—unless you want to stay here and help your dad with tactical coordination."

She glared at her husband. "Not a chance, but nice try."

"Don't blame me for offering. One can always dream that their stubborn spouse will see reason." Foley kept his eyes low as he offered his hand to

Ulysses. "We'll see you soon, sir."

Ulysses grabbed his hand and pulled him in close for a hug, a sign that he'd put aside any hard feelings he held in regard to Foley revealing his mental problems to Barr. "Be safe. And take care of my little girl."

"Yes, sir." Foley looked up at him. "I'll do my best."

"Bye, Dad." Ava waved, grabbed the pack containing her gear and her rifle, then followed Foley out to the tarmac.

Thursday evening, Ava carried her gear into the warehouse and stretched her neck. She'd spent the previous six hours in a refrigerated produce truck. She was chilled, sore and extremely tired from the arduous journey.

"We have cots set up for you at the rear of the warehouse." A man from the local resistance pointed to the back of the building. "A small area is partitioned off for the ladies."

"Thank you," she said wearily, "but I'm with my husband, so I'll be sleeping in the same bunk space as the guys."

Foley smiled at the man and followed Ava to the back. Bravo Platoon had already arrived and most members were sleeping on their cots. Bravo had traveled all together on a single migrant worker bus. Ava tiptoed through the large open area, trying not to wake any of the soldiers from Bravo as she and Foley searched for two cots near the wall.

Once they found a good spot, she whispered to Foley, "I'm going to get a shower. I feel grubby and

I'll sleep better."

Foley dug out his hygiene kit as quietly as possible. "Good idea. Once Charlie Platoon arrives, hot water may be in tight supply."

The two of them got cleaned up and returned to the cots where they soon fell fast asleep.

Ava awoke on the morning of the 4th. Foley was already up and gone from his cot. She stepped into her boots and crossed the empty dorm area. On the other side of the warehouse, a very simple meal of bread, peanut butter and jelly was available on a long fold-out table. She skipped the jelly and made herself a peanut butter sandwich. Next, Ava ladled a black liquid substance into a Styrofoam cup. It wasn't hot, and it didn't really smell like coffee, but that's what the label said, so she drank it. She scanned the round tables in the center of the room until she found her husband, then made her way toward him. "Good morning."

Foley sat at a table with seven other soldiers. His face was stressed. "Good morning."

She looked at the six men and the female soldier. All seemed worried. "What's wrong?"

"Charlie Platoon never showed up." Foley glanced up at her, then back down to the other people at his table.

Ava pulled up a chair from the table behind Foley's. "Where are they?"

Foley pressed his lips tightly and shook his head. "No one knows. We're under radio silence, so we can't call in or out. The resistance has back channels to Barr, so they've put a message out that troops from Charlie are missing. Still, even if he knew where they were, Barr couldn't do much to help them without compromising the greater mission. And it's not just us, it's all eight companies at risk if they deviate from the mission."

Ava had taken a couple bites of her sandwich but lost her appetite. "Do you think Charlie Platoon was captured?"

Foley crossed his hands. "We have to proceed under that assumption."

"Then that means they could talk. I know they're all committed, but you saw how far Markovich's interrogators went on my father. Most people can't stand that kind of abuse for very long." Ava looked at the front door of the warehouse, wondering when the regime might raid the location.

Kyle Thompson, Bravo's platoon leader, said, "We all went through the same training. Everyone knows how important this mission is. I think they can keep their mouths shut for a few more hours."

Ava didn't want to spread more despair but she hoped Thompson wasn't underestimating Markovich's ability to make the soldiers from Charlie talk. "Even if they keep quiet, if they were captured by the regime, Markovich will know an operation is underway."

"Maybe not," Foley replied. "He might assume Charlie was simply a recon team."

She didn't feel quite as optimistic. "Charlie was assigned to the level-one facility in the Travis County Jail. It's probably the most secure facility of the three in Austin. What are we going to do about that?"

Foley looked at Kyle Thompson. "We'll dedicate fifteen troops from Alpha and fifteen from Bravo to form a new Platoon. We'll call it Delta. They'll have to liberate the jail."

Ava's forehead creased. "That leaves only twenty-five troops each for Alpha and Bravo."

Foley nodded at the female soldier sitting at the table. "Jasmin Pierce cross-trained with Bravo and Charlie. She knows the plan for taking the jail. I'm putting her in charge of Delta. She'll get the others up to speed by tonight. We'll have to make do with what we have."

Ava gritted her teeth. The mission was precariously close to being destined to fail when it had been planned with such a stripped-down roster of troops. But now, the razor-thin margin for error was gone completely.

The rest of the day was spent by Ava watching the door with her rifle in hand. She watched the seconds tick by until the warehouse was discovered by the regime or Austin Company headed out to face certain death by attempting to invade three separate facilities with far too few fighters.

After sunset, Ava heard fireworks going off all around. She wondered how many of those were being lit off by resistance members who actually cherished the freedoms represented by the holiday.

She thought about what good cover the noise of the fireworks would have provided for the mission but saw the wisdom in a pre-dawn raid against troops who would likely be sleeping off the effects of this evening's revelry.

"You should try to get some rest." Foley walked

up behind her and massaged her shoulders.

She took her eyes off the front door only for a second. "Thanks, but I'd never be able to sleep. Even if we knew where Charlie Platoon was, I'd still be too amped up."

He took a bottle of water from the side pocket of his cargo pants and gave it to her. "Okay, but at least keep drinking. You need to be hydrated."

She opened it and took a sip. "I will."

He kissed her on top of her head. "We'll leave the safe house at 3:25 AM. Be ready by 3:00 for a final gear check."

"Sure thing." She watched him walk away, then turned her attention back to the front door.

The final hours before the raid crept by. Ava, entranced by staring at the door, began to nod off.

"Five minutes till final gear check." Foley patted her on the back.

Ava snapped out of her daze. "Yeah, I'll be right there." She hurried off to her bunk to collect her gear. She rushed to put on her tactical vest, which would be worn under an oversized windbreaker to hide her supply of extra pistol and rifle magazines. She'd wear a simple baseball cap, with her jeans pulled down over the tops of her combat boots. The entire company would be dressed in civilian attire meant to help them blend in and not give any warning to the enemy of the coming attack. Ava folded the stock of the AK-47 she'd be operating and placed it in her duffle bag. The rifle would stay concealed until the moment the attack on the level-two facility commenced. Once she was ready, Ava hurried to the front of the warehouse for final inspection.

Foley walked up the line inspecting the gear of each of the eighty men and women who were soon to depart on this treacherous assignment. He paid special attention to the suppressors on each of the rifles, making sure they were attached correctly. Once the battle began, noise wouldn't matter, but a few silent shots in the initial phase of the attack could give them just enough of an edge to actually be successful.

After a very short comms check, Foley bowed his head and said a prayer for the safety and success of Austin Company. Afterward, he looked up. "Godspeed everyone. Alpha Platoon, follow me!"

CHAPTER 25

Then Moses stood in the gate of the camp, and said, Who is on the Lord's side? let him come unto me. And all the sons of Levi gathered themselves together unto him. And he said unto them, Thus saith the Lord God of Israel, Put every man his sword by his side, and go in and out from gate to gate throughout the camp, and slay every man his brother, and every man his companion, and every man his neighbour.

Exodus 32:26-27

Alpha Platoon was broken into five smaller fire teams of five members each. Ava was assigned to

Team One with Scott, Carl, Elizabeth, and Foley as the team leader. Scott, Carl, and Elizabeth had all fought in the militia alongside Foley in the battle to liberate Boise. Team One would be responsible for getting to the main administration office where the cyanide-gas release trigger was housed.

The other four fireteams would be tasked with taking out the perimeter guards and securing the boundaries of the education facility until Alliance forces arrived. Captain Murphy would serve as the only medic for the Platoon.

Alpha Platoon was shuttled to the ORP, or objective rally point, by members of the resistance in six different vehicles, which left the safe house at staggered intervals. The ORP was a salvage yard located approximately 500 yards from Sanders Residential Education Facility. Ava, Foley, and the rest of Team One rode in an old dusty minivan. Their vehicle was the first to arrive at the ORP.

Ava exited the vehicle, waited for the others to get out, then shut the sliding door of the minivan as softly as possible.

One by one, the other vehicles dropped off the members of the remaining four teams at the ORP. Foley checked his watch. "3:55. Let's move out."

Ava said a silent prayer and followed Foley. They approached the glorified prison from the rear. Once they'd crossed the field between the junkyard and Sanders, Team Three split off and followed the fence toward the left of the administration building while Team Two tackled right. Unlike most detention centers, Sanders had only one row of fencing since it was a level-two facility. Three holes were cut in the fence by the platoon for multiple avenues of retreat in case they had to abort the mission. Teams Two and Three entered via the holes on the right and left. Teams One, Four, and Five entered through the center hole in the fence. Once inside the fence line, Foley pointed up at three surveillance cameras mounted along the edge of the roof. The building was a three-story facility, so the only way to neutralize the cameras was to shoot them. Foley took the camera on the right, Ava took the center one, and Carl shot out the last one.

"They'll know we're here," Foley whispered.

Ava heard the bolts of the suppressed AK-47s snapping from both sides of the buildings. The relative silence was soon broken by echoing gunfire.

"We've got heavy contact on the south side of the building!" cried a voice over Ava's radio earphone.

"Roger that, Team Three. I'm sending Four to back you up." Foley nodded at Octavio, the leader of Team Four.

Octavio led his troops quickly around the corner to assist those under heavy fire.

"Two, what's your status?" Foley asked over the radio.

"Hostiles down. Ready to proceed to the front, but we've got this service door over here that I don't want to turn my back on."

"Hang, on," Foley replied. "We'll cover the door." He released the mic button and addressed the team leader of Five. "You guys stay here until we know where you're needed."

"Roger." The man nodded.

Foley waved his hand for Ava and the rest of Team One to follow him. Ava hustled along the wall on the north side of the administration building. From her position, she could see the large detention center just across the parking lot from the administration building. She thought about the families housed in the giant jail—the men, women, and children whose lives depended on her being able to finish what she'd started.

Foley called over the radio again, "What's the status on the southside?"

"Hostiles clear."

Just then, the service door swung open with a loud kick and objects flying out. Ava instantly recognized them as flashbangs and closed her eyes.

BANG!

She dropped to one knee and opened her eyes. She could see, but the loud ring in her ears would keep her from being able to hear Foley's instructions for several seconds. The door opened in the opposite direction of Ava's position but in precisely the direction of Team Two. Gunfire rang out. Three soldiers from Team Two went down. The surviving members took cover around the next corner.

Ava grabbed the edge of the door with her left hand, and using the solid steel barrier as a shield, swung her rifle around with her right hand and began firing at the enemy troops inside the building. Foley ran around Ava and started shooting. Soon, the remaining troops from Team Two joined in the counter assault.

Ava saw Foley's mouth moving but was still temporarily deafened from the flashbang. She guessed he was calling for Team Five to come to the side door. Foley signaled to Ava to stack up behind him. She complied, and soon, Carl, Elizabeth, Scott and the soldiers from Team Two stacked up behind her. Foley held his hand up in the air, then suddenly dropped it and the group filed in through the door. Immediately, they began taking fire from the soldiers inside, who were shooting from inside the doorways of the offices along the hallway.

Foley stormed forward to the first doorway, shooting into the room as he arrived. Ava rushed behind him eliminating targets along the way. The entire team hustled to the first office, where Scott and Elizabeth held the entrance.

The first phase of the mission had been accomplished; they were inside the administration building.

Once inside the room, Ava looked Foley over. "You're hit!"

Blood was oozing from his forearm and shoulder. "Can't bake a cake without breaking some eggs." He winced in pain.

She huffed and quickly shed off the oversized windbreaker, which was covering her tactical vest. Ava reached for the medical kit attached to the right side of the vest.

Foley shook his head. "Not now. We've gotta get to the main office on the top level before the administrator gasses the hostages. We have to clear this floor, then try to get to the third story without taking on every hostile on the second floor."

The sound of gunfire erupted in the hallway as Team Five arrived to engage the remaining enemy fighters on the ground floor.

"Guys, Carl doesn't look good," Elizabeth's voice sounded distressed.

Ava looked at Carl who was slumped against the wall with his arm over his abdomen. No blood was visible through his tactical vest, but a dark red stain was appearing at the top of his pants. "Sit down. Let me take a look."

Carl shook his head. "Leave me here. Clear the building and then come back for me."

"That's not going to happen." Ava helped him slide down the wall to a seated position. She tugged his hand away from his stomach and unzipped his vest.

Foley looked on with sorrowful eyes. He pressed the button on his mic. "Five, what's your status?"

A man called out over the mic, "We thinned them out, but they're holed up in the offices down the hall. Is that your team in the first office on the left?"

"Roger," Foley replied. "We've got one man who's hit pretty bad. Doc, if you can hear me, we could use your help."

Captain Murphy called back. "I'm patching up a man from Team Three, then I'll be on around."

Ava pushed her mic button. "Hurry, he's not looking good."

Foley said over the radio, "Three and Four, I need you guys to split up and hold the perimeter. Three, take the southwest corner and focus on not letting anyone in or out of the front door. Octavio, have your guys cover the northeast corner and lockdown that service entrance. No one in or out."

"Roger," replied Octavio.

"We're holding the front," Team Three's leader said.

Foley pressed the mic key once more. "Five, try to take the office across from us. These walls are thin. We'll start shooting into the room next to us while Scott and Elizabeth cover the hallway for you guys to make entry."

The man's voice came back over the radio. "Just say when."

"Now!" Foley pointed to Ava who emptied a magazine into the wall, which stood between her team and the room next door.

Shots rang out all around her for several seconds, then a moment of odd silence came.

"Reload!" Foley shouted.

Ava tossed the spent magazine from her rifle on the floor and popped in a fresh one.

"Five, are you guys in?"

A different voice replied, "We're in, but our team leader is down. We lost another man, also. He took one in the face."

Captain Murphy rushed into the room and placed his rifle on the floor next to Carl, who had become unconscious. He quickly laid him out and cut away his shirt.

Ava looked at Murphy. His face told her all she needed to know. "Captain, if he's not going to make it, can you look at Foley?"

"You're hit?" Murphy asked.

"No big deal." Foley seemed more focused on the battle than his injury.

"At least let me put a compression bandage on your arm. It will take all but five seconds."

Foley glared at Ava. "Five seconds."

Murphy cut away Foley's sleeve and quickly bandaged both of his wounds. "Looks like they went through."

With his free hand, Foley pressed his mic button. "Five, we're going to advance to the room next to you. Lay down some cover fire into that room until we begin crossing. On my signal."

"Roger."

"Thanks." Foley reluctantly said to Captain Murphy. He looked at the rest of the team. "Ready?"

Ava and the others stacked up behind him.

"Hit 'em!" Foley called out to Team Five.

Gunfire rang out from across the hall.

"Go!" Foley ran across the hall, shooting as he went.

Ava did the same, targeting the door at the far end of the hall where she saw a muzzle flash. She watched a shooter fall face first into the doorway as she cleared the short distance to the next room. More shots came on her heels, but she couldn't worry about them. Inside the room riddled with bullet holes from Team Five's assault were three dead hostiles and two more who were taking cover behind a desk. Straightaway, Ava dropped to her knee to reduce her profile and shot directly into the desk. Foley and Scott flanked the desk and cut down the remaining two fighters in the room.

Elizabeth took a knee and held the doorway behind them.

Ava scanned the room. One of the remaining soldiers from Team Two was on the ground beside her foot, a growing puddle of blood covered the floor near his head. She looked around for the other man from Two. He was nowhere to be found.

"Another casualty in the hallway," Elizabeth said. "Multiple hits. I think he's already gone."

Foley's face was grim. He spoke over the radio. "Doc, we've got a guy down in the hall. You better hold off on helping him until we clear this floor. Otherwise, they'll just cut you down."

"No can do. I'll grab him and pull him into this office when you guys make your next move."

"Roger," Foley replied. "Team Five, are you ready to go?"

"Only three of us left, but I guess so."

"Same drill; run diagonally across the hall and take the next room. Go!"

Ava heard Team Five's boots stomping outside the door. Rifle fire echoed down the hallway.

"We're in," said the man's voice over the radio.

Then, an explosion of machine gun fire barreled throughout the building.

Foley pressed the mic key. "Five, what's your status?"

No one replied.

He repeated the request. "Five, anyone from your team, please respond."

Captain Murphy's voice was the next on the radio. "I think they adapted your tactic of shooting through the walls. I was getting stray bullets piercing the drywall all the way down here at the first office."

Foley quickly interrupted. "Then we have to assume the troops from Five are down and the enemy has their radios. Everyone, switch to the alternate secure channel."

Ava quickly adjusted the frequency on her radio.

"Octavio, I need your team to help us out in here." Foley made a quick magazine change.

"Not a good idea," said the team leader from Three. "We've got hostiles coming across the yard from the detention center."

Foley huffed. "Then both of you, get inside. Octavio, you guys help us get upstairs. Three, you guys hold that service door from inside."

Both teams acknowledged the order.

"We have to push through to that stairwell or we'll never stop the administrator from gassing the hostages. It's basically a suicide mission, but we have to try." Foley's gaze went from Elizabeth, to Scott, to Ava, showing his pain when his eyes met those of his wife.

"We're coming in the door now, boss," Octavio said.

Foley replied, "Follow us." He quickly glanced at his team. "Go!"

Foley led the way out the door and opened fire. Ava ran out directly behind him. Unlike her husband, she didn't spray the hall with bullets. Instead, she seized the opportunity provided by his cover fire to take calculated shots as targets became visible. They rushed toward the stairwell door exchanging bullets with the enemy while they moved.

Foley reached the door first and slung it open for the rest of his team. "Scott, take the lead. Run past the second floor. It's primarily housing for the guards. I expect most of them are already down here, but we could get some latecomers, so be careful. Nevertheless, we have to get by them and take the top floor."

Scott did not delay. Like Elizabeth and Ava, he had changed magazines while Foley handed out the instructions, then led the way up the stairs.

Elizabeth followed Scott, and Ava tailed her.

Octavio and one other man from his team came through the stairwell door.

"Where's the rest of your team?" Foley asked.

Ava turned around to see the woeful look on Octavio's face.

Foley offered a look of sympathy. "I'm going to need you to hold back anyone left on the second level."

"We'll do what we can, boss." Octavio swallowed hard and began climbing the stairs behind Foley.

Ava looked through the small opening in the door of the second story as she passed on her way up. Four more hostiles were emerging from their rooms. Octavio would have his work cut out for him.

Once they arrived on the third-floor landing, Foley pointed at Ava and Elizabeth. "You two, hold the stairwell. Don't let anyone else up here. We'll locate the main admin office and secure the gas release trigger."

"No, Foley! I don't want to get split up!" Ava protested.

"I'm going right down the hall. It should be the last door on the left." His smile was forced, which told her that he did not expect to live long enough to see her again.

"No!" Her voice became weak and shallow.

His departing grin persisted. "I need you to do this for me, Ava. I love you. I'll see you soon."

"Godspeed," Elizabeth said to Foley and Scott.

Ava felt frozen from grief while her husband marched off to certain doom.

Elizabeth gently put her arm on Ava's shoulder. "We've got a job to do."

Ava broke her gaze from Foley and turned to look down the stairwell. Gunfire broke out below her. Next, she heard the volley of bullets being exchanged between Foley and the guards of the main office. She watched the man below her on the second-floor stairwell landing fall, leaving Octavio by himself to keep fighting.

"I'm going to help Foley," Ava yelped.

Elizabeth frowned. "Okay. I guess if we're breaking rank anyway, I'll give Octavio a hand."

"Be safe." Ava readied her rifle and charged down the hall toward the barrage of rifle fire. The exchange ceased just before she walked through the door. No less than ten enemy soldiers lay strewn about the room like mobile homes after a tornado. One SJL guard had fallen out the window, impaling his chest with a large triangular shard of glass, which pointed to the ceiling like a crimson stalagmite. Three yards away from the door was

Scott's body, riddled with bullet holes. At the far end of the room was the administrator's desk. Foley's body was slumped against the desk between two dead hostiles and covered in blood. The entire scene was such a mess, she couldn't tell how much of the blood belonged to Foley and what was from the enemy soldiers.

Her attention was quickly drawn away from her motionless husband by a female's voice. The woman, who was obviously the administrator had not noticed Ava walk in the room behind her. The woman stood between the desk and the broken window looking out toward the detention center across the lawn. In one hand, she held a thin, silvery pistol. In the other, she held a small black box. The woman looked disheveled from the back. Her robe was untied, hanging loose on her razor-thin shoulders. Her short, jet-black hair was matted on one side where she'd been asleep. She spoke over the speakerphone with a raspy voice, hoarse as if from a hard night of drinking and smoking. "You guys should've had all of the prisoners corralled to the common areas by now. You need to finish that up and get over here. Trust me, you don't want to be anywhere near the detention center when I press this button. And there may be more of the attackers in the building."

"Are you okay, ma'am?" asked the voice over the speakerphone.

"Yeah, only two of them made it up here. They took out all of my personal SJL team. Carlton killed one of them before he died. The cute one was left standing in here by himself." The woman glanced down at Foley's unmoving body. "He didn't see me hiding behind the desk. I popped up and plugged him in the chest. He's finished, but still, hurry up and get your men up here." She picked up the office phone receiver and slammed it back down.

Ava's blood began to boil. Anger and rage seethed in her veins, in her eyes. This callous beast who'd killed her beloved, how could she be so arrogant? She'd make her pay for what she'd done to Foley. She'd make her pay for the way she'd spoken about it, bragged about killing the man Ava loved more than anything. And she'd make her feel fear like she'd never felt before. Ava would make this wretched woman's last moments the most dreadful seconds of her life. She leveled the AK-47 at the woman's head. "Turn around."

The woman froze, suddenly aware that she was not alone. Slowly, she pivoted to face her assailant. "Ava?" The woman's eyes grew wide as bucket lids. "You . . . you're . . . alive! You can't be! I watched you die! How are you here?"

Shock overtook Ava almost as much as it had the skinny woman before her. "Raquel! What are you doing here?"

Raquel snorted. "After you killed off my path to Hollywood celebrity status, administrator over one of these filth-ridden institutions was the best gig I could land, even with all the political capital I've worked so hard at building. At least this one was near all my old haunts and the people I know."

Raquel's eyes darted down at Foley, then back up. "I thought that one looked familiar. Well, at least he's out of his misery. He won't have to worry about being teased anymore by the little prude who hates life and can't stand to see anyone else having a good time either."

Ava kept the front bead of the iron sight trained on Raquel's chest. "For your information, we were married."

Raquel laughed mockingly. "Then I really saved him from a lifetime of torture."

"And now it's my turn to repay the favor. I'm going to put you out of everyone's misery."

Raquel slowly raised the black box, her thumb resting firmly against the red button. "And I'll send the people in that detention center to their grave. I know you well enough, Ava. For the rest of your life, you'll dream about all those people, the families, the mothers with their tiny babies in their arms while they died. The little boys and girls who will never laugh and play again because of you. They'll haunt you from this day forward."

Ava's finger could not have been any tighter against the trigger without making the rifle bark out the projectile which would end Raquel's life. She slowly brought the bead up to Raquel's head, knowing that unless the bullet pierced her brain before her finger could push that button, everything Raquel was saying was true. She'd never forgive herself if there was even the most remote chance that she could have done something differently. Ava ran the calculations in her head but she simply didn't know if she could kill her in time.

"Put down that gun, and I'll put down the remote." Raquel's antagonistic tone had died down. She seemed to be coming around to how dire the situation was between them.

Ava considered the deal.

"No," called a faint voice.

Ava glanced down only for a second. "Foley?"

Raquel slowly positioned the pistol in her right hand, aiming it at Foley's head. "What's with you people? You just won't die! But I tell you what, if you shoot me, I'll finish Prince Charming off so you can add his face to your list of ghosts who will be visiting you regularly in your nightmares. Put—the gun—down."

Ava shook her head. "No. Not unless you toss yours."

"Okay, we're negotiating. That's good. Let's say I toss my gun. Then what?"

Ava looked around the room. "Then I put my rifle down and you let Foley and the people in the detention center live. You can kill me or whatever you want."

"So how do we do this?" Raquel asked.

"Toss your gun out the window. Then, I'll dangle my rifle out the window, and you'll hold the remote out the window. We'll count to three and drop them both simultaneously."

Foley grunted his objection but didn't have the strength to formulate full words.

Raquel considered the offer. "I don't like it."

"It's the only alternative. Otherwise, I pull this trigger and put you down like 'Ol' Yeller." Ava faked a nod of complete confidence. "Then, whatever happens, I'll sleep just fine knowing I tried to reason with you but you refused to compromise. It's the only way I can be sure you won't gas the hostages the second I put down my rifle."

Raquel stood staring into Ava's eyes as if she were trying to see if she was bluffing.

"And time is running out. You've got until the count of ten to give me your answer. If you say nothing, I'll take that as a no, and I'll gun you down right here and right now."

Raquel tightened her jaw and flexed her arm holding the pistol at Foley's head.

"One, two, three, four." The pressure felt like so many needles pressing against Ava's skin, only from the inside rather than out.

"Five, six, seven." Beads of sweat formed on her brow.

Raquel took a deep breath and the color washed out of her face.

"Eight, nine . . ." Ava's nerves caused her hands to quiver, causing her to question how true her shot would be, making her wonder if she was sealing Foley's fate along with the men, women, and precious little children in the detention center just outside the bloody broken window.

"Wait!" Raquel screamed as Ava hit *Ten*.

Ava took a deep breath, ready to cry over the torment. "Time's up, Raquel. What's it going to be?"

"I'll do it."

"Exactly the way I said. No modifications."

Raquel gave a dull nod. "Exactly the way you said."

"Toss the gun. Out the window."

Raquel gradually moved the gun away from

Foley. She held it through the broken glass.

"Let it go." Ava kept her sights on Raquel's head.

Raquel growled as she allowed the pistol to slip away from her grip.

"Good. Now, take your thumb away from the button, turn the remote upside down, and hold it out the window."

"No way. I'm not falling for that one," Raquel argued.

"I'll take my finger off the trigger at the same time. It's the only way I know you won't push the button as soon as I lower my weapon!"

"Nope. I'm not doing that. You didn't specify."

Ava raised her voice. "Well, now I'm specifying. And the question of Foley living is no longer an issue since you ditched the gun. Do you really want to go back to the bargaining table with me?"

Raquel scoffed. "The question of Foley living is certainly still an issue, whether I have a gun or not. You better take another look at pretty boy."

Ava gritted her teeth, wanting to end this now. "Yeah, antagonize me while I have a rifle pointed at your face, Raquel. That's smart. Do what I said, or I'll blow your brains all over the wall."

Raquel tempered the attitude. "Okay. At the same time. I move my thumb and you move your finger off the trigger."

Ava nodded and placed her finger on the trigger guard while watching Raquel remove her thumb from the red button. "Out the window."

"At the same time," Raquel insisted.

Ava stepped over the leg of the body impaled in

the center of the window. She glacially held her rifle out the window as Raquel inverted the remote so she could not readily push the button.

There they stood. Raquel on one side, the bloody corpse of the SJL guard in the middle, and Ava on the other. Raquel held the remote out the window with her thumb and her forefinger. Ava dangled the rifle by the barrel below the silencer.

Ava nodded. Raquel lowered her chin in agreement.

"On three," Ava clarified.

Raquel acknowledged, "On three."

"One," the girls said in unison. "Two, three . . ."

Ava released the rifle, which dropped rapidly to the ground below.

Raquel did not release the remote. Rather she smiled at Ava with a devilish smile. All the evil in Raquel's soul pierced through her dark eyes, which were laughing with hideous malice.

Ava felt a firestorm of rage well up inside her instantly. She looked at the remote, which Raquel was already spinning around between her fingers. Ava knew she had less than a second before Raquel's thumb hit the button and killed every person inside the detention center with the deadly cyanide gas.

Ava didn't hesitate. With all of her fury and all of her strength, she grabbed Raquel by her hair. She clenched her fist in the matted jet-black mess. And with every ounce of her vigor, she thrust Raquel's head down against the jagged dagger of glass protruding from the corpse between them. She felt the shard pierce deep into Raquel's eye, but Ava plunged her weight onto the back of Raquel's head, driving the sharp point deeper into her brain. She turned to look out the window at Raquel's hand. Her body tensed up from the sudden trauma and her hand opened in an abrupt spasm. Ava watched the remote drop from Raquel's hand and land gently in the grass below—right beside her AK-47.

CHAPTER 26

When thou passest through the waters, I will be with thee; and through the rivers, they shall not overflow thee: when thou walkest through the fire, thou shalt not be burned; neither shall the flame kindle upon thee.

Isaiah 43:2

"We did it, baby! We stopped her." Ava knelt beside Foley.

Blood dripped from the corner of his mouth yet he still managed to force a smile. His breathing was labored and his voice was feeble. "You have to call it in to Altus. The encrypted sat phone is in the side pocket of my cargo pants."

She hurried to unzip his tactical vest. She ripped

the first aid kit from her vest and removed the EMT shears. "Sure, just as soon as we get you taken care of." Ava cut away his shirt to reveal the entry wound in Foley's chest. Blood spattered out of the hole with each of his tedious breaths.

"No, you have to call Altus first. The invasion is waiting on our report." His speech and expression showed his discomfort.

"They've waited this long. A few more minutes won't matter." Ava ripped open the packaging of the chest seal, wiped away the blood from Foley's wound, and placed the seal over the bullet hole.

Foley's breathing became increasingly shallow and his eyes closed.

Ava pressed the mic key on her radio. "Captain Murphy, Foley is hit in the chest. I put the ventilated seal on him, but he seems like he's fighting for air."

"Tension pneumothorax, do you have a decompression needle in your kit?"

"No, can you come? We're on the third floor."

"I'm hit in the leg," the medic replied. "The bleeding is controlled, but my stair-climbing abilities are hampered at the moment. Can you come down to me to get the needle?"

Ava couldn't fathom leaving Foley in this condition. "Octavio, Elizabeth, can one of you go to the captain and get a needle for me? Foley is in bad shape. I don't want to leave him."

"Roger," Elizabeth said.

Ava said a quick silent prayer for Foley, then retrieved the satellite phone from his pocket. She keyed in the numbers.

"HQ, go ahead."

She held back her tears. "This is Alpha Platoon, Austin Company. We've secured our objective but suffered heavy losses. We have multiple dead and severely injured. We won't be able to hold out long without support."

"Roger that, Alpha. We'll get to you when we can." The call terminated with an abrupt click.

Ava folded the antenna and looked helplessly at her husband. "God, I know you still work miracles. This wouldn't even be the first time you've blessed me with one for Foley, so my faith certainly isn't an issue here. But please, I'm begging you, save him from death once more, in Jesus' name."

Minutes later Octavio's voice came from behind. "Somebody ordered a doctor?"

Ava turned to see Elizabeth and Octavio panting heavily from carrying Captain Murphy up three flights of stairs. "Yes! Thank you, yes!" Ava moved out of the way so they could lower Murphy next to Foley.

Ava lifted her eyes to Heaven. "Thank you, Jesus!"

Ava called back over the radio, "Team Five, if there's any way possible for you to retrieve it, I've dropped something very important out the window."

The leader from Five called back, "Is it life-or-death important?"

"Yes." Ava didn't want to give too much information about the remote, in case the enemy was listening. "It's mission critical."

"Then we'll get it, but we've got hostiles outside

the building. Would it be possible for your team to provide cover fire from your location?"

Elizabeth answered, "Roger that, Team Five."

Ava gripped Foley's hand once more, then picked up his AK, following Elizabeth and Octavio to the broken window where Raquel's corpse was stacked on top of the fallen SJL soldier.

"I'll tell you what you're looking for when you're en route. Let me know when you're ready." Ava let go of the mic key.

"We'll go on your signal, but we need that cover fire."

"Okay, go!" Ava began sniping off every visible guard who had left the detention center and taken up positions around the admin building. Elizabeth and Octavio did likewise.

"What are we looking for?" Team Five's leader asked.

"West side of the building, directly below where we're shooting, you'll see an AK lying in the grass. Next to the rifle is a small black remote. We need to retrieve it at all costs." Ava resumed shooting.

"Then you'll have it." The leader's voice was obscured by a barrage of machine gun fire all around.

Ava kept her focus on the guards who were closing in on Team Five rather than paying attention to the remote below. She emptied the magazine of Foley's rifle then exchanged it for a fresh one.

Seconds later, Team Five's leader called back. "This is Sergeant Prindle, we have the device. Three good men lost their lives retrieving it."

"I'm sorry, Sergeant. But if the enemy had

located it, the hostages would have been gassed. I'm sending Octavio down to get the remote. We'll disassemble it and destroy it, so it can't fall into the wrong hands."

"I'm down to myself and one other soldier, so if you could send down a couple people to help hold the front door, I'd appreciate it," said Prindle.

Once again, Ava did not want to divulge too much information over the radio in case the enemy was listening in. "Roger." She looked at Elizabeth. "You and Octavio go downstairs, and you bring the remote back up."

She turned to Octavio. "Let Prindle know that it's only the seven of us alive and that Foley and the captain aren't in fighting condition."

A heavy crease came across Octavio's brow. "I'll tell him. I hope we don't have to hold this place too long."

Once they'd left, Ava squatted near her husband. "How is he?"

"He's breathing better. I gave him a fentanyl lollipop, so he'll be out for a while. Rest is the best thing for him until we can get him to a hospital."

"So, he's stable?"

Murphy offered an encouraging smile. "For now."

"How long can he stay like this?"

"A few hours."

Ava's stomach sank. "They said it could be tomorrow before the primary invasion force reaches Austin."

"We'll have to make a move before that."

Ava stood up and looked out the window. The

first hints of daylight were glowing softly in the sky. "SJL guards are still all over the place. We can't get out of here. And even if we could, we'd be abandoning the hostages."

Captain Murphy sighed. "I'm sure SJL backup will be arriving soon."

Ava grabbed the satellite phone again and punched in the number.

"HQ, go ahead."

"I need to speak with Colonel Barr, please."

"The colonel is indisposed. We've just activated Operation Lone Star."

"I'm the acting CO for Alpha Platoon, Austin Company. We've completed our mission, but we've lost all but seven people from our platoon. The hostages are not in immediate danger, but we're being surrounded by SJL troops. Once they neutralize us, they'll still have the hostages in the detention center. I'm guessing they probably have redundancies for releasing the gas manually. All of our sacrifices will be for nothing if we can't get reinforcements. Please, get this message to Colonel Barr."

"Ma'am, I'll do what I can to relay the message, but we've just committed all of the available Alliance resources to the invasion. I'm afraid there is very little he can do."

"Then can you patch me through to the Austin Company safe house? I know Barr has back-channel communications with the resistance members there. Maybe they can send help."

"I'm sorry, ma'am. The regime disabled all landlines, cell towers, and internet when we began the invasion. Markovich is even using jamming signals to interfere with radio frequencies. You may even begin to experience disruptions with your satellite phone."

"A lot of good it's doing me. Please, just get the message to the colonel for me."

"I'll do what I can." The call ended.

Murphy looked up at her. "Not good?"

She exhaled deeply. "We're on our own."

"Here's the remote." Elizabeth handed Ava the small device, which had cost so many lives.

Ava quickly took out her multitool and used the screwdriver to remove the back panel. She removed the battery, then used the wire cutters to snip the power supply. Afterward, she pulled out the circuit board and snapped it into pieces.

"Ava, you should take a look at this." Elizabeth stood by the broken window.

Ava peered through the broken glass. "Oh, no."

"What's happening?" Murphy inquired.

"Three armored personnel carriers just pulled into the lot," she replied.

Captain Murphy struggled to get up off the floor. "If you guys get me a chair, I can shoot from a stationary position."

Elizabeth quickly rolled the office chair around from behind the desk. "Should we move the bodies out of the way?"

Ava looked at Raquel and the dead SJL soldier. "No. They're not really hindering our ability to target, and they might even block a few bullets."

Ava pressed the mic key. "Octavio, you and the other two men head on up here. We've got company coming, and we're going to have to make a stand."

Sergeant Prindle replied, "We'd be better off trying to get out of the building, maybe find some cover or fall back to the ORP."

"Foley is unconscious and Captain Murphy can't walk. I'm not leaving them behind."

Prindle replied, "We're trapped in here. Nowhere to go. Staying here is equivalent to sealing our own coffins."

"I appreciate your commentary, Sergeant, but we're making our stand here. Get to the third floor, pronto. Collect as many grenades and as much ammo from the fallen soldiers as you can on your way up. We're going to need it."

Octavio replied, "Roger that."

Prindle, Octavio, and Dillon, the other survivor from Team Five soon arrived, carrying several full tactical vests they'd taken from the dead.

Ava pointed to Prindle. "You and Dillon stay in the stairwell. As soon as you hear SJL troops hit the first flight, start dropping grenades on them. Unless they brought a ladder, there's only one way up."

Sergeant Prindle seemed less than enthusiastic about Ava assuming the role of CO in Foley's absence, but because of her knowledge of Austin, the matter had been decided long ago at the outset of the planning stage. "Yes, ma'am. If I may offer a suggestion."

"Go ahead."

"That window will be a target for RPGs. You should move your wounded and munitions into the hallway."

She nodded. "Thank you, Sergeant. That's a

good call."

Ava motioned to Elizabeth. "Can you help Captain Murphy into the hall? And Octavio, we need to relocate Foley as well."

Murphy objected, "I'm no use in the hallway."

"I wouldn't say that. Your medical skills may soon be required." With Octavio's assistance, Ava tenderly picked up Foley and moved him.

Reluctantly, Murphy followed her directive.

Ava, Octavio, and Elizabeth hurried back to the broken window. Immediately, they began firing on the SJL soldiers exiting the personnel carriers. Six SJLs fell, then the vehicles sped away without unloading more troops.

Ava sprinted away from the broken window. "Hurry, they're headed to the south side of the building. We need to get to the corner office across the hall."

Ava rushed to the window, slamming the butt of her AK against the glass to provide an opening to begin attacking the troops who were pouring out of the personnel carriers. Elizabeth and Octavio were soon at her side shooting.

"Watch out!" Elizabeth screamed and pointed to the top hatch opening on the vehicle. "RPG!"

Octavio pulled Ava to the floor, just as the rocket-propelled grenade smashed into the wall, only inches away from the window. Chunks of the concrete block wall rained down on top of them. A cloud of dust filled the room. Ava's ears rang and she couldn't see because of the haze.

"You all okay in there?" Captain Murphy yelled.

"I think so," Elizabeth replied.

But, before Ava could get up, a second grenade struck the wall. Once again, smoke and debris permeated the air.

"We have to get to the hallway!" Octavio grabbed Ava by the back of her tactical vest and pulled her toward the door.

Elizabeth coughed and trailed close behind.

Seconds after they cleared the door, a direct hit from a grenade coming through the window shook the walls.

"How many did you kill?" Sergeant Prindle yelled from the stairwell.

"Nine total, I think." Ava wiped the powdery dust from around her eyes and mouth.

"That's a good start. Each one of those APCs probably carries eleven SJLs."

"Yeah, but there could have been fifteen or twenty guards left over from the detention center." Ava peeked around the side of the door frame into the room where she'd been moments before. The exterior wall was nearly gone and in its place was a gaping hole, which allowed her to see the vehicles sitting empty in the side parking lot.

"We've got our first contestants!" Sergeant Prindle yelled. "Fire in the hole!"

Ava watched him pull the pin from the grenade and toss it down the stairs. She heard it bounce off of several stairs while Prindle dove to the ground and covered his head.

KABOOM! The blast echoed off the walls of the stairwell.

Dillon looked down. "Got a couple of them." He readied the next grenade and waited for the next wave of soldiers to advance.

"Here they come!" Dillon pulled the pin and dropped the grenade.

BOOM! Once again, the explosion reverberated through the building.

Dillon stood back up with another grenade. "This is like shooting fish in a barrel." He pulled the pin.

A single rifle shot rang out from the stairwell below and Dillon collapsed backward, letting the grenade roll freely around on the landing.

Prindle scrambled past his fallen teammate to grab the explosive device and quickly chucked it over the rail.

BOOOM!

Sergeant Prindle pulled yet another pin and, looking over the rail, threw it down the stairs. POW!

KABOOM!

When Ava opened her eyes, Sergeant Prindle was also dead. She clamored to the stockpile of grenades near the stairwell door. Obviously, she couldn't look over the rail to see where or when to toss the grenades as that method had proven fatal for Dillon and Prindle, so she'd just have to keep pitching them down, one after the other, until she ran out.

With each successive explosion, the stash of grenades grew smaller. She looked at the last three remaining bombs. "Anyone have any ideas?"

Elizabeth suggested, "We can take cover inside the offices. Pick them off when they top the stairs."

Ava realized this was the end, but she wasn't going to give up without a fight. "Okay. Get

Captain Murphy and Foley in the last office. You and Octavio take the room across from them. I'll deploy the last three grenades, then I'll join the captain and Foley. I want to be by my husband's side when . . . the time comes."

Elizabeth forced a smile and nodded.

Ava tried to space out the remaining bombs to give the others time to get into position. She pulled the pin of the last grenade and hurled it down the stairwell.

BOOOM!

Ava darted to the office where Foley and Murphy were. She kissed her sleeping husband on the lips. "I love you, Foley Mitchem. It's been such an honor to be your wife."

She looked up at the captain who was in a seated position with his rifle tucked against his shoulder.

Murphy smiled at her. "I'm sorry it had to end like this."

"Me, too. But thank you for all of your help—with Dad, and with Foley. It has meant a lot to me."

"I'm glad I could be of service."

She nodded and shouldered her rifle.

CHAPTER 27

A thousand shall fall at thy side, and ten thousand at thy right hand; but it shall not come nigh thee. Only with thine eyes shalt thou behold and see the reward of the wicked.

Psalm 91:7-8

Machine gunfire reverberated up from the stairwell into the hallway. Ava leveled the front sight of the AK-47 just above the last stair at the end of the hall. As soon as the first SJL showed his head, she'd open fire. "We may very well meet our Maker today, but let's take as many of Markovich's troops with us as possible."

Murphy's jaw was set like a steel trap as he took

aim. "Let's do it."

The noise of battle continued to pour out of the stairwell, but Ava still didn't see anyone coming up the stairs.

Elizabeth yelled from across the hall, "What are they shooting at?"

"I don't know. I assumed they were laying down cover fire. Like maybe they thought we had shooters on the other floors." Ava turned to look at Murphy for his opinion.

The doctor simply shrugged. "Beats me."

"It's dying down." Octavio lifted his hand, signaling for the others to listen.

Ava tilted her head in curiosity. Moments later, only an occasional gunshot could be heard. "I'm going to look out the window."

"Keep your head low!" Captain Murphy warned.

She nodded and stood to look outside. Men in civilian clothing were opening the doors of the detention center. "Somebody is letting the hostages out of the prison. They're instructing the men to get the guns from dead soldiers."

"I've gotta see this." Elizabeth hurried across the hall into the office were Ava stood. "It's the resistance. It must be."

"We've still got to watch those stairs." Ava turned around to make sure the captain had his rifle ready.

"I'm on it," Murphy replied.

"Ava?" A voice called from the stairwell.

She turned, instantly recognizing the source. "Dad?"

Ulysses' face soon crested the top stair. "Are you

okay?"

"Yes." Overwhelmed by yet another brush with death, she lowered her weapon and rushed into her father's arms.

Ava cut the embrace short. "Foley is hurt badly. He needs surgery, and soon."

Ulysses looked toward the office. "Okay. We've got a trauma center set up nearby."

"Back at the safe house?"

"I'm with a different group of resistance fighters, so not the safe house you're thinking of. Colonel Barr sidelined me because of my episodes. I can't say I blame him, but I couldn't sit idly by while I knew you were in danger. I put together an off-the-books team—it's what I'm good at."

He glanced down the hall. "We need to move your husband now. More Social Justice Legion fighters are probably on the way here now. Help me get him down the stairs."

Ava called out as she led her father to the office where Foley lay fighting for his life, "Elizabeth, Octavio, can you guys help Captain Murphy back down the stairs? It looks like we might live after all."

Carefully, Ava and Ulysses carried Foley's limp body down three flights of stairs. Once they were outside, Ulysses pointed to the abandoned armored personnel carrier. "Let's take that vehicle. It'll give us some cover if we run into enemy troops. It also gives us plenty of room for Foley and the doc."

Ava got in and sat beside her husband. Octavio and Elizabeth gingerly assisted Captain Murphy into the vehicle while Ulysses located the keys to the APC.

"Come on, get in!" Ava offered her hand to Elizabeth.

Octavio looked at Elizabeth. "I think we're going to stay back. The hostages have guns to defend the compound until the Alliance forces arrive, but they're going to need leadership and direction. You take care of Foley. We'll catch up with you at the big celebration—when Texas officially becomes a member of the Alliance States."

"Thank you both; for everything." Ava nodded and pulled the door closed.

CHAPTER 28

Behold, I will do a new thing, now it shall spring forth; shall you not know it? I will even make a road in the wilderness and rivers in the desert. The beast of the field will honor Me, the jackals and the ostriches, because I give waters in the wilderness and rivers in the desert, to give drink to My people, My chosen. This people I have formed for Myself; they shall declare My praise.

Isaiah 43:19-21

Two weeks after the successful invasion of Texas by the Alliance States forces, Ava sat on the couch in Ulysses' living room. She held Foley's hand firmly, not wanting to ever be away from him again. Buckley sat on the other side of her. Ulysses stood at the edge of the sofa with his arms crossed, scowling at the dog who had taken his seat while he went to the kitchen for a glass of water.

Captain Murphy had agreed to come stay at the farm and keep an eye on Foley during the initial stages of his recovery. This allowed Foley to come home to recuperate rather than staying in the overcrowded, makeshift hospital at Altus. Murphy had voiced his regret over not being able to attend to the wounded coming off the battlefield, but with his own injury to care for, a single patient was about all he could handle. The captain sat on the loveseat next to Charity with his wounded leg propped up on one of the kitchen chairs.

Octavio and Elizabeth had come to visit and to give the captain a ride back to the base now that Foley was up and about. Elizabeth was in the large easy chair and Octavio sat next to her in another of the kitchen chairs, which he'd brought into the living room.

The group paid close attention to the television as they witnessed the most momentous event in US history since General Lee surrendered to General Grant at the Appomattox Court House ending the first American Civil War.

The Patriot News Network reporter narrated the scene being played out for all of America. "In a few minutes, roughly a hundred miles away from the Appomattox Court House, the Second American

Civil War will come to a much less conclusive end than the first.

"I'm here on the North Carolina side of Knotts Island. The large farmhouse you see behind me is situated right on the Virginia-North Carolina border. President Ross and Vice President Blackwell will be meeting here with General Secretary Markovich in what will be perhaps the most-tense two minutes ever recorded. They will sign the previously-agreed-upon ceasefire. In addition to the armistice, today will be the date of record on which two separate nations are born out of one.

"*E Pluribus Unum*, or *out of many one*, was the motto of the old United States, but today we will witness the opposite being manifested as, out of one, two countries emerge providing the political and geographical separation which has existed in the hearts and minds of two very different sorts of Americans for decades.

"Drastic governmental reorganizations have been taken by both sides with new flags representing each country. The United Alliance States has the flag most resembling the old Stars and Stripes. Eleven red and eleven white stripes represent the twenty-two states as do the twenty-two white stars on the field of blue, which remain in the top left corner. The United Alliance States has retained the Constitution and the Bill of Rights and the other active amendments except for the 16th Amendment. The UAS Congress also added language to the 14th Amendment granting at conception, the full rights and protections provided to all UAS citizens.

Additionally, they have stripped away all legal decisions by the Supreme Court. The UAS Congress has also vowed to pass legislation which will restrain the judicial branch from creating new laws through interpretation and legal precedent.

"The new flag for the People's Republic of America replaces the red and white stripes with solid red. The blue field in the top left corner has been replaced with white which serves as a background to a single red star representing the socialist progressivism embraced by the country's leadership. The PRA Politburo has abandoned the founding documents in their entirety and has adopted new models, which have been personally hand-crafted by General Secretary Markovich under the guidance of billionaire investor George Szabos and a special advisory committee from the UN.

"Reporters have been restricted from attending the signing for security purposes, but we will be airing the live feed provided by President Ross' administration.

"Okay, I'm getting a message from my producer, both parties have arrived, we'll go to the signing now."

The television cut to a scene inside the old farmhouse. A long wooden table was the centerpiece of a large formal dining room. Markovich walked in, flanked by his security team, which all wore red armbands. Next, President Ross hobbled into the room. His skin was pale, his eyes sunken, and his appearance gaunt. It would be a long time before he fully recovered from his period of incarceration and abuse at the hands of the man sitting across from him. Vice-President Blackwell escorted Ross into the room, steadying him by his arm, as if he were too debilitated to stand on his own. Ross' emaciated jaw was locked tightly as he glared across the table with a deliberate snarl for his communist counterpart. Blackwell helped him to his chair, then sat down beside him.

In a very unceremonious fashion, a piece of paper was signed by Markovich, then passed across the table for Ross and Blackwell's signatures. Once finished, both parties quickly exited the residence as if neither trusted the other to not blow up the house. The war had officially been put on hold, but the animosity between the two sides would linger for ages.

"Well that's that, I suppose." Ava scratched Buckley on top of his head.

Octavio stood. "We should probably get going. Are you ready Captain Murphy?"

Murphy nodded and Charity helped him up. He turned to Ava. "How long until you close on your farm in Texas?"

She looked at Foley and then her dad. "I'm not sure. It was my old boss' place. He was killed by Markovich's men and the farm went to his brother. The probate courts are a little backed up, as you can imagine, but the brother said we could move in and rent it from him at a reasonable rate whenever we want. We need to find a buyer for this place first. We'd love to have you come visit once we're settled in."

Charity helped him to the door. "That could be a

while. Maybe you should pop in and check to see how Foley's doing in a week or two."

Ava thought that sounded like a curious request to be coming from Charity, but she didn't say anything about it.

"You folks take care of yourselves and thank you for the hospitality." The captain waved and then turned his attention back to Charity. "You can come visit me at Altus. It's not that far."

"Maybe I'll do that." Charity smiled, then blushed when she noticed Ava looking.

Ava stood by the door and waved. Buckley ran out the door in pursuit of the action. Charity escorted the captain out and helped him into the back seat of Octavio's car. She turned to Foley. "Those two have a thing going! Did you know that?"

"What, you didn't?" He smiled.

The landline phone rang and Ulysses walked to the kitchen to answer it. "Hello? Yes, one second. Ava, it's for you."

"I'm not home."

"Oh, I think you might be. It's the Vice President."

Ava looked at Foley with big eyes. "I'll be right back."

He grinned. "Take your time. I'll be here when you get back."

She tried to cushion her excitement but still scurried to the phone. "Vice President Blackwell, what a pleasant surprise."

"Ava, I wanted to call and thank you once more. I know today wasn't the best outcome we could hope for, but I'm afraid that without your dedication and perseverance, it would have been much worse. I'm here with someone else who wants to express his gratitude as well. Hang on one moment."

Ava waited quietly.

"Mrs. Mitchem, this country owes you a debt that can never be repaid." Ross' voice was frail and hushed. "I, myself may have never seen my family again had it not been for your bravery. The entire time I was being held by Markovich, I never lost hope. I always believed God would use patriots like you to secure a homeland for the remnant of true Americans."

She grinned from ear to ear. "Thank you, Mr. President, but I'm afraid you're ascribing an undue amount of credit to me. It was a team effort." She pulled the long cord of the old-fashioned wall phone into the living room where she could see Foley and Ulysses. "My father, my husband, and all the people who lost their lives in this conflict, they're the real heroes."

"You're all heroes, Ava. But please, pass along my appreciation to your father and husband. I understand they both went through a lot during the war. How are they?"

"Foley was shot a few times. God gave me more than one miracle with him. He's recovering nicely. My dad was tortured, he had severe PTSD episodes from this conflict as well as the three decades he spent in a Chinese prison. He's doing much better. By the grace of God, I think we're all going to be okay."

"Very good. I'll let you get back to them. Thank

you again and God bless."

"Thank you, Mr. President. We were all so glad to see you come home. Goodbye." Ava hung up and returned to the living room. Ulysses had retaken his seat on the couch in Buckley's absence.

Ava sat down between her father and husband, putting one arm around each of them. The girl who thought she'd never meet her real father, never be able to trust a man, who thought she'd never see Texas again, would soon be back in the Lone Star State with her loving dad and her faithful husband.

DON'T PANIC!

Inevitably, books like this will wake folks up to the need to be prepared, or cause those of us who are already prepared to take inventory of our preparations. New preppers can find the task of getting prepared for an economic collapse, EMP, or societal breakdown to be a source of great anxiety. It shouldn't be. By following an organized plan and setting a goal of getting a little more prepared each day, you can do it.

I always try to include a few prepper tips in my novels, but they're fiction and not a comprehensive plan to get prepared. Now that you're motivated to start prepping, the last thing I want to do is leave you frustrated, not knowing what to do next. So I'd like to offer you a free PDF copy of *The Seven Step Survival Plan.*

For the new prepper, *The Seven Step Survival Plan* provides a blueprint that prioritizes the different aspects of preparedness and breaks them down into achievable goals. For seasoned preppers who often get overweight in one particular area of preparedness, *The Seven Step Survival Plan* provides basic guidelines to help keep their plan in balance, and ensures they're not missing any critical segments of a well-adjusted survival strategy.

To get your **FREE** copy of *The Seven Step Survival Plan*, go to **PrepperRecon.com** and click the FREE PDF banner, just below the menu bar, at the top of the home page.

Thank you for reading
Ava's Crucible, Book Three:
United We Stand

Reviews are the best way to help get the book noticed. If you liked the book, please take a moment to leave a five-star review on Amazon and Goodreads.

I love hearing from readers! So whether it's to say you enjoyed the book, to point out a typo that we missed, or asked to be notified when new books are released, drop me a line.

prepperrecon@gmail.com

Stay tuned to **PrepperRecon.com** for the latest news about my upcoming books, and great interviews on the **Prepper Recon Podcast**.

If you've enjoyed Ava's Crucible, you'll love my end-times thriller series, *The Days of Noah*

Tennessee public school teacher, Noah Parker, like many in the United States, has been asleep at the wheel. During his complacency, the founding precepts of America have been slowly, systematically destroyed by a conspiracy that dates back hundreds of years.

Cassandra Parker, Noah's wife, has diligently followed end-times prophecy and the shifting tide against freedom in America. Noah has tried to avoid the subject, but when charges are filed against him for deviating from the approved curriculum in his school, he quickly understands the seriousness of the situation. The signs can no longer be ignored, and Noah is forced to prepare for the cataclysmic period of financial and political upheaval ahead.

Meanwhile, in an off-site CIA facility outside of Langley, rookie analyst Everett Carroll discovers he's not being told the whole truth. He's instructed to disregard troubling information uncovered by his research. Everett ignores his directive and keeps digging. What he finds goes against everything he's been taught to believe. Unfortunately, his curiosity doesn't escape the attention of his superiors, and it may cost him his life.

Watch through the eyes of Noah Parker and Everett Carroll as the world descends into chaos, a global empire takes shape, ancient writings are fulfilled, and the last days fall upon the once-great United States of America.

If you have an affinity for the prophetic don't miss my EMP survival series, *Seven Cows, Ugly and Gaunt*

In **Book One: Behold Darkness and Sorrow**, Daniel Walker begins having prophetic dreams about the judgment coming upon America for rejecting God. Through one of his dreams, Daniel learns of an imminent threat of an EMP attack which will wipe out America's electric grid and most all computerized devices, sending the country into a technological dark age.

Living in a nation where all life-sustaining systems of support are completely dependent on electricity and computers, the odds for survival are dismal. Municipal water services, retail food distribution, police, fire, EMS and all emergency services will come to a screeching halt.

If they want to live, Daniel and his friends must focus on faith, wits and preparation to be ready . . . before the lights go out.

You'll also enjoy my first series,

The Economic Collapse Chronicles

The series begins with *Book One: American Exit Strategy*. Matt and Karen Bair thought they were prepared for anything, but can they survive a total collapse of the economic system? If they want to live through the crisis, they'll have to think fast and move quickly. In a world where all the rules have changed, and savagery is law, those who hesitate pay with their very lives.

When funds are no longer available for government programs, widespread civil unrest erupts across the country. Matt and Karen are forced to move to a more remote location and their level of preparedness is revealed as being much less adequate than they believed prior to the crisis. Civil instability erupts into civil war and Americans are forced to choose a side. Don't miss this action-packed, post-apocalyptic tale about survival after the total collapse of America.

ABOUT THE AUTHOR

Mark Goodwin is a Christian constitutional author and the host of the popular Prepper Recon Podcast which interviews patriots, preppers, and economists each week on PrepperRecon.com to help people prepare for the coming storm. Mark holds a degree in accounting and monitors macro-economic conditions to stay up-to-date with the ongoing global meltdown. He is an avid student of the Holy Bible and spends several hours every week devoted to the study of Scripture and the prophecies contained therein. The troubling trends in the moral, social, political, and financial landscapes have prompted Mark to conduct extensive research within the arena of preparedness. He weaves his knowledge of biblical prophecy, economics, politics, prepping, and survival into an action-packed tapestry of post-apocalyptic fiction. Having been a sinner saved by grace himself, the story of redemption is a prominent theme in all of Mark's writings.

"He brought me up also out of an horrible pit, out of the miry clay, and set my feet upon a rock, and established my goings." Psalm 40:2

45085272R00165

Made in the USA
Columbia, SC
23 December 2018